PREPARING *for* PEACE

Reformers Unanimous International

PO Box 15732, Rockford, IL 61132
Visit our website at www.reformu.com.
Printed in Canada
Cover design by Jeremy N. Jones

Curington, Steven B., 1965-
Preparing for Peace: Overcoming Strife Through the Peace of the Hid-N-Life
Steven Curington.

ISBN 978-1-61623-562-8

STEVEN B. CURINGTON

PREPARING *for* PEACE

Overcoming Strife Through the Peace of the Hid-N-Life

CONTENTS

Special Thanks:

To our editing team, led by my good friends Chris Lemke and Tom Siebert, with heartfelt appreciation to Wendy Burks, Kay Sharp and Beth Wilson for their work as the grammar team.

Dedication:

This book consists of many excerpts from the greatest of books—my Bible. My Bible is without question His great prescription for obtaining and maintaining peace with God, peace with self and peace with others. It is my love for His Law that has given me a peace I never found growing up in deference to my Bible or as a young adult in rebellion to this Holy Book. But it was as a man of middle age that I learned to love my Holy Bible, and it is the love for my Bible that gave me my great release of peace. I hope to love it more and more each day, that someday I can say: Nothing shall offend me. I dedicate this book to my Bible. "Great peace have they which love thy law: and nothing shall offend them" (Ps. 119:165).

— Psalm 29:11 —

The LORD will give strength unto his people; the LORD will bless his people with peace.

PREFACE

NO PEACE, NO RELEASE

A Hyperbole on the Demise of Serenity

by Steven B. Curington

Satan called an impromptu meeting at the headquarters of his principality. There he met with his ruling powers, his top-level commanders of authority. In silent attendance were the rulers of the darkness of this world taking copious minutes for the demonic followers who wreak havoc on his behalf. Frustrated, Satan opened his address with this realization:

"We cannot stop Christians from reading their Bibles," he said. "The more we try to do it, the more they will commit to memory. We can't keep Christians from going to church. The more we try, the deeper underground they will meet. We can't keep them from knowing the Truth, for He has promised and will deliver His Spirit in order to produce the catalyst for this intimacy. Finally, with that said, we cannot stop them from forming a personal intimate relationship with Jesus Christ.

"But my fellow warriors," the prince of darkness continued, "once they gain that connection with Jesus, they will have peace with God. That peace with God will give them peace within themselves. This will empower them to live a serene life of peace with others. At that stage, any power we could ever hope to wield over them would be broken.

"So, we must create a diversion. We must create something that will appear to be intimate, something that will lead them to reject this peace that passes their understanding. It will not look like war. It will instead look like peace. But it will feel like turmoil. I want to call it apathy. It will be their personal righteousness. It will be a personally empowered self-righteousness. So here is my plan for self-righteous man:

"We will allow them to think peace comes through rituals of service and services. So we will let them go to their churches. We will let them have their covered-dish dinners. But we steal their personal quiet time, so they don't have time to develop a relationship with Jesus.

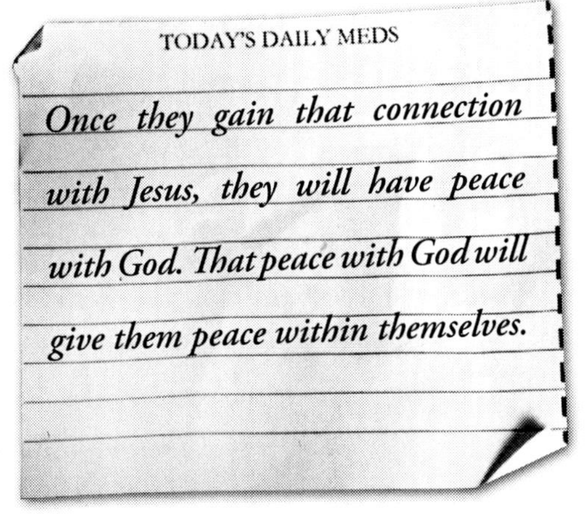

"This is what I want ALL my powers and rulers to empower your followers to do," the devil demanded. "I want you to distract them; that way they will be unable to maintain a vital connection with their Lord on a daily basis. This will keep them from gaining valuable communication from Him during their day.

"How shall we do this?" one demon shouted. Satan replied: "Keep them busy with unimportant things that will be non-essential to the personification of His life. Give them things they can do in their own power that have no need of His resurrection power. Then lead them to create innumerable schemes to occupy their minds and convince them through emotional stimulation that if they spend and spend, they will find peace. But, then, stand by and wait for when they need to borrow and borrow. Give them whatever they need, no matter how little chance they have to afford it. This will turn their false peace into worry. The worry will persuade the men to put their wives to work for long hours," Satan added, gleefully. "Use condemnation, jealousy and a combination of greed and fear to stimulate the husbands to work 6 to 7 days each week, 10 to 12 hours a day, so they can afford their empty lifestyles that give them temporal peace of the soul. They will become addicted to this cycle. But there will be no way out.

"If we are successful, we can keep them from spending time with their children. This will cause their families to fall apart, and their fragmented homes will no longer offer any escape whatsoever from the pressures of their work. They will seek peace from those they love, but find only turmoil. This will lead to confusion and difficulty to reason and think properly. I will take over!

"As the prince of the power of the air waves, I will over- stimulate their minds so that they cannot hear. I will use oppression to entice them to play their radios or media players at work and while driving. I will prepare entertainment that will keep their TVs, DVDs and PCs going constantly. This will jam their minds and break any hope for a meaningful union with Christ. Oh, and yes" the devil devised, "I will fill their coffee tables with magazines and newspapers. Pound their minds with the news 24 hours a day. Invade their driving moments with billboards. Flood their mailboxes with junk, offering free products, phony services and false hopes.

"They will look for satisfaction in anything physically, because there will be NO peace spiritually. Then I will place thin and beautiful models on the magazines and TV stations so the men will believe that outward beauty brings happiness. This will surely lead them to be dissatisfied with their wives.

"As for the wife, her work will weary her. We can easily keep these weaker vessels too tired to love their husbands at night. They don't know it yet, but if they don't give their husbands the love they need, their spouses will find a way to get it elsewhere. And that will fragment their families even quicker. We shall learn to divide before they can multiple. This will conquer them quickly!"

The evil one went on: "Let's add in some joyful-but-stressful times that must be observed. We will grant them a Santa Clause in order to distract them from teaching their children the real meaning of Christmas. We will offer them an Easter bunny, so they won't talk about Jesus' resurrection or comprehend His power over their sins. In their recreation, let us weary them with selfish indulgences that they may learn to rest by living even more excessively. They will return from their recreation exhausted. Doing so will keep them too busy to go out in nature and reflect on God's creation. In order to keep them busy and destroy their reflections, let us instead entice them with amusement parks, sporting events, plays, concerts, and movies. In an effort to afford some sort of peace, let them exchange busy for busier. And to those who acclaim to fame, we will honor them with the accolades of being the busiest!

"Now, as for their spiritual fellowship, they gotta have it or they will seek Christ for intimacy. This doctrine will replace Christ. If they can spend time with God's people, who are equally at turmoil with their families and at odds with the world, they will find solace in their secret place, but it will not be serenity. It's simply stupidity.

"However, while they are attending these church-sponsored

events, let us seal the deal. We will involve them in gossip and small talk, so that they leave with troubled consciences. The leadership will crowd their pathetic and limited lives with so many good causes that they will have no time to seek power from Jesus to do any of it! Soon they will be working in their own strength, sacrificing their health and family for the good of the cause."

"It will work!" the demons of destruction shouted in unison. "It will work! It is quite a plan!" And as they headed out for war, they asked one simple question: "What does BUSY mean, our dreadful Angel of Light?"

"When will you ever learn?" the Serpent hissed. "It sssssimply stands for:

B-eing

U-under

S-atan's

Y-oke

Under my yoke, there will be no hope. And where there is no peace, there will be no release."

INTRODUCTION

RU

WAR

This book is about peace. It is about peace in the midst of temptations as well as peace in the midst of trials, tribulations, turmoil, tumults and tragedy. But we cannot discuss peace without understanding the primary tool the devil uses to disrupt our peace and place us in battles and ultimately in bondage. The *tool* is turmoil but the *technique* is temptation. You see God allows adversity into our lives so that He might perfect us, or conform us into the image of His obedient Son.

However, adversity only enters in our life when God allows Satan a form of limited access to us. No matter how limited Satan's access may be, the devil always accepts the task. As a matter of fact, he has most likely been requesting the task for a period longer than we could conceive. I believe the devil regularly requests permission to create havoc in our lives; for he is the creator of war and the instigator of warfare. General William Tecumseh Sherman said, "War is hell." No, it's not. War is *from* Hell! But God has a plan—a goal, if you will—for allowing us to face the adversity of battle. God's goal in allowing adversity is for us to be *perfected*; Satan's plan is for God to be *rejected.*

At Reformers Unanimous, we call this Adversity University. God does not want one class, one semester or one year of this educational process to give Satan any territorial advantage over us. No, quite the contrary, He wants every adverse moment we experience to bring Him glory. The battlefield, thus, is my life and your life. God wants us to protect this territory for His glory.

Sometimes, in the face of adversity, we "give place to the devil." The word *topos* is where we get the word *topography*; it is territory. When we give place to the devil, we lose valuable real estate that needs to be taken back. Whenever an enemy takes valuable territory that belongs to another, we must recognize that it is not friendly fire but an all-out war.

Many people tend to think that warfare is about killing people. No! It's not. It's about territory. It's almost always about capturing land. There may be a hatred that would lead one to kill his enemy, but most every country that has gone to war has done so to either conquer, set free, take back or triumph in the possession of another country's claim to territory. That is the devils goal.

In June 1967, the state of Israel won a miraculous six-day war against Egypt, Jordan and Syria. Vastly outmanned and outgunned, Israel quickly reclaimed the Sinai Peninsula, the Golan Heights, the West Bank and the Gaza Strip—all territory that God had promised the tiny nation through its forefather Abraham (Genesis 12:6-7). With God, we comprise a majority over any foe, and He will enable us to reclaim territory that the enemy has taken from us. Even Noah and his family, who were the only righteous people on the planet, went into the ark a minority and came out a majority!

Friends, the battle between good and evil is bigger than you and bigger than me. But when the good prevails, it is because the battle was fought over my dead body. When my body refuses to sacrifice itself for the good of His glory, then evil has triumphed and more territory is lost to Satan's ruling authority.

It is a sad commentary on Christian living today that many of us never even think in battle terminology. We are not trained in battle tactics; nor do we even acknowledge the tools used to taunt us into turmoil with the enemy.

On March 22, 2003, the United States and its allies launched a massive aerial attack against Iraq. This relentless missile assault was dubbed a "shock and awe" campaign designed to convince Saddam Hussein to surrender even before a ground invasion of his country was underway. Satan, the prince of the air, also tries to defeat us with such shock-and-awe tactics.

However, God will empower us to prevail and to bring Him glory. His glory is *dependent* upon our victory. But our victory is contingent upon our ability to remain at peace with the "tools" the devil uses to create division, turmoil and sometimes even all-out war. What are those tools? People! The devil wants us to hate and ferociously fight any offending flesh and blood that enters our space and creates turmoil.

But God wants us to love and serve all flesh and blood. He tells us in the Holy Bible that He wants us to seek peace with all men (Hebrews 12:14), to even pursue it with our lives. He wants us at peace with one another. It is that pursuit to maintain peace among all people that brings God the most glory and takes back the territory being torn apart by the tempter.

That's right. The devil is the tempter, and his primary technique is to disturb our peace. He will tempt us to respond improperly, out from under the prompting influence of the actions and reactions of the fruit of the Holy Ghost. Thus, upon our blaming the behaviors of others, he will create turmoil in our hearts, and we will subsequently create turmoil with our words. Once this turmoil is running rampant, the peace of God and the God of Peace are no longer dwelling in our hearts. Thus, in the battlefields of our minds, we have been rendered prisoners of spiritual warfare.

We must learn the truths concerning God's empowering and calling for peace; and we must submit to them. And in His Book, learn them we shall! Peace is the entire focus of this book. Chapter one will explain how we can prepare for peace by understanding Satan's battlefield technique of temptations.

I told you previously that Satan's technique for turmoil is temptation. But God's battlefield technique for restoring serenity to the warfare that the devil wages on our mind is to turn those tumultuous temptations into Spirit-led examinations.

This book will explore three counter-insurgent strategies we should implement to thwart the devil's shock-and-awe attempts to destroy us and collaterally damage those we love.

They are as follows:

Satanic Temptations vs. Spiritual Examinations

Self Dependence vs. Faithful Independence

Instigating Turmoil vs. Making Peace

We will begin by comparing temptation with examination. For these are the techniques used to deliver the weaponry for our battle. Satanic temptation delivers turmoil to the embattled, but Godly examination delivers peace to the entombed. From there we will discuss battlefield tools of peace and turmoil almost exclusively. One will advance warfare. The other makes "war fair".

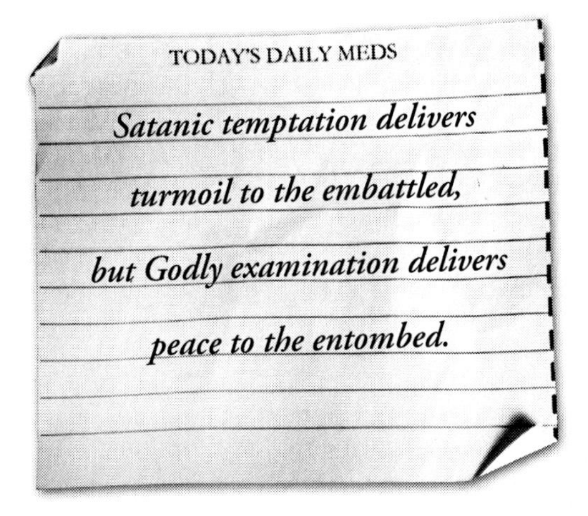

ONE

RU READY FOR YOUR TEMPTATION EXAMINATION?

I am not an expert on the subject of temptation. However, I have experienced a lot of temptation in my life, just like any other Christian. I also work every day, all day, with others who are fighting it almost exclusively in their lives. Many people ask me how we at Reformers Unanimous teach addicted people how to overcome a temptation. We teach the addicted how to overcome a temptation the same way that we teach born-again believers how to overcome, endure or escape a temptation. By developing a personal relationship with the Lord, that's how! But let's see what the Bible says about myriad temptations and our need to consider them a mere examination from the One who longs to enjoy a deep abiding relation with us.

James 5:19-20

"Brethren, if **any of you** do err from the truth, and one convert him; Let him know, that he which converteth the sinner from the error of his way shall save a soul from death, and shall hide a multitude of sins."

Notice that the apostle James uses the salutation *brethren,* indicating he is writing to his fellow believers. So this message is for us Christians, not just the unsaved addict. James is preaching to the choir, but sometimes the choir needs to be converted.

Now the word *err* literally means to *wander.* And James uses the word *truth* to refer to Our Lord Jesus Christ, who said: "I am the way, the truth, and the life..." (John 14:6). So when we err from the truth, we are wandering away from "the way" of Jesus and ultimately from God Himself.

James then alludes to the one who *converts* someone who has wandered away from the truth. When we think about conversion, we usually think about someone being converted from a sinner to a saint. When we are converted, our souls are saved from hell. That's the first conversion of a Christian, changing your position from an unbeliever to a believer.

But that's not the kind of conversion—or change of position—that James is talking about here. This type of conversion is when we change our disposition. This means we turn back to Christ *after* we have turned away from Him as a result of yielding to a temptation to sin.

The *one* mentioned here refers to someone in the church who is willing to invest in "any of you brethren" who are struggling. He is suggesting that we be the kind of Christian who will *help* rather than hinder or hurt the tempted. This is the mature believer who will not only help save someone from a premature physical death but most assuredly from a spiritual one. He or she hopefully hails from a local body of believers who will actively pursue peace and prevent their fellows from giving into temptation and the "multitude of sins" that would surely follow.

But more important than fixing those who fail in the midst of temptation is training everyone how to handle it. We have so many churched people who want to *escape* temptation (I Corinthians 10:13), but what we need are some James 1:12 Christians who can *endure* temptation and qualify for the crown of life reserved for those who are willing to endure temptation, and reject the battle balm of sin.

Let's look at a scriptural passage that better defines the temptation that leads to erroneous thinking; for wrong thoughts are the interference of the enemy that he uses to scramble our frequency of communication from the Great Commander. It is stinking thinking that always leads the "saved to misbehave."

I Peter 1:3-7

"Blessed be the God and Father of our Lord Jesus Christ, which according to his abundant mercy hath begotten us again unto a lively hope by the resurrection of Jesus Christ from the dead, To an inheritance incorruptible, and undefiled, and that fadeth not away, reserved in heaven for you, Who are kept by the power of God through faith unto salvation ready to be revealed in the last time. Wherein ye **greatly rejoice**, though now **for a season**, if **need be**, ye are in heaviness through **manifold temptations**: That the **trial of your faith**, being much more **precious** than of gold that perisheth, though it be tried with fire, might be found unto praise and honour and glory at the appearing of Jesus Christ:"

The apostle Peter is telling us here how great it is to be a Christian. We have an inheritance reserved in heaven that does not fade away, he writes. We are kept by the power of God. That word *kept* means *protected*. We have a protection around us when we submit to the power of God through faith unto salvation. Our salvation is ready to be revealed in the last time. This is all good news. You will not hear it on CNN, MSNBC or Fox, but it is the best news you will ever hear.

We are to greatly rejoice in this greatest of all news, Peter states, even though we are now necessarily in a season of heaviness through manifold temptations. You see, God may have determined that this season of temptation may be needed. Peter says "if need be...." We are sometimes going through these temptations because we are living like Peter when he was allowed to be sifted by the devil. Sometimes we need to be sifted, too! In other words, our future ministry is dependent upon the pressures of personal development, and personal development rises up from the ashes of disappointment.

Now I am sure most of us can learn to accept temptation. But how can we learn to yearn for it? You may say: What?! Learn to yearn for it? Why would anyone yearn for temptation? But I have learned, as Peter teaches us here, that temptation has great reciprocal benefits.

Let's look deeper into our passage so we may better understand. Next we see the word *rejoice* and the word *temptation* in the same sentence. That may seem like an oxymoron or contradiction in terms; but in God's language, it is not contradictory.

Rejoice is an Old English word for the modern English words *repeatable joy*. It is joy that repeats itself. We experience joy, and as a result of that joy, another round of joy is kick-started. It's being in a state of perpetual joy, despite the difficulties of life.

So a temptation is intended by God to have a reciprocal effect that produces joy over and over again. Do you experience joy in your temptations? Before I learned this spiritual lesson, I did not ever experience joy, let alone repeatable joy, whenever I was tempted. However, Peter clearly says: "Wherein ye greatly rejoice, though now for a season, if need be, ye are in heaviness through manifold temptations:" (v.6).

Now then, all of a sudden, we see a punctuation mark in the Bible. Please understand there is great theology in the punctuations of the Bible. Note the colon following the word *temptations*. A colon is a punctuation that precedes an explanation. He is saying that we are rejoicing because **right now** we may *need* to be in manifold, or various, temptations.

And then Peter explains *why* we are rejoicing in our temptation: "That the trial of your faith, being much more **precious** than of gold that perisheth, though it be tried with fire, might be found unto praise and honour and glory at the appearing of Jesus Christ:" (v.7).

So Peter is clearly defining temptation as a trial of our faith. This is not the only time that the Holy Bible equates temptation with a test of faith. James 1:2-3 states, "My brethren, count it all joy when ye fall into divers **temptations**: Knowing *this*, **that the trying of your faith** worketh patience." God knows that we are slow learners, so His Holy Spirit often inspired multiple authors of the Bible to repeat important spiritual principles. We must learn to see temptation as a trying of our faith. Thus, it's not the *consequence* of a vulnerable sinner but *evidence* of a venerable saint!

TODAY'S DAILY MEDS

A trial is nothing more than a personal examination of where we are placing our confidence.

In this instance, the word *trial* means examination, i.e., an examination of our faith. *Faith* is the old English word for the modern English word *confidence*. So what God is really saying identically through both Peter and James is that He is putting our confidence in Him on trial by allowing temptation to enter our lives. A trial is nothing more than a personal examination of where we are placing our confidence. So, in other words, what the devil intends to be a temptation, God intends to be an examination—an examination of temptation.

Thomas à Kempis, author of the classic, *The Imitation of Christ*, said: "We usually know what we can do, but temptation shows us who we are."[1] Paul teaches us we don't even know our own hearts, but we need to discern our hearts using the Holy Bible. God searches our hearts, and puts us on trial so that *we* might know our hearts and see ourselves like He does—from the inside out!

The heart is our meditator, the dwelling place of our short thoughts and long meditations. Your mind is where you store your memory. It's like a DVD. Your heart is the DVD player. It plays your very own home movies, so to speak. However, the Bible says that our hearts are "deceitful above all things, and desperately wicked" (Jeremiah 17:9).

In other words, our hearts deceive us so much that we don't even know how wicked our thinking can be. We are so conditioned to the negative viewing pleasures of our hearts that we don't even wince when our home movies are rated suitable for only *immature* audiences! So God reveals the home movies of our hearts, and he does so through difficult examinations of our faith. He's showing us where our hearts truly are.

Now that raises a question: Is God examining *our* faith or is God examining someone else's faith through temptation? When we received the Lord Jesus Christ as our resurrected Savior, we also received His Holy Spirit. And when we received the Holy Spirit, we received nine unique characteristics called the *fruit of the Spirit* (Galatians 5:22-23). These are love, joy, peace, longsuffering, kindness, goodness, faith, meekness and temperance.

The first fruit of the Spirit is love. Before I was saved, I thought I really knew how to love people well. But as a human, my love for others was flawed. Now that I am a Christian, I have God's love in me. But I still can choose to turn back to my old, flawed conditional love that had selfish thoughts of return from those whom I had loved. God, however, would not have given me His selfless love if He wanted me to rely on the selfish love that I had before I was saved. He wants me to love others with His love.

What about my joy? I was happy back then, but now I have God's joy. I can yield to my own old joy or I can experience God's inexpressible joy. The same is true for peace, and for that matter, all of the fruit of the Spirit.

Faith, the seventh fruit, is a free gift from God. It takes a measure of *our* human faith to receive salvation. But once we are saved, we are given the faith of God. We will discuss His faith vs. my faith in greater detail later. It is dispiriting to hear a born-again believer say: "I wish I had more faith." You don't need any more faith. When the apostles asked Our Lord to increase their faith, they were not talking quantitatively but *durationally*. They wanted to increase the duration of their faith in difficult circumstances. They didn't need any *more* faith because they had all the faith they would ever need; they had the faith of the Lord Jesus Christ embodied within their spirit in the form of His Spirit. Likewise, Christian, you have God's faith—and that's all the faith you need. We merely need to yield to God's faith in the face of difficult circumstances.

The apostle Paul wrote, "I am crucified with Christ, nevertheless

I live; yet not I, but Christ liveth in me: And the life which I now live in the flesh I live by faith in the Son of God who loved me and gave Himself for me" (Galatians 2:20). If Christ lives in us, then we must have His faith. God does not want us to **do** *better*; He wants us to **be** *deader*! He wants us to be dead so that through His Son, we can have access to His faith.

We are saved by God's grace through *our* faith (Ephesians 2:8). As a result, we then receive *God's* faith through His indwelling Holy Spirit. When we begin to revert back to our fleshly personal faith, we are exercising our *confidence* in our own power, not God's. The fruit of my efforts could never equal a smidgen of God's faith. And the results of yielding to God's faith give me far more power than my meager faith can muster! It's like trying to use a flashlight battery to electrify our homes rather than connecting to the area power grid. (But even that analogy falls short because God's power is infinite.)

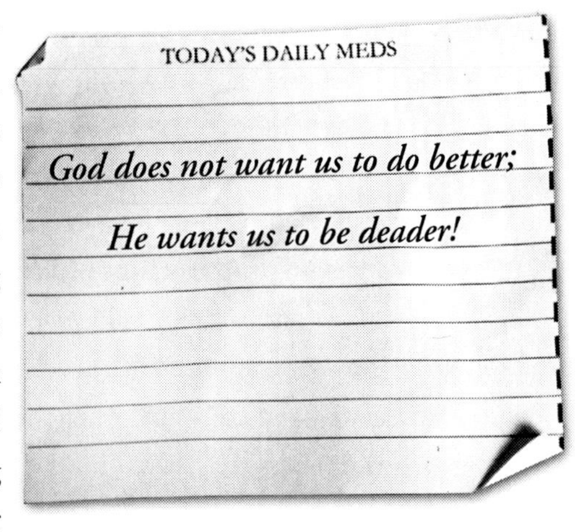

However, many of us just don't always know when we are empowered by our own faith rather than by God's faith. We sure would like to know, but we are often too ignorant to figure it out. So God allows the enemy limited access to us. Thus, a temptation will enter our lives—through his permissive will.

People often ask me: "Brother Curington, are you saying that

God is in charge of temptation?" Yes, I'm saying that God is in charge of temptation. I'm not saying that God tempts anybody; I'm saying that the Bible says that Jesus Christ was led by the Spirit into the wilderness to be tempted by the devil (Matthew 4:1). Would you say that Jesus Christ followed an evil spirit? No, so obviously the apostle is referring to the Holy Spirit.

Moreover, Jesus Christ Himself said that when we pray, we should ask Our Father to "lead us not into temptation" (Matthew 6:13). God does not present the temptation to sin—Satan does—but God permits the temptation to take place. Every temptation of the devil is nothing more than an examination from God, an examination of temptation.

If you are yielding to His faith in times of temptation, it will come with a reward and simply build *more* faith. And it will cause you to rejoice in the face of difficult circumstances, just as the many disciples experienced and exclaimed when they spoke of adversity and suffering. When done in His faith, it produces rejoicing—repeatable joy. But when you are yielding to *your* faith, then you are acting in your own power. And that is a very frustrating place to be. But when you begin to fail in the face of temptation, i.e., God's examination, you will recognize it and realize that your relationship with Him is weak. You will need to go back to the drawing board to regain that intimacy. It is that drawing board whereby we draw nigh to Him and He to us (James 4:8). Thus, we regain our peace that there is nothing between our soul and our Savior, so that His blessed face we may see.

But, apparently, a lot of Christians need to go back to the drawing board. A *Christianity Today* survey concluded that nearly 40 percent of pastors confessed to a struggle with pornography.[2] There are increasing rates of divorce, abortion and alcoholism in the church. This is the result of Christians exercising human, not godly, faith when faced with temptation.

In I Peter 1:7, the apostle writes further that "the trial of your faith" is "much more precious" than gold that perishes. What does that mean? In the past, when I experienced trials of my faith through temptation, I didn't consider them to be precious. I sometimes still don't. Those who would consider them precious are exercising the same type of faith as the apostle Paul, who said he could "take pleasure in infirmities, in reproaches, in necessities, in persecutions, in distresses" (II Corinthians 12:10). People like Paul and Silas sang songs of praise while in prison (Acts 16:25) but I don't sing praise songs when I get so much as a flat tire! What's up with that?

Our Lord Himself commanded us to "rejoice and be exceedingly glad" when we are reviled and persecuted as well as when people "say all manner of evil against" us (Matthew 5:11-12).

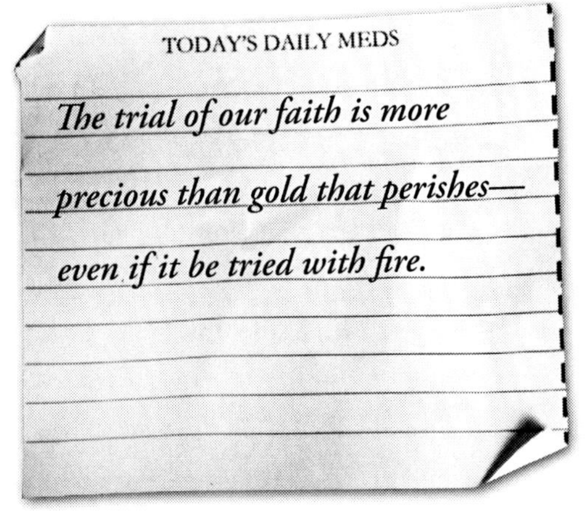

And there *are* those who rejoice in habitually hard circumstances. When they are under extreme hardship, they are able to yield to the faith that lies within them. And by yielding to that faith, they experience a supernatural joy and encouragement that is more precious to them than any amount of paycheck they could receive.

So Peter is saying that the trial of our faith is more precious than gold that perishes—*even if it be tried with fire.* This man, also known as Simon Peter, was speaking from firsthand experience. For he knew what it was like to have his faith tried by the edge of a fire. He had been to the Refiner's Diner and learned to *savor the flavor* of God's favor! Yes, indeed. Peter knew a little about fires, didn't he? You will remember a few of them. . .

Remember the story that begins in Luke 22:31? Jesus is speaking to Simon Peter. "And the Lord said, Simon, Simon, behold, Satan hath desired to have you, that he may sift you as wheat:" Now our Lord knew this because all of our access to temptation goes through a permissive God upon request. Do you remember the story of Job? He was given over to Satan by the hand of God (Job 1:8). Satan went to Him, and God said: "Hast thou considered my servant Job...?" And here in Luke's gospel, we see Jesus advising Peter that Satan is seeking *permission* to have access to him. (And, by the way, Jesus is going to give it to him!)

"But I have prayed for thee," Jesus tells Peter (v.32). Prayed *what* for him—that his faith would fail? Not! But rather "...that thy faith fail not:" In other words, our Lord said: Hey, I hope your faith doesn't fail. Why is Jesus saying this? Is it because He doesn't know the outcome? No, it's because Peter doesn't know the reason for the temptation. In this prayer request we see God's rationale for allowing Satan access to Peter. His faith was weak. It was human faith, and God wanted Peter to experience something. What was it He wanted Peter to experience? A conversion, that's what! But not *to* Christ. That had already happened. A conversion *back to* Christ would be a better way of saying it.

So our Lord said He prayed that Peter would not fail, adding, "and when thou art *converted....*" There's that **same word** we saw in

James 5:19. So Simon Peter had not yet *converted* to Christianity? No, he was a believer. However, he was going to wander from the way and was going to be sifted. Jesus was praying that when that sifting happened, Peter would be strong in faith, and if not, that he would be converted back to the Way, the Truth and the Life. Just like we Christians today need to be converted back to God following a sinful shortcoming.

"And when thou art converted, strengthen thy brethren" (Luke 22:32). In other words, Jesus is telling Peter: When you see that you have blown it, you will convert back to My way and prevent others from blowing it in the face of their temptations. It sounds like Peter was going to have a ministry to the falling brethren as a result of a fall, huh?

Of course, Peter didn't quite get it yet. He didn't realize that he would soon be singing his own rendition of Frank Sinatra's *I Did it My Way,* instead of following God's way.

"And he said unto him, Lord, I am ready to go with thee both into prison, and to death" (v. 33). To which Jesus responded: "... Peter, the cock shall not crow this day, before that thou shalt thrice deny that thou knowest me."

God knows beforehand when we are going to sin because He is omniscient; and He also knows when we are going to be tempted because He has given the devil advance liberty to tempt us.

"Pray that ye enter not into temptation," Our Lord warns Peter and the other disciples (v. 40), repeating the admonition a second time after He had prayed at the Mount of Olives (v. 46). He concluded that Peter's spirit was willing, but his flesh was weak (Matthew 26:41). Jesus saw the temptation coming, he knew Peter's weaknesses, and He warned him how many times? Yep, three!

A Fire That Emptied Peter: Luke 22:54-62

"Then took they him, and led him, and brought him into the high priest's house. And Peter followed afar off. And **when they had kindled a fire** in the midst of the hall, and were set down together, Peter sat down among them. But a certain maid beheld him as he sat by the fire, and earnestly looked upon him, and said, This man was also with him. And he denied him, saying, **Woman, I know him not**. And after a little while another saw him, and said, Thou art also of them. And Peter said, **Man, I am not**. And about the space of one hour after another confidently affirmed, saying, Of a truth this fellow also was with him: for he is a Galilaean. And Peter said, **Man, I know not what thou sayest**, And immediately, while he yet spake, the cock crew. And the Lord turned, and looked upon Peter. And Peter remembered the word of the Lord, how he had said unto him, Before the cock crow, thou shalt deny me thrice. **And Peter went out, and wept bitterly**."

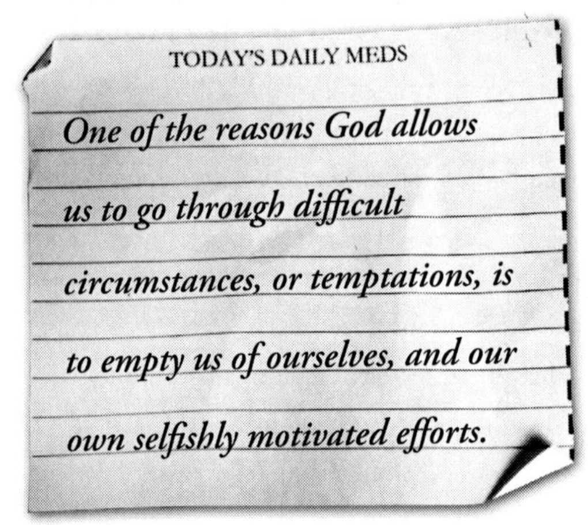

This was a temptation by fire that absolutely *emptied* Peter. It emptied him of his pride, and the self-sufficiency of who he thought he was. In Peter's own false humility, he had boastfully proclaimed to Jesus that he was ready to go with Him to die.

Whoops! Now we find Peter, a short time later, adamantly refusing to even admit that he knows Jesus, while he warms around a fire with a bunch of women! This is a man who did not rejoice in temptation but rather rejected the threat that Jesus had thrice warned him about, yea, even telling him in advance that he would blow it.

"Oh no, I won't," Peter seemed to say. This was a man full of pride. And God said, so to speak: "The devil's got a temptation. I call it an examination. Here you go. Let's blow it. Let's get you emptied of who you really are."

One of the reasons God allows us to go through difficult circumstances, or temptations, is to empty us of ourselves, and our own selfishly motivated efforts.

And, you know, this isn't the only fire that Peter went through. He went through another "fiery trial" as he called it in I Peter, another testing, another temptation—that is to say—more examinations! After failing his exam miserably and being emptied of himself, he rejoined the rest of the disciples, who decided not to attend the crucifixion out of *faith*, or I should say, *fear*!

Peter actually went back to his former occupation. He hid a bit here and hid a bit there. But we see a miraculously different scenario in John 20:19. Now, all of a sudden, Jesus shows Himself to His disciples, and in doing so, gives them something they never had before: the in-dwelling Spirit of God breathed upon them! It would produce the fruit of the Spirit, the first of which would be the love of the Lord Jesus Christ. Next would be the joy of the Lord that would be our strength, followed by the peace of God that would pass all understanding, and then the seventh fruit, which would be the *faith* of the Lord Jesus Christ. Peter's faith, found in the soul of his human reasoning, is no longer necessary when His faith enters into His spirit. Let's read from another gospel.

John 20:19-22

"Then the same day at evening, being the first day of the week, when the doors were shut where the disciples were assembled for fear of the Jews, came Jesus and stood in the midst, and saith unto them, Peace be unto you. And when he had so said, he showed unto them his hands and his side. Then were the disciples glad, when they saw the Lord. Then said Jesus to them again, Peace be unto you: as my Father hath sent me, even so send I you. And when he had said this, he breathed on them, and saith unto them, Receive ye the Holy Ghost."

Many Christians believe the disciples received the Holy Ghost on the day of Pentecost, following Our Lord's ascension into heaven (Acts 2). But they actually experienced the *indwelling* of the Holy Spirit right here in John 20, just after Jesus was resurrected.

Shortly thereafter, Peter was ready for his next trial by fire. Do you remember this fire?

A Fire That Enlisted Peter: John 21:1-9

"After these things Jesus shewed himself again to the disciples at the sea of Tiberias; and on this wise shewed he himself. There were together Simon Peter, and Thomas called Didymus, and Nathanael of Cana in Galilee, and the sons of Zebedee, and two other of his disciples. Simon Peter saith unto them, I go a fishing. They say unto him, We also go with thee. They went forth, and entered into a ship immediately; and that night they caught nothing. But when the morning was now come, Jesus stood on the shore: but the disciples knew not that it was Jesus. Then Jesus saith unto them, Children, have ye any meat? They answered him, No. And he said unto them, Cast the net on the right side of the ship, and ye shall find. They cast therefore, and now they were not able to draw it for the multitude of fishes. Therefore that disciple whom Jesus loved saith unto Peter, It is the Lord. Now when Simon Peter heard that it was the Lord, he girt his fisher's coat unto him, (for he was naked,) and did cast himself into the sea. And the other disciples came in a little ship; (for they were not far from land, but as it were two hundred cubits,) dragging the net with fishes. As soon then as they were come to land, **they saw a fire** of coals there, and fish laid thereon, and bread."

When Peter arrived on the shore, Jesus was awaiting. With a critique? Nope! With an "I told you so"? Nope! With a "that'll teach you to deny me"? Nope! He was waiting to call him to full-time Christian service! That's what!

This is when Jesus asked him three times, the same number of times of the denial: Peter, do you love me? Feed my lambs. Do you love me? Feed my sheep. Do you love me? Feed my sheep (v. 15-17). Sure, he questioned Peter for the purpose of reminding Peter what had *emptied* him. When Peter answered in the voice of a man strengthened by the Holy Spirit of Faith, God *enlisted* Peter! In the U.S. Army, a soldier enlists and then is emptied with a shaved head and boot camp. But in the Lord's Army, God empties us before He enlists us.

We saw the first fire emptied Peter, but here we see he faced yet another fire. (Aren't you thankful for the fire of second chances?) Here was a man who thought he would do anything for the Lord Jesus. He went through an examination, what the devil calls a temptation. And he failed miserably, wept bitterly but got back up. And when Jesus showed Himself to him, all of a sudden, he became alive. Yes, Peter must have thought: This stuff is real! I knew it was real!

So we see a man who, as a result of an examination of temptation, is doing just a little bit better. What changed? I'll tell you what changed. This time he succumbed to the Spirit that was in him.

Now he had the power of the Holy Spirit living within him; he subsequently had God's faith. So he jumped out of the water, and there was another fire. It was the fire that enlisted him. But it wasn't the last fire that Peter experienced. Do you remember Peter's third and final fire? It was his most popular and most powerful fire. It was what my six-year-old son calls a "triery fial." In I Peter, the apostle would call it a fiery trial.

A Fire that Empowered Peter: Acts 2: 1-4

"And when the day of Pentecost was fully come, they were all with one accord in one place. And suddenly there came a sudden from heaven as of a rushing mighty wind, and it filled all the house where they were sitting. And there appeared unto them **<u>cloven tongues like as of fire</u>**, and it sat upon each of them. And they were all filled with the Holy Ghost, and began to speak with other tongues, as the Spirit gave them utterance."

Surely this WAS an empowering fire. For Peter, having been initially *emptied* of his pride, was subsequently *enlisted* into his ministry and now effectively *empowered* for his ministry by the Holy Ghost. In retrospect, I guess Peter did know a little bit about fiery trials after all, didn't he?

So did the apostle pass his examinations of temptations? We need only read his God-inspired writings to find the answer:

I Peter 4:12-14

"Beloved, **think it not strange** concerning the **<u>fiery trial which is to try you</u>**, as though some **strange thing happened** unto you: **<u>But rejoice</u>**, inasmuch as ye are **partakers of Christ's sufferings**; that, when his glory shall be revealed, ye may be glad also with exceeding joy. **If ye be reproached** for the name of Christ, **happy *are ye***; for the Spirit of glory and of God ***resteth* upon you**: on their part he is evil spoken of, but on your part he is glorified." (Emphasis mine)

These verses clearly teach us that Peter concluded the Refiner's Diner to serve on a fire for the finer! He indicated that not only was it more precious than gold, but it brought happiness and rejoicing. Peter had learned that temptation viewed as an examination was actually an opportunity to gain God's favor. And Peter, no matter how difficult things got, learned to savor the flavor of favor!

He realized, as we teach in this book, that we wrestle not against flesh and blood, but we have only one adversary and that adversary waits patiently to sift us. He waits until we are as self-righteous as ever and as confident in self as we can be. Then he will pounce. Shock and awe. Peter put it this way.

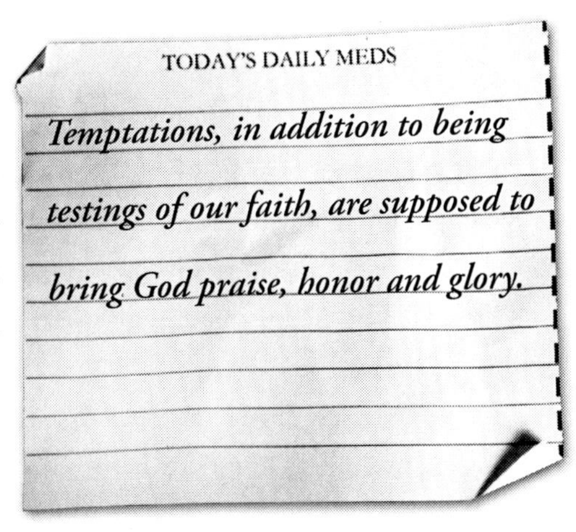

I Peter 5:8

"Be sober, be vigilant; because *your* adversary the devil, as a roaring lion, walketh about, seeking whom he **may** devour:"

Having endured three transformative fires, Peter now understands that the devil has no power to tempt him without God's permission. Notice he says the devil seeks whom he *may* desire, not whom he *can* desire.

And does Simon Peter now realize that temptation is a testing of his faith and, therefore, a time for joy? Another look at this epistle answers the question with a resounding YES!

I Peter 1:7-8

"That the **trial of your faith**, being much **more precious** than of gold that perisheth, though it be **tried with fire**, might be found unto praise and honour and glory at the appearing of Jesus Christ: Whom having not seen, ye love; in whom, though now ye see him not, yet believing, ye **rejoice with joy unspeakable and full of glory**:"

Temptations, in addition to being testings of our faith, are supposed to bring God praise, honor and glory. Peter gets this. But I don't know if *we* always look at temptations that way. I don't know if we always recognize them as examinations. Do you? Do you consider temptations of your faith, or confidence, to be enjoyable and worth repeating for the sake of rejoicing? That would seem to be a difficult thing to acknowledge. But not so for our first-century Christians, whose personal faith *must* have been stronger than ours, having personally witnessed it all! But yet we, 2,000 years removed, actually have more faith, or confidence, in our own self-righteous efforts than in His righteous efforts—His faith. What a sad state of current affairs.

But for that to change, we need to change our perceptions of these our darkest hours. We need to remember now that God's intentions are to reveal weaknesses in our Christian walks, whatever areas in which we might not be committed to Him, whatever areas of our life that we are living in our own power instead of His indwelling power.

Peter is our role model. Following his three trials by fire, he healed a lame man, led 3,000 people to the Lord with a single sermon, helped found the first church, and continued through his words and deeds to advance the cause and kingdom of Our Lord.

TWO

RU COUNTING?

I was excited when I first saw that another apostle, James, had confirmed the spiritual truth that Peter had taught in his first epistle, and which we've already studied in the first chapter, about temptations being examinations of faith.

James 1:2-4

"My brethren, **count it all joy** when ye fall into divers **temptations**: Knowing this, that the **trying of your faith** worketh patience, But let patience have her perfect work, that ye may be perfect and entire, wanting nothing."

Count it all what? Joy! James is using the same word that Peter did. That's not surprising since they were both inspired by the same God!

The word *count* here means *to consider.* Consider it all joy when you fall into *divers*—again, the same meaning as Peter's word *manifold*—or various temptations.

Now what exactly *is* a temptation? Is it something sinful that you want? Nope. Peter taught, as James says, that if you would just count it joy to resist that temptation, you will receive patience. And that patience will have its perfect work, and you will be made entire or whole.

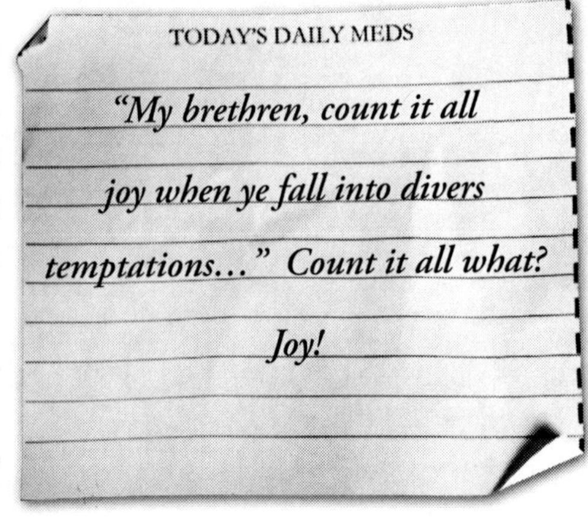

Let's look further at the epistle of James, for further explanation of temptation examinations.

James 1:14-15

"But every man is tempted, when he is drawn away of his own lust, and enticed. Then when lust hath **conceived**, it bringeth forth sin: and sin, when it is finished, bringeth forth death."

From this verse, we discover that Satan's standard operational procedure for initiating temptation into our lives is to, first, deceptively draw us away from the Spirit-filled, abundant Christian life. How does he do this? He uses our own lusts, or desires. What else would be so effective other than our own deep-rooted desires that we ourselves have molded into our personal weaknesses over the course of our lives—our very own designer desires?

Nothing! And, unfortunately, the enemy knows this! Satan next uses intuitively placed stimuli, or outside influences, to *entice* our desires. To *entice* means to *influence to evil.* So what is this saying, then? Well, the enemy has studied each of us to know what our weak links are, and then places us into circumstances that will make those weaknesses manifest themselves in the hope of spoiling our testimonies or otherwise furthering his wicked agenda.

In the epic film *The Godfather*, Sonny Corleone's weak link was his hot temper. His enemies knew this, so they set him up by having his brother-in-law Carlo beat up his wife, Sonny's sister Connie. So when Sonny drives out to avenge his sister's beating, he is machine-gunned down at the causeway. This is how Satan works. He studies our potentially fatal flaws and then attacks them. Shock and awe.

But, glory to God, the devastation of temptation can be avoided, my friend. Looking back at our key verse in James, we see that up to this point we have only been enticed, or "instigated to evil." At this juncture, sin has not yet occurred. But it is at this point that we must yield to a fruit of the Spirit, faith, to avoid falling into sin. This all-important pivotal moment is what I call the meditation of temptation. This process will bring this study full-circle and hopefully blow your mind, as it did mine!

James tells us that we will be drawn away and enticed by our own desires and that "when lust hath **conceived**, it bringeth forth sin… " We have learned that the word *conceived*, in this context, means to *frame in the mind*. So James is telling us that it is only when we allow our lusts, or imaginations (stored images), to be framed in our mind that sin actually occurs. I don't know about you, but this encourages me a great deal, my friend! We have an option to stop the sin from occurring right here and now.

So James teaches us that first we experience an instigation to evil through some outside stimulus, or oppression, that is brought about by one of our designer desires. This, as we have seen, is the first precursor to sin, and it lies within our body. The body will then initiate a peace process with the soul. The soul is made up of our mind, will and emotions. Our soul then has the opportunity, at this very instance, to cast down the wicked imagination that has formed, or to dwell upon it—framing it in the mind. If we cast down this bad thought we have victory, but if we frame it in our minds, we have just brought forth sin.

I don't know about you, but most people I know find their happiness by giving into temptation. However, this is not where we need, nor want, to be! You will certainly experience a fleeting happiness by giving into temptation that comes and goes; but if you endure temptation, you'll find joy and happiness that lasts forever! This is something you don't want to miss out on.

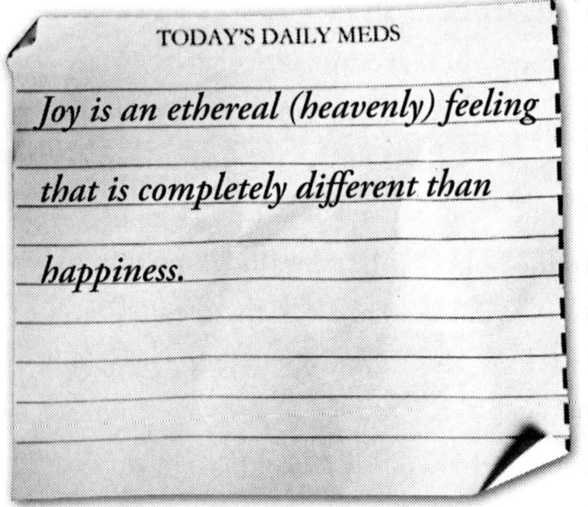

Joy is an ethereal (heavenly) feeling that is completely different than happiness. You can only find joy by yielding to the Spirit of God. Joy will produce within us endorphins (pleasure chemicals) in the brain that are 100-percent addictive. Thus, joy becomes repeatable because when you enjoy something, it produces an increase in the neurotransmitter serotonin that the brain will seek to maintain.

So we can see that enduring temptation is, in fact, an addictive behavior! This dovetails nicely into the Theory of Multiplication of Temptation, for we have seen that the more victories we experience, the more we will be tempted!

Many of us have gained victory over a majority of our external sins, but God sees everything we have framed in our minds. The Bible tells us that it is what's on the inside of man that will ultimately defile him (Matthew 15:11). All throughout Scripture we see that sin always originates in the mind. God views a sinful thought, which we have chosen to frame in our minds, just the same as if we choose to engage, or act upon, that thought. This is a difficult truth that takes a measure of faith to accept; but accept it we must, friend!

Jesus equated sinful thinking with sin itself when he said: "But I say unto you, That whosoever looketh on a woman to lust after her hath committed adultery with her already in his heart" (Matthew 5:28).

When God sees a wrong thought framed in our mind—something that we may get away with in front of our spouse, our children, our employer, etc.—he sees a conceptual sin that will lead Him to put us through a personal examination so that we may discover our error, and therefore, grow spiritually. So we see that when we are enticed to evil and fail to follow the prompting of the Holy Spirit, and likewise fail to follow the intuition of the Word of God, the Lord will allow us to experience an examination of temptation! We can avoid this often-painful process, however, if we simply refuse to allow ourselves to frame in our minds the sinful thoughts that are stirred up within us from an instigation of evil.

When we fail to exercise the faith granted to us by the Holy Spirit, and instead substitute our own faith for it, allowing ourselves to conceptualize sinful thoughts, we are essentially saying to the Lord that we have confidence that what we are doing is okay and acceptable—and that there will be no judgment rendered for it. We rationalize to ourselves that just thinking sinfully is okay as long as we don't follow through on such a thought. However, my friend, we are wrong every time! The Bible says that if you think it, you did it. Period!

Oh, and what about that judgment thing? We most certainly will experience judgment in the form of a God-ordained fiery trial, or an examination of temptation, just like Peter did three times over making these very same mistakes. If this happens though, we are not to faint in our time of adversity. Instead, like Peter, we are to endure these fiery trials and receive the "crown of life" that is promised to us.

If this does not excite you, brothers and sisters, I don't know what will. Through these truths we see that God has developed a system where He uses an often-eschewed concept, temptation, to perform a number of wonderful things in our Christian lives. If we gain victory over our temptations, we have seen that we will experience a never-ending joy—or rejoicing. This will promote the peace for which this book was written.

But if we fall short—like Peter initially did—God will use the temptation as an examination so that we may learn from the experience and eventually regain our peace through victory. Believe it or not, when we experience temptation, it is essentially a win-win situation, but only if we allow God to work through it. He wants to use our temptations, friend. Won't you let Him?

Going back to one of our key verses, we read, "...and sin, when it is finished, bringeth forth death" (James 1:15). On a more somber note, we know from this verse that if we fail to yield to the fruit of the Spirit, faith, and we don't allow God to live through our lives during times of temptation, then we will potentially fall victim to a premature physical death and a most-certain spiritual death as a result of our erroneous ways.

The Lord will allow temptation into our lives so that He may be glorified through us. However, if we stubbornly refuse to embrace the Lord's conversion work, the enemy is lying not far behind and seeking whom he may devour. And devour, he most certainly will.

Remember good ol' Principle #2 of the Reformers Unanimous Ten Principles: Every sin has its origin in our hearts! By using the meditation of temptation, we can prevent these sick and malicious thoughts from ever making that 18-inch journey from our heads to our hearts.

James closes his exposition on temptation with this admonition: "Do not err, my beloved brethren." To err means to wander. The apostle is beseeching us to not wander from the reality of these truths.

In our next chapter, our focus will change from the techniques of temptations vs. examinations, to the tools of turmoil vs. peace. We will learn how not to slack during the devil's shock-and-awe attacks. From this point forward, we will be studying spiritual warfare and how we can come to believe that any war we fight in the Spirit will surely be more than fair!

THREE

RU SLACK DURING ATTACK?

If you have truly come to embrace and even occasionally experience the Spirit-filled life, you have undoubtedly realized an ever-increasing amount of turmoil in life. We often experience division, discord or discomfort because of people, places, things and other earthly entities. While living godly lives, it seems we have an uncanny propensity for attracting trouble. And all the while, we are striving to live for God by yielding and obeying to His every known desire. So I ask you, my friend, what gives? Why are things so hard for those of us who have such a passion for being and doing right?

In answering that question, I would like to share with you a few stories and corresponding truths that have occurred in my life. The Lord has allowed me to discern, through these incidents, the driving force behind all of my circumstances.

The Word of God is very clear about Christian adversity. The Bible pointedly tells us that such battles are of a spiritual nature, hence, our often-misunderstood cliché: spiritual warfare.

WOULD LIKE INFORMATION ON

- ❐ How to begin a relationship with Christ
- ❐ How to join this Church Family
- ❐ Senior's Activities
- ❐ Women's Activities
- ❐ Men's Activities
- ❐ Care Groups
- ❐ Women's Bible Studies
- ❐ Family Recreation Activities
- ❐ Young Adult Ministry

CONNECTING CARD

Date: ____________________

Name(s)________________________________

____

Children's Name(s) and Age(s)

____

____

Address: ________________________________

My friend, what exactly is spiritual warfare? In this chapter, I will answer that question and demonstrate exactly why it is imperative that we not slack during an attack!

Ephesians 6:12

"For we wrestle not against flesh and blood, but against principalities, against powers, against the rulers of the darkness of this world, against spiritual wickedness in high places."

What the apostle Paul is teaching us here is that the root of our life's stressors is not people, nor is it any other physical or worldly object or circumstance. But, rather, he clearly explains that the issues with which we struggle are of a spiritual nature. It is pivotal for us to understand and accept the fact that our primary adversary is none other than Satan himself. Knowing this, we must face life's challenges by *faith* that our God is far more powerful than any opposing force.

TODAY'S DAILY MEDS

The Word of God is very clear about Christian adversity. The Bible pointedly tells us that such battles are of a spiritual nature, hence, our often-misunderstood cliché: spiritual warfare.

This verse also tells us that our adversary, the devil, has a vast array of demonic players at his disposal to use against us. For starters, our verse mentions principalities. The word *principality* simply means *a prince's territory*. Worldly speaking, we know that Crown Prince Abdullah controls the country of Saudi Arabia, a reasonably sized territory. Spiritually speaking, we see that Satan also is a prince of a territory, but according to the Bible, his territory is "this [entire] world!"

Satan is known as the prince of darkness as well as an angel of light. This means that he presents himself in both overwhelmingly evil manifestations *and* in deceptively innocent ways.

Bernard Madoff's clients innocently thought they were placing their savings into the hands of a highly successful investor with a sterling reputation. But the devil had deceived these investors through this wicked deviser, and Bernie *made off* with $50-billion worth of other people's money.

Scripture also tells us that Satan is the prince of the air. If he is the prince of the air, then he must obviously have reign over the air *waves.* That's right. Satan rules most forms of mass communication in this world. No wonder radio and television have become so corrupt. In addition to the graphic sex and gratuitous violence on television, we even have TV shows called *Hell Date* and *Hell's Kitchen.*

But Satan, the prince, does not operate alone. He stands atop a strong organizational pyramid that makes a Fortune 500 company look like a recently shuttered mom-and-pop resale shop.

Strong, situated and empowered beneath him is a diverse chain of command. Directly underneath the prince there are what the Bible calls *powers.* Powers is an Old English word for the modern English word *authority.* By the very nature of the word *authority,* we know that these entities must be fairly high up the chain, and indeed they are. These authorities preside over a conglomeration of demons.

Paul goes on to write in verse 12 that "we wrestle against rulers of the darkness of this world..." *Rulers* is the Old English word for the modern English word *leaders.* And we know one cannot be a leader absent of followers; so obviously, underneath these leaders there is a contingent of demonic followers.

A typical chain of command in the business world is: 1-3, 3-5, 5-7. That is, one person manages three people, those three people manage five people, those five people manage seven people, and so on. So taking this model—which is surely inferior to a supernatural model—and applying it to Satan's forces, we find that on any given day we can face up to 66 demonic soldiers.

And you say you don't have time to put on your armor in the morning?! No wonder we get so many whippings! My friends, knowing this, how can we possibly justify resisting a daily, instructional talk with God each morning that ends with a meditation of tactical strategies to overcome the devil? After all, that is the only means of defense against our very, very formidable foe.

Furthermore, we must be fully prepared to fight someone who is fully prepared to fight us. And when we fail to prepare accordingly, we leave ourselves vulnerable to regular annihilation. Imagine the outcome of a battle when one side's commanding officer fails to plan a strategy. Instead, he decides to just 'wing it' and hope for the best. Not only will *he* be destroyed, but also those who follow him. What an egregious tragedy it is, my friends, when we allow those who follow us to remain ill-prepared.

Even the military generals who planned the 2003 invasion of Iraq now concede that we did not adequately strategize to pacify the country after the fall of Saddam Hussein. And the tragic result of this lack of strategic planning was thousands of U.S., coalition and civilian casualties.

Depending on where we are in our spiritual maturity, we will face different degrees of opposition. If we are baby Christians, we most likely will wrestle primarily with the enemy's followers. However, as we mature and God gains continuous victories for us over demonic oppression, the enemy will begin to challenge us with increasingly formidable spiritual devils. In other words, new levels bring new devils.

As one is called into high-ranking Christian leadership, he may eventually be challenged by the prince himself. Look at Adam, Job, Peter and our Lord Jesus Christ. And then consider the modern-day Christian leaders who have been tempted by Satan and thereby tainted by scandal. This, my friends, is why it is so imperative that we pray for our pastors.

And it is also for this reason that I exhort you, brethren, to never underestimate the value of preparation. It has to be personal, practical and tactical. Advance with confidence as you prepare for power over the prince.

Demonic Oppression

If you have been born again, you undoubtedly have come to occasionally experience some form of demonic oppression. Now the devil is very deceptive and attempts to hide the fact that he is actually attacking us. It is very rare that we will face a situation and say, "Wow! That was surely a demonic moment!"

> TODAY'S DAILY MEDS
>
> *Never underestimate the value of preparation. It has to be personal, practical and tactical.*

However, I recall one such occasion that took place early in my ministry. At the time, about 80 people were attending our Friday-night addictions program. On this particular day, I was travelling home on Sunday afternoon from a weekend vacation with my family when I received a phone call from a student in my class whom we'll call Joe. He was a good man with a wife, two children and a steady job at an automobile assembly plant.

However, about every 6 months or so, Joe would go off the deep end and use drugs for an extended time. After one such binge he called me, and as I answered the phone, I realized that I was speaking to a very strung-out and troubled man. It was obvious what had happened to Joe: he had been out using for many days, wanted desperately to pull out of his crisis but could not muster the strength to do it alone.

Sensing the urgency of the situation, I agreed to meet Joe later that night after church at a local coffee shop. Imagine my surprise when later that evening I walked into church and saw him sitting in the back row, agitated and sweating profusely. I proceeded to walk back and spend a few minutes with him.

It seemed very odd to me that he would leave a dope house and come directly to church. Throughout my years of addiction, church was the last place I would want to go following a binge. So I asked him what happened and why he showed up at church. To this day, Joe's response to my question rests eerily upon my heart. He said:

"I'd been binging for days, and earlier today, after I spoke with you, some guy snuck up on me and took a picture of me. He then ran off laughing. The moment the flash went off, I felt something come over me. As I felt this presence on me, I took off! I ran for hours trying to get away from *it*, but I can't seem to shake it or this feeling!"

At that point, I prayed briefly with Joe and then told him that I would see him later at his house. With a white face and an obviously spooked demeanor, I returned back to my wife.

After church, I dropped off my wife and kids at home and drove the three blocks to Joe's home. I knocked on the door and got no answer, so I decided to just let myself in. I searched his house in an attempt to locate him, but to no avail. Finally, as an afterthought, I decided to check the basement. Sure enough, there he was sitting on the cold concrete floor. Though he had not used drugs all day, he had perspiration dripping from the features of his face and had eaten nothing. He was in desperate straits and deeply oppressed.

The Holy Spirit immediately told me what to do. I picked him up, placed him in a kneeling position, and began to cry out the very blood of Jesus upon this man. As I lifted my voice calling the dark spiritual forces to leave him alone, he began to cry and squirm. But within seconds he was calmed, within minutes he was eating, and within an hour he was at peace with God and chuckling with me.

I had never in my life seen anything like that, nor have I since then, and I pray I never will. After Joe had calmed down, I stood there in a state of utter shock over what had just happened. It was very clear that we had just eradicated a demonic force from our presence.

Satisfied with his condition, I left his house and began driving the few blocks to my home. As I got about a block away from my house, I began to feel peculiar. An inexplicable sense of anxiety swept over me, and nausea began to well up in my throat. Soon thereafter, I realized what was happening. It hit me! The demonic spirit that had oppressed Joe was beginning to oppress me.

Immediately, I pulled the car off into the grass and launched into a fervent prayer of desperation. As I began to sweat, I rolled down the car window, allowing fresh air to circulate throughout the vehicle. I pleaded for protection from God and separation from this demonic presence. Suddenly, I felt a calming influence that overwhelmed that external pressure. It was real; I know it was real!

This story is a clear-cut example of a high-level spiritual attack. I don't know who earned it— Joe or me—but I know who endured it—Joe *and* me! In this case, there was absolutely no ambiguity concerning the source of the oppression that Joe, and then I, had felt.

A Personal Attack

I recently experienced a similar incident, albeit somewhat less intense. My wife Lori and I were blessed with a trip to Florida. We were excited because this was going to be the first time we would be able to spend extended quality time away from the children in many years.

While in Florida, Lori asked if she could get her hair "island braided." She had this done years before, and we both liked it, so I said: "Sure, why not." After looking and asking around, sure enough, we found a place that would braid her hair in such a style.

As we entered the salon, we were surprised to see a very dingy looking interior with one chair and a cracked piece of glass substituting for a mirror. Outside, the usually busy streets were dead and nearly vacant, since it was the off-season. The only passersby seemed to be vagrants of some sort, or otherwise people living a hard-knocks lifestyle.

It was about 6 p.m., and the female stylist agreed to braid my wife's hair, saying that it would take a couple of hours. (As it turned out, it took four.)

As Lori was preparing to sit in the chair, I went out to park the car. Upon my return, I could just sense that this hair stylist was deeply troubled. She kept going on and on about how badly she hated everything in her life. Lori, who is usually not a very vocal person, knew what this woman needed and had already begun to meekly share the gospel with her.

Before long, Lori and the hair stylist had a good rapport going. It quickly became clear to me that a woman who was typically nasty had taken to my wife and was treating her very kindly. Things were going well—for now, anyway.

But it could not have been more than 20 minutes later when a shaky looking older man came poking his head in the salon. He looked around suspiciously for a few moments and left without speaking a word. This re-occurred with increasing frequency over the next hour or two. Each time the man showed up, I could visibly see the hair stylist become more tense and agitated.

About three hours into the braiding, Lori and I were both getting tired. At this point, a very cordial looking woman entered the salon and greeted the stylist with a kind salutation. They spoke for a minute or two, and then the woman turned to leave.

All of a sudden, the stylist went absolutely berserk. Her friend had been standing there smoking a cigarette the whole time without the stylist uttering a word of objection. But apparently, her friend's movement toward the door triggered the stylist's verbal tirade against her.

She then proceeded to throw an object across the room and began to pursue her friend, screaming and cursing along the way. Needless to say, Lori and I were shocked. The situation eventually died off, and the friend left without further incident. The stylist then returned to Lori without a word and began to finish braiding her hair.

As she was working the strands of hair, I could tell she was being overly rough by the painful winces streaking across Lori's face. Tears began to well up in my wife's eyes, and that did it for me. I had seen enough. So I said, "Ma'am, you're making my wife uncomfortable. Would you mind calming down?"

The stylist turned with a snarling curl upon her lip and stared down at me, as I was reading my book in a chair. A moment later, she unleashed a second verbal assault—this one even fiercer than the first! And it was directed at me! Her voice escalated proportionally with the foulness of her language, and it did not take long before a half-dozen of her vagrant "friends" closed in on the scene as if to assist in this lady's aggressive behavior.

This threw me into defensive mode, so I jumped up from my chair, desperately trying to recall the moves used in a Bruce Lee movie I had recently watched. I was sure I was going to have to physically defend my wife and me. Just then, a thought occurred to me: I did not want to be an aggressor in any way and undermine my wife's witnessing to this woman.

My guard came down, and I was able to resolve the situation with humble, calming words. I told the stylist, "You just finish my wife's hair, and I'll stand over here by the door." Ten minutes later, she finished and I paid her, adding a generous gratuity.

As we were walking out the door, the stylist said something that caught me off-guard. She said, "You guys just need to pray for me." At that point, I was 100-percent certain that what we had just encountered was nothing less than a demonic attack. Satan was fighting my wife's efforts to share the gospel. Little did I know that this particular battle was far from over.

That night Lori was visibly shaken. But I assumed that to be normal, considering the circumstances, so we retired early for the evening. The next day, Lori, who is typically joyful and perky in the mornings, awoke with an anger that completely betrayed her character. This demeanor persisted and effectively ruined our day. I couldn't sense what was going on, and she wouldn't tell me anything either. It was terribly frustrating, to be perfectly honest.

That night, I took Lori out to a quiet little seafood place that was as docile and separated from the world as one could have hoped. The only people in the restaurant were a few senior citizens who were minding their own business and not infringing upon our privacy at all.

However, Lori could not take it. She felt as if the people in the room were staring at her. As our appetizers arrived tableside, I threw some money on the table and pulled Lori out of the restaurant. When we exited to the back alley, I noticed an inordinate amount of perspiration upon her skin and tautness in her muscles. I knew then what I was seeing. All I could think to do was to put my hands on her and begin to pray for her. It wasn't long before her spirit calmed, and we began to talk through the issue. It soon became apparent what had happened.

The day before, as my wife encountered the troubled hairstylist. That same demonic force that troubled that hairstylist was now bringing oppression upon my wife . Ever since that incident, my wife had been tormented with feelings of anger and discontent—just like the stylist was the day before.

Finally, we prayed again and peace filled her heart. Lori said she was content with my menu selections, so we returned to the restaurant for a phenomenal evening, and then to our room. All seemed to be well. But later, as I was drifting off to sleep that night, I felt my wife squirming in the sheets next to me. When I asked her what was wrong, she replied: "I'm not doing so well. Will you pray with me again?"

So, I began to pray with her. Afterwards, she thanked me, but I could tell that she was still bothered. I did not know what else to do at this point, so I just started singing *Victory in Jesus* in a soft, calm and soothing tone. I sang to her until she fell asleep.

The next morning, my wife was fine, and she thanked me appreciatively. And, as far as I can tell, she has been fine ever since. One thing is certain, however, it was not easy to shake off that demonic level of devil!

The two previous illustrations are obvious examples of satanic activity. Now, let me be clear: I do not believe in satanic *possession* of a believer, but I do believe in demonizing *oppression* of believers.

This is what the apostle Paul is telling us when he says, "We wrestle..." We are engaged in a perpetual war against our enemy, and our only weapon is the sword of the Spirit, which is the word of God (Ephesians 6:17). Unfortunately, our enemy will very rarely allow his demonic attacks to be so easily recognized. Most of the time, he will disguise his efforts through myriad clever tactics.

Bill Wilson, co-founder of Alcoholics Anonymous, described alcohol as "cunning, baffling and powerful."1 But he could have easily been describing the devil.

Thus, I want to share with you some signs that can alert us to the fact that we—or someone whom we love—are under a spiritual attack. Knowing these signs can help us to avoid being slack during our attack. After all, the worst mistake one can make is to not know who their enemy is and begin to fight another fellow soldier. Soldiers fight better when the enemy

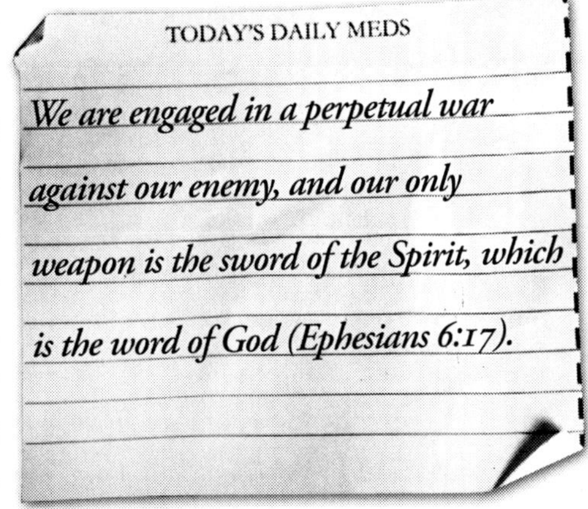

line is in front of them, not between them. Moreover, by knowing and being able to recognize these signs, you will be able to avoid many interpersonal problems in your life.

For instance, when my wife was going through the previously described spiritual oppression, I did not know what was actually occurring. Because of this, the devil was able to gain small amounts of victory as he had my wife behave in ways that caused division between us. Had I truly known from the beginning who our adversary was, I would have been able to be more patient toward her and focus my defense against the source of the problem—the devil.

By recognizing our real foe, we can give our loved ones a break. We will realize that it's actually the enemy who is seeking to destroy our relationships by placing enmity between ourselves and others.

The first spiritual principle I want to point out is how we may use our walk as an indicator of our stability to engage in warfare. Ephesians 6:10 begins, "Finally, my brethren, be strong in the Lord...." The #1 sign that we are engaged in and unprepared for an attack is when we notice our walk with God is in a weakened state.

The word *in* means *surrounded by the limits of.* So when we are consistently placing ourselves within God's boundaries, and in the power of His Word, we are strong. Our enemy is very smart, and he knows each one of us extremely well.

Satan, therefore, is not going to launch a spiritual attack against us until he is able to weaken our defenses. How does he do this? He does this, my friend, by methodically distracting us from diligence in our commitment to "personal trainer time" with Jesus.

If you find that you have not been as faithful as you should be in your God-and-I time, or even in your meditations throughout the day, brace yourself for an attack. I can assure you that you are either in the midst of one, or one is soon coming!

Now, allow me to caution you here. Just because you wake up and read your Bible every morning does not mean you are walking with God. I once met a man who for 43 straight years awoke at 3:30 a.m. every day and read his Bible until 5 a.m.

He *thought* that he had a terrific walk with the Lord. However, this very man brought great shame to himself when he was caught in immoral behavior. My friends, how does a man who reads his Bible for an hour and a half each and every day for 43 years engage in such behavior? The answer is that his *talk* with God did not translate into a solid *walk* with God.

People engage in praise and prayer, and they get into the Word, but their communication with the Lord is only one way. God doesn't want to hear a monologue. He desires a dialogue, too. Our talks with God must be two-way to put us in position to successfully walk with God.

One-way communication with the Lord serves only to polish our armor. But we sometimes fail to actually *place* it on! It is the two-way communication that dresses us fully with the protection of our spiritual battle gear. And, when God speaks to you, take copious notes.

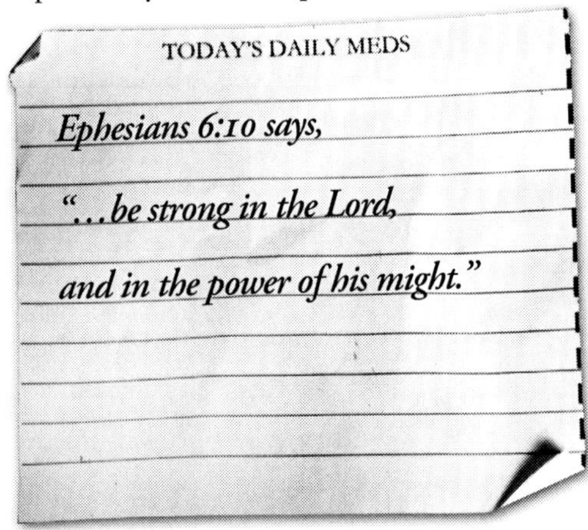

A Power Vacuum

The second indicator that you are—or are about to be—subject to a spiritual attack is when you find that the Lord's power is absent from your life. The second part of Ephesians 6:10 says, "...

be strong in the Lord, and in the power of his might." We see that we are told to revel in His mighty power, and more importantly, we are to display God's power. God blesses everybody with their own unique gift mix; but in order to really accomplish great things for Him, we must rely upon Him to be the power source in our lives.

For years, the ministry of Reformers Unanimous has grown and prospered. And like any Christian, I would occasionally question how much of the success could be attributed to me, and how much was a result of the Lord. I'll tell you my friends: I will *never* make that mistake again.

During this past year, I discovered firsthand what it is like having God's power absent from my life. As I pushed on through periods of unexplainable spiritual dearth, I obtained a newfound appreciation for what the Lord has actually done *through* me and *through* our staff to build this ministry. It has become perfectly clear that the success of RU has nothing to do with me. It is all Him!

This raises the question: How can one know if he has God's power in his life? Well, one way is to knowingly and experientially have had His power, and then to periodically lose it, as I sensed happened to me. Otherwise, I believe that the Holy Spirit is fairly clear with us regarding this. If you are lacking God's power, your Christian life will undoubtedly be lacking in victories. If this is where you find yourself, friend, you best prepare yourself because the enemy will not be far behind.

Satan is a liar and a coward. He will not take us on at our strongest. Oh no, he will wait until we are operating in our own power, then he will strike. As it is normal for us to occasionally drift away at times from the Lord's power, we must make it a point to recognize that we are doing so and prepare ourselves for the inevitable attack that is to come on these occasions.

Thirdly, a spiritual attack may be either occurring or imminent in your life if you have been consistently failing to refresh your armor daily. The Bible tells us in Ephesians 6:11 to "put on the whole armor of God, that ye may be able to stand against the wiles of the devil." The key here is that we must put on *new* armor each and every day.

Imagine going to work one day wearing your very best suit. As you walk into the office, your coworkers all take notice and compliment you on your nice-looking outfit. All day long, your dress seems to impress those whom you are around. In this case, you succeeded in dressing yourself properly—for the day.

But notice that by wearing that suit you were only successful for that day. If you were to arrive back at work the following day wearing the very same suit, do you think people would be as impressed with your style? Of course not. And this, my friends, is exactly how the devil views our spiritual armor. When we spend time with the Lord in solid two-way communication, effectively putting on our armor each and every day, we impress our enemy with the fact that we are prepared for that day. We are dressed for success. Thus, we keep Satan at bay.

Finally, Paul tells us in the second half of verse 11 that if all is well and done properly, we "...may be able to stand against the wiles of the devil." *Wiles* is the Old English word for the modern English word *schemes*. Now, by the very nature of schemes, they are executed in a deceptive manner. In other words, one does not know when he is in the midst of a scheme.

Instead, it is not until one has been *scammed* that he can look back and say that he was the victim of a scheme, or wile. So if you find yourself frequently ending up on the wrong side of righteousness and looking back scratching your head, wondering what just happened, I can guarantee you, my friend, you either just got burnt by a spiritual attack or are in the midst of one.

Granted, you are probably wondering right about now what good it possibly does to be able to identify a spiritual attack *after* it occurs. After all, our goal is to identify that we are in danger of experiencing an assault and then preventing it. But, my friend, it is also important for us to understand what exactly the origin of these relatively minor falls is. It is not the people around us who cause such problems to occur, but rather it is the dark forces engaging us in a never-ending battle.

So why, pray tell, do we insist on blaming those around us? Too often we will unleash our fury upon our innocent loved ones simply because we cannot comprehend the true origin of an attack. If we understand the real nature of the assault on us—a spiritual attack for which we did not prepare—it will help us to immediately take steps to gain victory over it. If we know this truth and fail to obey its teaching when attacked by another, we should sense a need to apologize. For this *devil* is only coming at this *rebel* because he senses I am *disabled.*

By realizing these key indicators of the presence of the enemy, we can rightly focus our attention upon things that will help us to prevail against our true adversary—the devil.

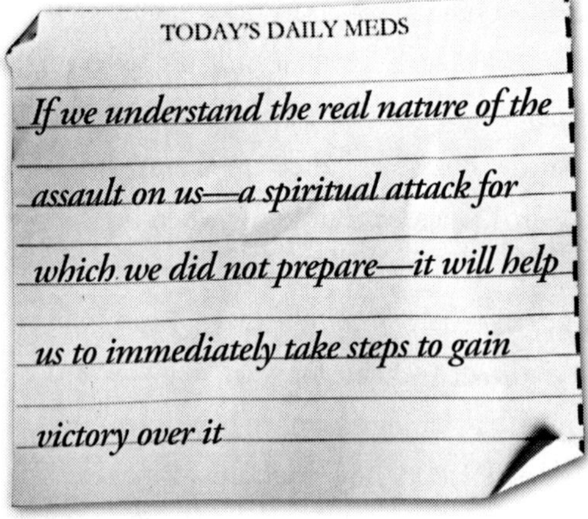
TODAY'S DAILY MEDS

If we understand the real nature of the assault on us—a spiritual attack for which we did not prepare—it will help us to immediately take steps to gain victory over it

My friends, it is my hope and prayer that you will take what we have learned and apply it to your lives so that you may be better prepared in advance, or more quickly recover, while in a wiles of Ol' Scratch ! After all…we must never slack during an attack!

In our next chapter, we will discuss demonic devices of the devil. We will begin by asking you this question: "Are you ignorant of the devil's devices?"

FOUR

RU IGNORANT OF DEMONIC DEVICES?

Having been in church all but ten years of my life, I have had the opportunity to watch many young Christians grow into adults. Our pastor, Dr. Paul Kingsbury, has faithfully preached the Word to them day in and day out throughout their lives. He has made it his life's work to pour every ounce of effort into discipling his church members to become active, vibrant Christians.

Dr. Kingsbury is second to none when it comes to developing lay leaders within his congregation. But despite his best efforts, we still have a gross majority in our church that go on to battlefield inadequacy. Despite his unmatched skill and his leadership team's ministry, many kids still manage to get off track.

As a third-party observer and former "Christian-school kid gone bad", it is very painful for me to watch as the parents of a wayward child shift most or all of the blame on our pastor, criticizing him for their child's failures. What these parents fail to realize, my friend, is that **we wrestle not against flesh and blood!** It is simply a matter of displaced frustration. The Bible tells us that people do not fail us as much as we allow spiritual forces to defeat us.

If we know this, and acknowledge it in our lives, then we will avoid making the error of blaming those dearest to us for life's unfortunate circumstances. If we can master this meditation, we will spare our churches and families from a great deal of interpersonal division and discord.

In the previous chapter, we looked at Biblical signs that indicate we are either in the midst of a spiritual attack, or are about to experience one. In this chapter, we will key into one particular area of spiritual warfare: vulnerability.

II Corinthians 2:5-11

"But if any have caused grief, he hath not grieved me, but in part: that I may not overcharge you all. Sufficient to such a man is this punishment, which was inflicted of many. So that contrariwise ye ought rather to forgive him, and comfort him, lest perhaps such a one should be swallowed up with overmuch sorrow. Wherefore I beseech you that ye would confirm your love toward him. For to this end also did I write, that I might know the proof of you, whether ye be obedient in all things. To whom ye forgive anything, I forgive also: for if I forgave any thing, to whom I forgave it, for your sakes forgave I it in the person of Christ; **lest Satan should get an advantage of us: for we are not ignorant of his devices."**

In this passage, Paul is alluding to I Corinthians 5, where we learn of a young man in Corinth who was caught up in an immoral relationship with his mother-in-law. At that time, Paul rebuked the church for not taking this man's sin seriously, and called for them to cast him from the fellowship. The Corinthians heeded this advice and removed him from the church.

However, in II Corinthians 2, we see that this man had turned his life around—which is the intended outcome of such discipline. He responds properly to the church discipline imposed upon him and is eventually in position to be restored.

This man now appeared to be in line with God's will, but yet many of the church members refused to restore him. They could find no mercy for this repentant believer, and a spirit of forgiveness was all but out of the question. It is for this reason that Paul exhorts the church of Corinth to forgive this man.

He says, "Wherefore I beseech you that ye would confirm your love toward him…To whom ye forgive anything, I forgive also: for if I forgave any thing, to whom I forgave it, for your sakes forgave I it in the person of Christ…"

The verse that follows holds the key truth that I wish to focus on in this chapter. In verse 11, he continues, "lest Satan should *get an advantage of us*: for <u>we are not ignorant of his devices</u>."

Now, given all that we have seen about Satan, we most certainly cannot afford to give him any advantage in our perpetual battle against him. No way can we allow him one inch with which he may maneuver against us. Note, however, the second half of verse 11: "… for we are not ignorant of his devices." Now, in my opinion, Paul was being a bit presumptuous when making this conclusion. I feel many Christians, including myself, at times *are* quite ignorant of the devil's devices.

If I were to ask most church congregations that I am blessed to address whether they felt ignorant, or instead, privy to Satan's devices, I am confident that I would receive an aggregate blank stare.

Although the Word of God sheds light upon some of Satan's tactics, most churched people unintentionally overlook or are commonly unaware of these satanic tactics.

I would speculate that this is the tact of a very capable opponent who seeks to keep us ignorant by shielding us from these devices. In the following paragraphs, I want to expose six of these demonic devices that I have found and to which Paul may be referring. It is my objective to help you, our readers, say with confidence that you "are not ignorant of his devices." By knowing these devices, Paul stated, we can avoid giving the devil any advantage over us.

Device No. 1:

The devil seeks to *drive us to despair*. He will often achieve this by destroying our confidence—not only our own self-confidence, but even more so our confidence in God! The Latin derivative of the word *confidence* is *con fideo*, or *with faith*. The devil attempted to persuade Jesus to question His own faith in God's goodness while tempting Him in the wilderness.

Satan instigated Jesus by taunting Him, essentially saying: "If thou be the Son of God, if you really have control over this, why don't you do something other than what God wants and get out of here?" The devil attempted to drive Him to despair. Jesus, however "a hungered," was quickly restored by

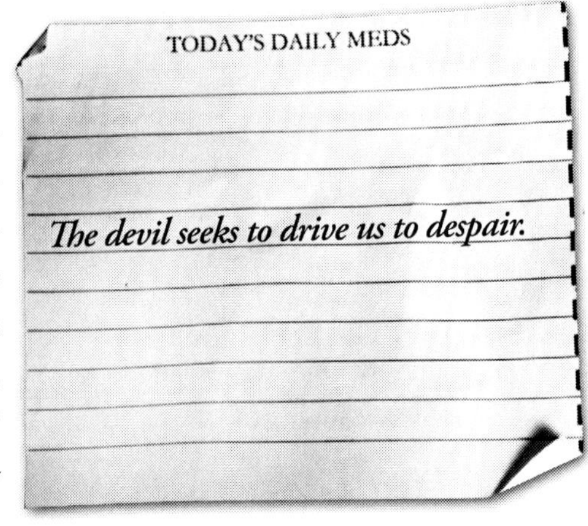

His faith when He said: "Get thee hence, Satan" (Matthew 4:10).

The devil plays the same trick on us. He wants us to despair from lost opportunities, neglected responsibilities, or our futile attempts to succeed through self-effort. Whether frustrated while serving God in our own power or completely rebelling and experiencing the consequences thereof, Satan wants us to despair that we are incapable of gaining God's mercy.

My friends, confession toward God and repentance from the world will surely be met with God's longsuffering mercy. Judgment is reserved for that day far away; but as repentant children, we need not despair, Jesus is there!

Or as Christian songwriter John M. Moore so beautifully put it:

Days are filled with sorrow and care,
Hearts are lonely and drear;
Burdens are lifted at Calvary,
Jesus is very near.

Burdens are lifted at Calvary, Calvary, Calvary.
Burdens are lifted at Calvary, Jesus is very near.

Cast your care on Jesus today,
Leave your worry and fear;
Burdens are lifted at Calvary,
Jesus is very near.

Burdens are lifted at Calvary, Calvary, Calvary.
Burdens are lifted at Calvary, Jesus is very near.

Troubled soul, the Saviour can see,
Ev'ry heartache and tear;
Burdens are lifted at Calvary,
Jesus is very near.

Burdens are lifted at Calvary, Calvary, Calvary.
Burdens are lifted at Calvary, Jesus is very near.[1]

Device No. 2:

The devil seeks to *make us presume*. Presumption is destroying our ministries. The framings of personal perceptions of self, or critical presumptions of others, are a tactical technique the devil uses to spread not only the kind of despair listed above but also discord and division among the brethren. Moreover, presumptuous thinking leads to the competitive performance-based Christianity that Paul predicted would be the death knell for our personal ability to win the world to Christ.

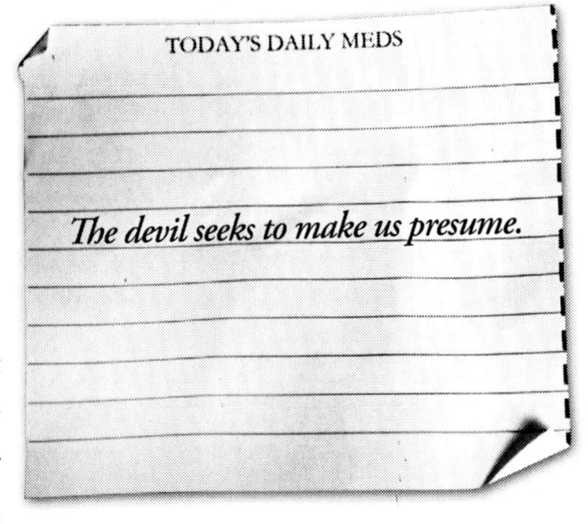

Philippians 2:14-15

"Do all things without murmurings and disputings: That ye may be blameless and harmless, the sons of God, without rebuke, in the midst of a crooked and perverse nation, among whom ye shine as lights in the world;"

Think about today's conflicts in Christendom. There are arguments about who has the biggest mega-church, the most effective ministries, and the most money? As long as there is presumptuous thinking, there will be an unnecessary *competitive* performance among God's people. The success of this demonic tactic is why we carry such blame among the lost and viewing public. God will someday reveal the harm we have done to those closest to us who have yet to see His light emanate from us.

How does this critical position affect our disposition? Satan often places in our hearts an attempt to discern another person's motives. This process is seldom or even never beneficial to our meditations. My friends, I can promise you most perceptions are straight from the devil. It's nothing but wicked, negative thinking! How can anyone, with a limited point of view, logically assume what kind of thinking lies behind *another* person's actions? The only viable conclusion is we are led through satanic oppression to do so! The turmoil caused by such behavior allows the enemy to gain a foothold into our minds. That foothold can become a stronghold and eventually it will morph into a stranglehold and destroy a life.

But if we are more aware of our tendency to cooperate with this satanic strategy, we may be able to catch ourselves in the act, cast down that negative, critical, pessimistic or competitive thought, and terminate the enemy's plan before it fully develops. We must never presume to know what is going on in others' lives, let alone in their minds! If Satan can't destroy us by appearing to lift us up through *reflections* of prideful adequacy or superiority, he will seek to tear us down by terrorizing us with *perceptions* of inadequacy and inferiority to others.

Device No. 3:

The devil seeks to tempt us *to uneasiness*. We all go through dry times in our walk with God. There are peaks and valleys that we experience; we never stay the same. The Christian life is an alive, dynamic experience that is in an ever-changing state. When we are young in our spiritual development and just beginning our Hid-N-Life pilgrimage, we tend to still lack grace. We maintain strong human tendencies toward "soul" control of the body.

However, when a Christian is in this early stage, the Lord—in His goodness—is often quick to impart undeserved, supernatural illumination to us. This is when His abundant grace allows Him to overlook our preference to "do good" in the flesh. We must recognize it will not always be this easy. As we grow into a more perfect man in God's amazing grace, it becomes more of *a maze of grace*. It seems as if Christ frequently leaves us to ourselves to find His grace in amazing ways.

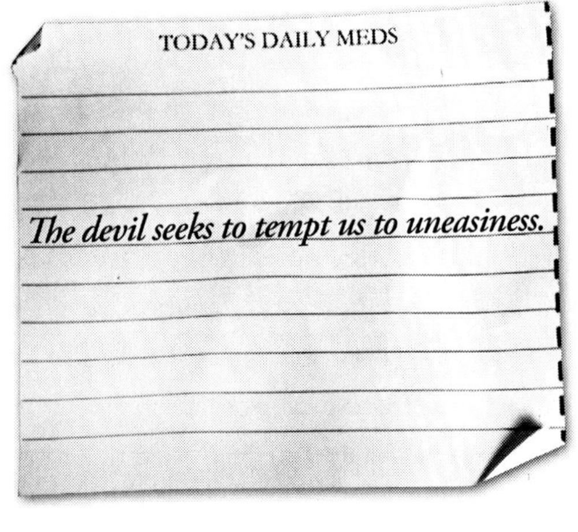

During this time, He seemingly permits an awful deadness in our spirit. If we do not sense this stagnation or dehydration, it can lead to a personal dread that tends to overwhelm us. Satan is then able to sense our moment of dread and vex our righteous soul to impatience in the turmoil of our temporary tribulations.

The devil achieves this by inculcating in us fear, which is his most effective weapon of mass destruction. If he can get us to feel afraid, he can get us to pick up a drink, a drug or even a gun.

The Bible states that "God hath not given us the spirit of fear" (II Timothy 1:7). Well, if God doesn't give us the spirit of fear, then who does? There is no love, much less peace, in fear! A common church acrostic for FEAR is: False Evidence Appearing Real. The devil presents phony evidence to make us feel afraid, very afraid.

It is normal for the Lord to allow us to experience this sense of false dread and deadness so we may reach a new level of dependence on Him and in Him. It is not necessarily a result of sin in our lives but rather it is often in preparation for the Lord's plan for our lives. This season of unrest is designed to strengthen our intimacy with the Lord. It is an imperative step in the Christian life.

This winter of discontent symbolizes our time in the tomb. We are not experiencing our cross for we are free of the conviction of any known sin at this time; however, we have also yet to be risen with Christ. It is a time of loneliness that drives us to Jesus. However, the devil sees our expressions of dearth and attempts to make us uneasy, to trouble us, to cause us to leave the fellowship of His tomb prematurely and ineffectually. He will do this by driving us into situations where we experience blasphemous and unbelieving thoughts, thereby causing our faith to weaken if we do not take appropriate measure. Such thoughts can cause torment in our hearts that can afford Satan an advantage over us in battle.

Device No. 4:

The devil further seeks to tempt us so he may *distract us from worship*. He may do this even by luring us to occupy most of our time with church activities. This may cause us to neglect our prayer and Bible study, and thereby neglect our kingdom work. I've heard people say, "I didn't get much out of the worship service today." I find these words to be quite blasphemous. Worship is not something we get. God "gets" from worship! We are to give worship to Him.

The in-dwelling Spirit of the Lord provides us with three valuable stimulations. Each is dependent upon the other. Those stimulations are conviction, worship and intuition. When we are under conviction, it is God's design for us to repent of a particular wrong, i.e., sin. When we delay or refuse to confess and repent of that which He has convicted us, it grieves the Spirit of God. A grievous Spirit will weaken our worship.

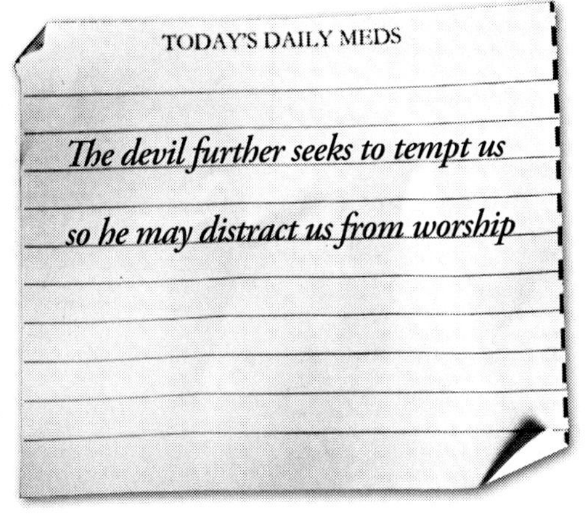

Weakened worship then staves off the intuitive leading of the Holy Ghost. This renders us "soulical" believers, destined to develop our soul (character) but unable to develop spiritually—until we repent of this cycle.

If the devil can bring us into sin, he can overwhelm our conviction with his own condemnation. We know that condemnation does not come from God (Romans 8:1); it comes from the devil. He has this access as a result of our unwillingness to *conform* to the convictions of the Holy Ghost.

If you are not living *in* Christ Jesus, then you will surely experience condemnation. When in condemnation, we reject the Spirit's conviction. That's how Satan keeps us in sin, out from under Him, and distracted from meaningful worship in our spirit. This device of the devil is seldom understood.

We must simply resist the condemnation that leads us to use euphemisms like: "I just can't do it" or "I've always been this way" or "I'm just like my mom" or "It's all their fault." Then we can properly affirm the Holy Spirit's convictions, which say: "You can do all things through Christ" (Philippians 4:13) and "Greater is He that is in you, than he that is in the world" (I John 4:4) and "He which hath begun a good work in you will perform it until the day of Jesus Christ" (Philippians 1:6).

These promises are for those who confess their sins, are forgiven of their sins and, thus, are cleansed of all unrighteousness. This position changes our disposition and allows us to return to worship in the Spirit (Philippians 3:3) and to experience the dynamic intuitive leading of the Holy Ghost in the important decisions of life!

The enemy hates when we seek the Lord and frequently will attempt to keep us from doing so. Have you ever sat down with your Bible and a nice hot cup of coffee, only to come to feel as if the Lord has failed to show up for the appointment? This sometimes is due to simple lack of discipline on our part, but it can sometimes be another device of the devil: outside pressure on the mind to stimulate broken concentration of the heart. Once again we have been distracted from our worship.

Satan also will at times put slanderous and blasphemous thoughts into our heads—like he did to Ananias and Sapphira in Acts 5:3—so that we will lie not only to man, but to the Holy Ghost! These distracting tendencies destroy our worship and render God's Word dry and powerless to us. Again, our worship is hindered.

While we are in the midst of worshipping, the devil will often assault us with false perceptions that cause us to question God or to think of things past or future. In this distraction, he might stunt our studies or stymie us from the hearing of faith. Satan is also a master at distracting our worship of God by creating dangerous perceptions through timely and deceitful questions. He did it to Adam and Eve, and he even tried it with Jesus.

Just as he used the lawyer to sow discord amongst the brethren by posing inappropriate questions that were geared to challenge Jesus' authority (Matthew 22:34-40), he will also use others to do the same in our lives—especially in times when we are seeking God with desperation. It is vitally important that we realize our worship is not dry because God is mad at us. He loves us and wants clear communication with us. But our worship is stunted because of the enemy who is distracting us.

The Lord understands that the devil attacks us in this manner, and He likewise extends the grace necessary to prevail against the demonic assault. But, of course, this grace is contingent upon whether or not we acknowledge that we are actually facing a device of the devil. If we fail to do so, we will most certainly provide the enemy with an advantage over us in our endless war.

Device No 5:

The devil seeks to tempt us *with carnal friends and relatives.* Many people I know claim that their friends are only strong, vibrant Christians. Allow me to break it to you: this generally is not true. The devil is very effective at blinding us to the true nature of those whom we have befriended. If we develop an unhealthy friendship—or soul-tie—with somebody, we will often overlook certain flaws in them that could become a stumbling block to our own spiritual progress.

Consider this: does the Bible say, "Whereas by one woman sin entered into the world?" No, it doesn't. It says, "Whereas by one man…" (Romans 5:12).

The devil tempted Eve to convince her husband to violate the one command that the Lord had given to him prior to Eve being created. And it was by this method that Satan introduced sin into the world. You see, the devil loves to use those close to us to marginalize many wrongdoings and weaken the Spirit-given conviction we have toward certain sins.

We see in the book of Job an example of another wife who is deceived into coaxing her husband into sin. After myriad tragedies in Job's life, Satan was able to get into the head of Job's wife and convince her to pressure her husband to simply "curse God and die" (Job 2:9). Wow! What an encourager she must have been?! In this case the devil's tactic was ultimately unsuccessful as Job withstood his wife's wrong instigation and instead brought glory to the Lord.

Yet another exemplar is Peter. In today's ministry world, he would be classified as one of Jesus' staff members. Now as a member of Jesus' staff, Peter was persuaded by the devil to say to his Boss: "Lord, spare Yourself."

The enemy put these words into Peter's heart and prompted him to speak them to Jesus in an attempt to veer away from His plan. Again, however, Jesus in His perfectness responded to Peter perfectly by saying, "Get thee behind Me, Satan" (Matthew 16:23).

You see, He recognized that it was indeed Satan who was speaking through Peter's mouth, and He called him out on it. How amazing!

Finally, take Judas Iscariot, for example. The Bible tells us the **devil put it into Judas' heart** to betray Jesus (John 13:2). Remember that Psalm 41:9 had foreshadowed the fact that Jesus would be betrayed by His "own familiar friend." Dissected and defined, what this phrase actually means is "friend of all friends," or his "best friend."

So, essentially, what we see here is the devil convincing a person to betray his best friend, effectively putting Him to death. Granted, Jesus obviously allowed this to occur, as He could have foiled Satan's plan at any time if He chose to. But instead He allowed the devil to work through Judas.

This, my friends, is an invaluable insight into one of the enemy's more effective devices. Be wary of friends and relatives; they can quickly become Psalm 1:1 Christians—ungodly counselors, habitual sinners or scornful critics. If they do, Satan will seek to use them as devices to advance *his* agenda for your life. Failure to exercise caution in following your heart in relationships will most definitely provide the devil with an advantage over you.

Device No. 6:

The devil also seeks to *lull us into complacency by withdrawing from us*. After tempting Jesus in the wilderness, the devil left Him for a season. It is along these lines that the Bible encourages us in Galatians 5:1 to "Stand fast therefore in the liberty wherewith Christ hath made us free, and be not entangled again with the yoke of bondage."

Paul tells us this so that we will remain vigilant in anticipation of the enemy, even when we are free from his presence. Paul tells us this because he knows that demonic forces will tend to walk away from us until our guard is down. And the moment we are vulnerable, he is right there ready to wreak havoc upon our lives once more.

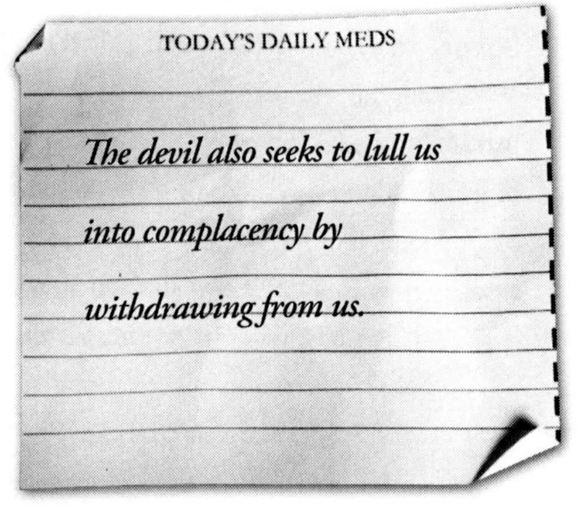

I Corinthians 10:12 says, "Wherefore let him that thinketh he standeth take heed lest he fall." This is Paul yet again cautioning us from becoming overconfident in our upright position when we find satanic oppression absent in our lives. Just like a prizefighter competing in a championship bout, the devil will do everything he can to win.

One strategy a smart boxer will employ is observing his opponent with patience until his guard goes down, or he becomes focused elsewhere. And when he senses this, WHAM! That's when that punch will come.

Satan's ploy here is not unlike the fabled "rope-a-dope" technique that Muhammad Ali used against heavily favored champion George Foreman in 1974. For seven rounds, Ali let Foreman pummel him with punches. And then, after fooling Foreman into thinking he was weakened, Ali leaped off the ropes in the eighth round and proceeded to batter Foreman at will and took back the heavyweight title with a technical knockout.

But the devil is even quicker and craftier than Ali in his prime. We must therefore be diligent in keeping our guard up, even when we feel that we are safe from the enemy and at a peak in our spiritual walk. If we are not careful in this manner, we once again offer up a free advantage to the devil—one we definitely cannot afford to concede.

Now that we have learned a little bit about our enemy and are less ignorant of his devices, let us now focus on the Biblical answer to combating these dark devices of the devil in this demonic world.

The tactical answers to spiritual warfare, and the advance preparation required to distance you from the devil's devices, are found in Paul's letter to the Ephesians. In the latter chapters of this book of the Bible, Paul goes into great detail regarding the armor of God that is to defend us from the enemy.

Allow me to briefly introduce one element of this armor that I feel is not only overlooked in our arsenal, but also underappreciated in terms of effectiveness. I am referring to "the preparation of the gospel of peace" (Ephesians 6:16).

That is right, my friends. Peace! Don't get me wrong. I am no hippie, but at the same time, how can you experience warfare when you are actually at peace? I am not speaking of peace with the enemy, for that will not happen in this life.

I am referring to being at peace with God. It takes preparation, advance preparation. And it is this advance preparation that prepares us to advance deeper into enemy territory, all the while at peace with the one who fights on our behalf. For after all, the battle is the Lord's.

So we will be learning how to give peace with God a chance to bring you peace in the midst of your storms!

FIVE

RU AT PEACE

In the previous chapter, we discussed six of the devil's devices that he uses to gain advantage over us in the perpetual battles of spiritual warfare. These devices are daunting and taunting. Although the defensive weapons of *our* warfare may be mighty, we must ensure they do not become worldly but remain wonderfully made.

Do you recall the devastated but repentant young man who sought to be restored to his church fellowship, but his brethren were unable to be at peace with him? This created an environment of turmoil that Paul concluded would unknowingly and ignorantly expose them to satanic devices.

In this chapter, I want to express how God uses peace, or for our purposes—the preparation of the gospel of peace—in order to thwart the devil's goal of creating turmoil.

It is, after all, Satan's nature to create a tumultuous environment in which to wage warfare. The Bible says, "...God is not the author of confusion, but of peace..." (I Corinthians 14:33). So if there is confusion in our lives, it is writ large in the devil's handwriting.

Remember also that the world is Satan's principality, so he will always enjoy home-field advantage. Moreover, we face not so much the devil himself but his delegated powers (authorities), leaders (rulers) and followers. So we have an entire demonic force squaring off against us. Therefore, we must take proactive measures to stand any chance of gaining or maintaining our victory over the wiles of the devil.

TODAY'S DAILY MEDS

God is not the author of confusion, but of peace..." (I Corinthians 14:33).

There is no better way to prepare for spiritual battle than to embrace the Gospel of Peace! We do this, my friends, by engaging in the power granted to us by Jesus Himself: the power of the promises of His spoken Word found throughout the New Testament explanations of sanctification.

However, we must abide in not only the Good News of Promises nor in just the Good News of Justification, but in the Good News throughout the Gospel and prophesied throughout the Old Testament. That is how we can resist devils until they flee.

This Good News is about God's redeeming grace, the new covenant, whereby Christ does the work of the Christian life. It is the Good News of His forgiveness and cleansing for sins past as well as for sins present. This Good News also includes the hope of an abundant new life.

Yesterday's newspaper may be only good for wrapping fish,

but this Good News is all wrapped up in the threefold promises of salvation: justification, sanctification and God's glorification. That is what is meant by the good news of the Good News. Wow! What a Good Newscast!

With a view of seeing all things working together for Good News, we can proactively prepare ourselves. Let us now look at how God intends for us to capitalize on this advance preparation of His Gospel of Peace.

Peace as Our Protective Weapon

In every circumstance of life there are often multiple perspectives from which situations can be viewed. But in reality, most everyone chooses one of two particular ways. As the adage goes, "There are two sides to every coin." That is, every bad thought has an opposing good thought. This is what I call the principle of negative neutralities, a negative versus a neutral or positive outlook.

There are those who most often portray life's events in a positive light, and those who see most all circumstances from a negative, or at best, neutral point of view. This means they remain silently indifferent, but far from positive in their perspectives. It's the age-old question: Is the glass half-empty or half-full? Well, for real gloom-and-doom negativists, the glass is always completely *empty*.

Regardless of whether or not one is outwardly negative, or just simply silent, it leaves them in an equally vulnerable position to be attacked meditationally from the enemy. One of the most detrimental tendencies I've observed among apathetic Christians is a propensity toward negative neutrality in the meditations of life.

The Bible states, "...whatsoever things are true, whatsoever things are honest, whatsoever things are just, whatsoever things are pure, whatsoever things are lovely, whatsoever things are of good report: if there be any virtue, and if there be any praise, think on these things" (Philippians 4:8).

Despite the apostle Paul's clear instruction that we will have no value (be any virtue) or no commendation (be any praise) if we think negatively, many of God's people will attempt to create value and expect commendation for their efforts in life, while at the same time exchanging the truth for the lies in our perceptions; the honest for the dishonest in our communications; justice for injustice in our people dealings; purity for impurity in our motives; the lovely for the ugly in our harsh rhetoric toward those most important to us; and a good report for an evil report of one another.

Paul's words here are not intended to be exceptional examples of how to properly perceive things, but they are to be the norm among God's people. Not so in today's church. I would propose that we cannot think Philippians 4:8 thoughts unless we reject negative perceptions and neutral expressions in the circumstances of life!

As British statesman Edmund Burke noted: "All that is necessary for the triumph of evil is for good men to do nothing."[1] Neutrality is negativism. Jesus said that if we are neither hot nor cold but lukewarm, He will spit us out of His mouth (Revelation 3:16).

When believers choose negative thinking in bad situations or neutral thinking in the midst of things considered good, Satan will attempt to impose outside pressure, or oppression, upon us so that he can create a mindset of turmoil.

Our neutral thinking—as well as negative, pessimistic, critical and competitive thoughts—is fertile soil for seeds of apathy, bitterness, rebellion and rejection. If the enemy succeeds in this game of mind control, my friends, we will have a very difficult time spreading the

Gospel of Peace.

One of the most crucial things we can do is *dwell well.* That is, we perceive things internally and then purposely portray them externally in a positive and uplifting manner. My friends, we must continuously reflect on our thinking to determine if we measure up to Paul's exhortation. It does us no good to simply memorize this verse. Oh no, we must adhere to it in our meditations!

Furthermore, it does us no good to meditate upon this verse if we fail to yield to it in the face of our most difficult circumstances. As we examine our thoughts, we must ask ourselves if we are negative, or even silently neutral, when we find ourselves in a tight spot. Or do we instead choose in advance to prepare ourselves so that we may be prompted to perceive adversity properly and portray it in a positive manner.

We are incapable of spreading the Gospel of Peace absent a proactive preparation to portray a positive outlook. Conversely, if we are always looking at things from an optimistic viewpoint, then we are willing to share that viewpoint while others may be attacking us and thereby defuse a vast majority of the devil's "turmoil tools" of weaponry.

By maintaining this optimistic viewpoint, we greatly limit the enemy's power against us. Though many people decry the power of positive thinking, I consider it a better resource than the weaknesses of negative thinking! Better yet, I suggest that Biblical speaking triumphs over negative thinking. But Biblical speaking will require proactive preparations and submission to the Spirit's persuasive promptings.

Preparation: The Shodding of the Feet

When breaking down the armor of God in Ephesians 6:15, Paul advises us to have our "feet shod with the preparation of the gospel of peace;" The word shod means to wrap. Now what in the world does wrapping our feet have to do with peace? Understand that Paul's illustration of our battlefield armor was most probably conceived while he spent time in a Roman prison. It is quite possible that as he peered through the dark dungeon at the Roman centurion guards, he formed metaphors in his mind about the various pieces of armor with which they were adorned.

Judging by his pointed references to it, Paul was particularly enamored by the armor piece upon the feet of the guards. As Paul wrote his epistles to various churches, he drew a parallel between the armor of the Roman soldier and the protection afforded to us through Jesus Christ.

As the jailed apostle was sitting in his cell, he could have very well looked up and pondered: "My Lord has provided me with a helmet of salvation, a breastplate of righteousness and shield of faith."

And then he may have looked down at the soldiers' feet and said, "We need the preparation of the Gospel of Peace!" Paul was quite perceptive in noting that the Gospel of Peace needed the advance preparation of wrapping to protect the Christian soldier.

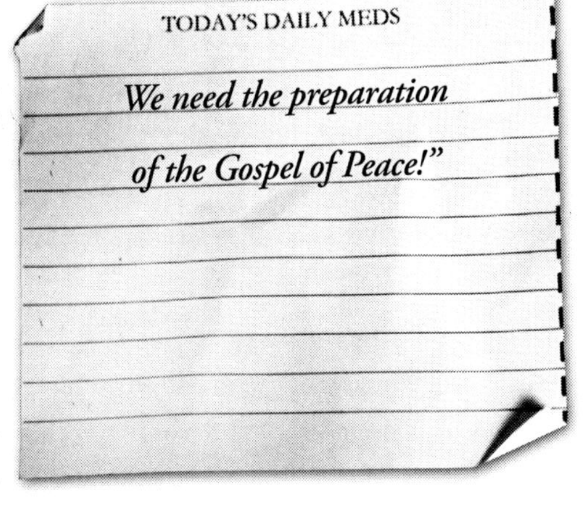

A football player takes only a few moments to put on his protective helmet and shoulder pads, but as for his feet and ankles and knees and elbows—they are a different story. It takes a lengthy measure of advance preparation in the form of time and tape to wrap these vulnerable parts of the body for the warfare he is about to engage in on the gridiron.

Likewise, my friends, it is unequivocally necessary that we, as Christian soldiers, make advance preparation in key areas of vulnerability and protect them with the Gospel of Peace to avoid or win the devil's war games.

The Roman soldiers, like our gridiron greats of old, surely spent quality time properly preparing their feet for battle. They knew that without the faculty of their feet, they would be left entirely vulnerable. It is likewise with us that if we fail to wrap our feet in advance preparation with the Gospel of Peace, we will be left wide open to the devices of the devil.

The Roman soldiers would shod, or wrap, their feet with many layers of thick cloth, fully covering the sandal. On the underside of the sandal they would apply what were called "graves of brass," similar to a brass plate, which would then also be wrapped in cloth to keep it secure and protect the bottom of the foot.

You see, in the time of the apostle Paul, it was common for an army to apply "shards," or sharp objects intended to impale the foot, in the anticipated pathways of the opposing forces. With these objects camouflaged in the path of an advancing army, the enemy would be vulnerable in two ways.

First, if they were unaware of this battle tactic, they would soon be injured and rendered incapable to advance or even retreat. They would be dead or become POWs. Secondly, if they knew of the tactic but were unprepared by failing to prepare their feet, they would be forced to focus on the pathway and thereby lose focus of their enemy.

To counter this tactic, the Romans developed a means of *prior preparation* by which they were able to safeguard their feet. Paul, having had ample opportunity to ascertain these facts, then brilliantly likened this piece of armor to our need for an advanced "preparation of the gospel of peace," prior to any spiritual attack.

Now how, pray tell, did Paul dream up this analogy? The simple answer is that he knew that by shodding their feet, the Romans were able to have peace of mind about the welfare of their footing as they engaged in battle.

Imagine a U.S. soldier fighting in a battle during, say, the Vietnam War. As he is engaging the enemy, searching the jungle foliage for signs of activity, the last thing the soldier would want to do is look down at his feet prior to every step.

Rather, the soldier requires confidence in his footwear protection so that he may advance without having to focus anywhere but *onward*! Knowing this, Paul realized it is exactly the same for us as we interact as natural men and women within the spiritual realm in which we have been placed, hence, the likening of the Gospel of Peace to the Roman foot armor.

My friends, I am not painting an evil, spooky war story complete with silly gimmicks to make the battle seem realistic. This is not *Saving Private Ryan*. It is saving people from dyin'! Spiritual warfare is very real and we must realize that we engage against demonic forces on a daily basis. Remember, we war not against flesh and blood!

Knowing this, we must choose "thoughts of peace and not of evil" in order to facilitate "an expected end" (Jeremiah 29:11). Therefore, we must prepare our hearts for peace. The only way to do this is by what Paul calls the shodding of the feet. Walking, working or warring without this "shodding" will cause us to wrestle with flesh and blood in our *soul*—when the Lord intends for our *spirit* to battle the spiritual influences surrounding us.

Remember the cartoon character Pogo? He famously said: "We have found the enemy, and he is us!" Oh, my friends, if only those cartoon writers knew how true this really is! We are our own worst enemies. We are the architects of our adversity.

The Bible tells us that the Gospel of Peace will be enjoyed as it enjoins; it will create a harmony between us and ourselves (our soul and spirit); between us and God (our spirits and His Spirit); and then as a result of that, between us and others (our soul and the souls of others).

A thorough study of God's Word will show us that God considers peace to be an imperative that is implemented by his *foot* soldiers!

Notice what Jesus taught us regarding demonic warfare.

Mark 6:1-11

TODAY'S DAILY MEDS

The Gospel of Peace will be enjoyed as it enjoins; it will create a harmony between us and ourselves (our soul and spirit); between us and God (our spirits and His Spirit); and then as a result of that, between us and others (our soul and the souls of others).

"And he went out from thence, and came into his own country; and his disciples **follo**w him. And when the Sabbath day was come, he began to teach in the synagogue: and many hearing him were astonished, saying, From whence hath this man these things? And what wisdom is this which is given unto him, that even such mighty works are wrought by his hands? Is not this the carpenter, the son of Mary, the brother of James, and Joses, and of Juda, and Simon? And are not his sisters here with us? And they were offended at him. But Jesus said unto them, A prophet is not without honour, but in his own country, and among his own kin, and in his own house. **And He could there do no mighty work**, save that he laid his hands upon a few sick folk, and healed them. And he marveled because of their unbelief. And he went round about the villages, teaching. And he called unto him the twelve, and began to send them forth by two and two; and **gave them power over unclean spirits**; And commanded them that they should take nothing for the journey, save a staff only; no scrip, no bread, no money in their purse: **But be shod with sandals**; And not put on two coats. And he said unto them, In what place soever ye enter into an house, there abide till ye depart from that place. And whosoever shall not receive you, nor hear you, when ye depart thence, shake off the dust **under your feet** for a testimony against them. Verily I say unto you, It shall be more tolerable for Sodom and Gomorraha in the day of judgment, than for that city."

Let us pause and notice a few interesting aspects about this passage. First, can we consider how amazing it will be for us when we get to heaven and can hear Jesus teach—live and in person—like these folk of His day? The Bible says the people in the synagogue were "astonished." They knew not from where this Man nor His wisdom came.

Secondly, our passage notes that the people were shocked at Jesus' insights because they knew Him as nothing more than a lowly carpenter. To see a carpenter display what appeared to be a rather scholarly Biblical education would have been rare in that day. In this passage, the people who heard Jesus speak were amazed to hear such things from who they thought was a simple man from simple means.

Thirdly, the people noted that this Man was none other than

the "son of Mary, the brother of James, and Joses, and of Juda..." This was yet another allusion to our Lord's low repute. His brothers had some sort of bad reputation, ostensibly for their kinship. The brothers were known, but Jesus, their eldest brother, was unknown.

In Bible times, this would have been very odd. The oldest was always the most notable child. Those who heard Jesus speak on this day were blown away, albeit a little curious as to how He came to possess such incredible wisdom, given His background.

If that were not enough, those who heard Jesus' proclamation noted with disdain the level of nerve that Jesus had to preach *amongst* His own people. May this be a lesson to those of us who are teaching among our own within the church. Though we know that we cannot expect the world to respect our salvation, it is sometimes even "the churched" who fail to fully respect our regeneration.

When we get right with the Lord, there is always an element of expectation on our part that our social group will embrace and equally accept what Jesus is doing in our lives. Unfortunately, as was the case with Jesus because of His heritage, this doesn't always happen. Like Jesus, we must therefore prepare ourselves for peace in the midst of our very own people's skepticism. Overcoming this will take patience and perseverance.

White House aide Charles Colson was sent to federal prison for his role in the Watergate scandal. When he got out, his conversion to Christ was met with widespread skepticism. But today Colson is widely respected as an award-winning Christian author and founder of Prison Fellowship, which ministers in more than 30 countries. He has obviously persevered.

Displaying peace in the face of skeptics will allow Christ to demonstrate His power through us in our lives. As a believer, performing your ministries at peace with other people will be *proof* to those who knew your former creature. They will eventually become comfortable with His "new creation." This is equally important to those unsaved friends in the world whom we pray will accept the Good News of the Gospel of Justification.

Finally, but most importantly, we see in this story the fact that the people who heard Jesus had such limited faith, coupled with a spirit of incredulity toward this message of peace from the ultimate Peacemaker. They scoffed that the One who could "do all things" could do "**no mighty work**, save that he laid His hands upon a few sick folk, and healed them."

So we can conclude that even Jesus has *self-imposed* limitations on His power as a result of the disbelief of those around Him and of us as well. That's right! Though Jesus could do all things, His mighty works were limited. When we are properly prepared and empowered to spread the Gospel of Peace, the only thing that will limit our effectiveness is disbelief on the part of the people to whom we are attempting to minister.

Because of negative, critical and competitive thinking, it would have taken even Jesus Himself time to build credibility among the pessimists. It is critical for us to realize people are critical! We must keep this in mind as we go forward in our work for the Lord, for there will always be naysayers.

Another reason why it is absolutely imperative that we administer the Gospel of Peace is so that we may minister in a meek humble way to those who are both scorners and nonbelievers. Our minded *platitudes* offered to their high-minded *attitudes* will defeat their pre-established spirits of division, discord, haughtiness and pride. This pride that brings division among the ranks of God's army is another well-warring tactic of the devil.

So, this raises the question: What did Jesus then do to promote peace with these unbelieving scoffers? Well, in the face of this opposition, we see in verse 11, He simply took on a particularly peaceful persona and taught his disciples to do the same. That persona was expressed in the Biblical injunction: "If you're not going to believe me, *shake off the dust under your* ***feet*** *for a testimony* ***against them...*** "

He didn't say argue with them, criticize them or even rebuke them. He simply said walk away and allow none of their disbelief to remain embedded in you or on you. For if it is on your foot, it will be figuratively on your mind. If it's on your feet, it hurts your peace.

He was cautioning them to make peace and remain at peace with themselves. But as the Bible notes, He taught that even this act of peace making must be done with unprecedented meekness and a spirit of humility.

Jesus was only able to react this way in the face of such adversity because He was *fully prepared* to distribute a Gospel of Peace! Clearly, Jesus was operating with His feet fully shod.

TODAY'S DAILY MEDS

In Hebrews 12:14, we are enjoined to "follow peace with all men... But we can't get a grip on what the devil's got gripped if all we do is gripe with one another!

I am not advocating making peace with the devil. This is, in fact, an all-out war with the devil! But we are to be at peace with God, peace with ourselves and peace with our fellow man, whether they are saved or unsaved.

In Hebrews 12:14, we are enjoined to "follow peace with all men…" Tell that to many Christian criticizers today and you will be labeled a *compromiser*. Why? Because they think we wrestle against flesh and blood. Men and women are not our enemy. Other church members are our fellow soldiers. Other like-minded churches are from the same army, just a different infantry. And other denominations that teach salvation by grace alone are part of my armed services, albeit a different division.

Additionally, the unsaved are *not* the enemy! They are the captured people for whom Christ died. They are prisoners of war who need to be released from the devil's jail. But we can't get a grip on what the devil's got gripped if all we do is gripe with one another!

All of these insights into our Savior's words are important for us to comprehend; however, the key to this passage lies in the following verses.

Mark 6:8-9_

"And commanded them that they should take nothing for their journey, save a **staff** only; no scrip, no bread, no money in their purse: But be **shod with sandals**; and not put on two coats."

Jesus commanded the 12 apostles to go forth, 2 by 2, in order to effectively spread the Gospel. His instructions about what to take along with them were very clear. He tells them to take a staff only, and to remember to be shod with sandals.

Now, my friends, there is great significance to these specific instructions. Notice that the end of verse 7 states that Jesus "gave them power over unclean spirits." Our Lord then explains what to take along with them; in essence, He is telling them **what is needed to have power over unclean spirits**! He specifically tells them that food, money, clothing and prepared speeches are of no concern or benefit. The only items that Jesus tells them they need are **a staff and feet shod with sandals**.

You see, a staff is a Biblical symbol for comfort. "…thy rod and thy staff, they comfort me" (Psalm 23:4). Jesus tells them that they will need a measure of comfort to effectively minister in the presence of demonic warfare. Also, we see that Jesus is extremely dogmatic in demanding that they have their peace derived only from **fully shod feet**.

Just as Paul later teaches in his epistles, Jesus teaches His disciples to properly prepare their feet with the Gospel of Peace for whatever house they enter to dwell. Moreover, Jesus said the apostles were to *remain* at only one home the whole time they were in a city until the day they left town.

That would require only one thing: Peace! You can't stay in people's homes for long until turmoil follows your every move. Jesus taught us to cast out demons and to win the battle of spiritual warfare against demonic forces. We would need to be comforted by a staff that would later be our comforting Holy Ghost. And He taught us to prepare ourselves to make peace with people with whom we would congregate and reconcile in ministry. Make no mistake about it. In this obscure passage, Jesus taught us more than anyone that in order to overcome unclean spirits and demonic devices, one must be entirely devoted toward PEACE!

SIX

RU RECONCILING?

Devotion to peace will require us to embrace a new ministry opportunity. It is one of tranquility in the face of adversity. It is the ministry of reconciliation. This ministry is not only your responsibility; as you embrace this new ministry, you will see that it is an enjoyable opportunity!

Our Ministry of Peace

We as Christians have one primary ministry—the ministry of Peace. Recall in chapter four we discussed some of the devil's devices, alluded to in II Corinthians 2:11. We saw how the devil operates through our ignorance of his devices. It's how he is able to gain an advantage over us. But this, my friends, is only the first step: understanding the enemy's operatives. How do we also gain an advantage over him? A few chapters later, in his second letter to the Corinthians in chapter 5, Paul provides us with a solution.

In verse 17, Paul writes: "Therefore if any man be in Christ, he is a new creature: old things are passed away; behold, all things are become new." Now, if you have been in church for any amount of time, undoubtedly you have heard this verse more times than you could number. You may very well even be able to quote it. Indeed, this is a solid promise to hang upon our hearts but, again, this verse alone does not provide us with any tangible steps for us to take in order to make this truth happen in our lives.

This is why the following verse begins with the conjunction "and"—because verse 17 was never intended to stand by itself! Rather, Paul sought to show us *how* to become a new creature in Christ in verses 18-21:

"And all things are of (or, belong to) God, who hath reconciled us to himself by Jesus Christ, and hath **given to us** the **ministry of reconciliation**; To wit, that God was in Christ, reconciling the world unto himself, not imputing their trespasses unto them; and **hath committed unto** us the **word of reconciliation**. Now then we are ambassadors for Christ, as though God did beseech you by us; we pray you in Christ's stead, be ye reconciled to God. For he hath made him to be sin for us, who knew no sin; that we might be made the righteousness of God in him."

The word *reconciled* means *to be called back into a union.* Reconciliation is synonymous with peace, which is nothing more than preparing yourself to be at peace so that you can prepare others for peace.

The peace movement of the 1960s was unsuccessful because most of the participants, although well intentioned, did not have peace themselves. That kind of inner peace, the peace that surpasses all understanding, can only come from Jesus Himself.

Reconciliation means *to bring two offended parties back into union with one another.* Peace is *defined as joining parties into harmony.* Reconciliation is *rejoining parties back into union.* Both peace and reconciliation are very similar.

Making Peace with God

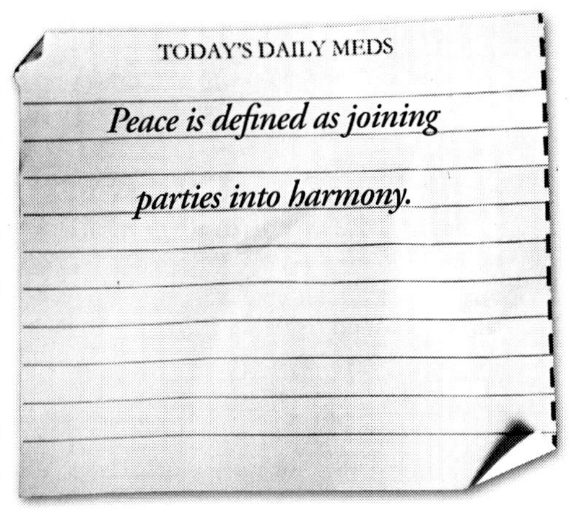

Verse 18 tells us that God *reconciled* us back into harmony with Himself by way of Jesus Christ. He teaches us here that it is God the Father who does the reconciling, but it is Jesus who made it possible. Our verse goes on to say, "and hath given to us the ministry of reconciliation..."

Paul is telling us that now we have been brought back into harmony with God through the peacemaking ministry of Jesus. We are thus charged with the very same ministry of peacemaking among others to cause them to come to Jesus (reconciliation) or to come back to Jesus (make peace with Him). When we are successful, then we can bring them to God. How amazing! Utilizing Jesus, God brought us to reconciliation. Now, God wants to utilize us to bring others to Jesus so they may be brought ultimately to Him.

Jesus came and died on the cross so that we may be restored unto God; now all we have to do is bring people to Jesus! If that doesn't put a charge under you, my friends, I don't know what will! But it will require peace. Turmoil and full-fledged war with others will never bring people to Christ.

And, most assuredly, when you are at war within yourself and within your own flesh, no one will be capable of looking to you to receive this ministry because you are in need of this ministry yourself. Be at peace and thus promote peace!

Again, I say, reconciliation is bringing two offended parties into harmony and union with one another. Reconciliation is a joining; peace is a re-joining.

Now, look at verse 19. Paul says: "To wit, that God was in Christ, reconciling the world unto himself, not imputing their trespasses unto them…" Let us stop right there. What does that mean? When people wronged Jesus, He did not declare war but instead He declared peace.

How did He do this? Notice the end of the verse, "…and hath committed unto us the *word* of reconciliation." It is *our* properly prompted words in the face of *their* trespasses that will promote peace.

Now where do these proper words come from? They come from our thoughts. We recall that Scripture tells us "out of the abundance of the heart the mouth speaketh" (Matthew 12:34). So, we see here that if we will *think* thoughts of peace, we can be more prompted by our preparations of the heart to *speak* words of peace.

This is how we can embrace the charge that has been committed unto us, which is "…the *word* of reconciliation." That the single "word" is peace. Peace with others, peace with ourselves and peace with God. It is all done through the Lord Jesus Christ!

In his book *Peace with God*, Billy Graham writes a profound sentence: "I know men who would write a check for a million dollars if they could find some peace. Millions are searching for it. Every time they get close to finding the peace found only in Christ, Satan steers them away. He blinds them. He throws up a smoke screen. He bluffs them. And they miss it! But we Christians have found it! It is ours now forever. We have found the secret of life."1

Paul puts it this way in verse 20: "Now then we are ambassadors for Christ, as though God did beseech (beg) you by us: we pray you in Christ's stead, be ye reconciled to God." Here we see Paul pleading with us to stop battling with God ourselves, for He hath reconciled us back into peaceful harmony with our Creator. But nonetheless, we often keep turning away from this union and creating a division with Him, thus making us incapable of bringing others into reconciliation with Him .

Paul is literally begging us to put an end to this pattern of defeat. He goes on to say in verse 21: "For he (God the Father) hath made him (Jesus) to be sin for us, who knew no sin; that we might be made the righteousness of God in him."

Here, he is calling us to be at full peace with God, for absent of peace with God, we cannot possibly bring others into a position of peace with God.

This, my friend, is how we may fight spiritual battles using peace. We see that our ministry of reconciliation comes from the proclamation of Good News in the face of bad news. It's being able to see the glass as half-full rather than half-empty; it's being able to see the shiny side of the coin rather than the dull side of the coin. It's putting away our position of negative neutrality and exchanging it for a position of positive portrayal. It is having an attitude of gratitude toward God. And the only way to do this is to be prepared with—you guessed it—the Gospel of Peace.

God in His Word often speaks using these three words: feet,

peace and gospel. We saw it above and in our "preparation passages" found in Ephesians and again in Romans 10:13-15, where we read,

"For whosoever shall call upon the name of the Lord shall be saved. How then shall they call on him in whom they have not believed? And how shall they believe in him of whom they have not heard? And **how shall they hear without a preacher**? And how shall they preach, except they be sent? As it is written, **How beautiful are the feet** of them that **preach the gospel of PEACE**, and bring glad tidings of good things."

Here we see once again that it is by our *words* of Good News that we are able to bring people to Christ, and we have already seen that it is Christ who shall reconcile them to God. But, Paul asks: "How shall they hear without a preacher?" The word *preacher* does not mean *pastor*; it means *proclaimer*. A preacher is simply a proclaimer of a combination of words that are really both Good News and the promotion of peace; for it is the Good News of Peace!

Notice that Paul does not say "how beautiful are the feet of those that preach the Gospel" of standards, or music, or anything else; but rather he says it's those who preach the Gospel of Peace who have beautifully precious feet! Feet shod with the preparation necessary to proclaim words of peace that will bring reconciliation between God and man.

Isaiah 52 is the final chapter that I wish to cite regarding the importance of the Gospel of Peace as it pertains to our feet and preaching. But first, I want to preface by saying that the prophet Isaiah wrote these words, as they were inspired unto him by God, about 700 years before Christ was born.

Isaiah 52:7 says, "**How beautiful** upon the mountains are **the feet** of him that bringeth **good tidings**, that **publisheth peace**; that bringeth good tidings of good, that **publisheth salvation**; that saith unto Zion, Thy God Reigneth!"

Note, my friends, that the bearing of good tidings is not a Santa Claus message; it is a Salvation message! According to Webster's 1828 dictionary, the word *publish* used in this context means *to proclaim.*

So we see that Isaiah, long before Paul's day, recognized the same truth: the "proclamation of peace" is preeminent in the presentation of the salvation message. In fact, Isaiah repeats himself to this end in the latter half of verse seven: "...that publisheth salvation..." Again, I say, the proclamation of peace is one in the same with proclaiming the way to salvation! Can you see the importance of this truth?

Furthermore, we see here that Isaiah is not only referring to the justification element of salvation (having our sin debt paid for us, thus receiving eternal life) but also the element of sanctification (having Christ living through us while on earth) that comes with salvation.

How do we know this? Because Isaiah writes, "...that saith unto Zion..." He doesn't say "unto Sinai" but rather "unto Zion." Study of Scripture will show that it is from Sinai that we get "rules from God," but it is from Zion that we are granted "a relationship with God."

Isaiah is very clear in making the distinction that Jesus reigneth upon Zion. This is why Isaiah writes that he bringeth "good tidings." It truly is Good News! We no longer are slaves to the law, but are now set free by the liberty found in Christ Jesus! If that's not Good News, then I know not what is!

To me, this is the best news I've ever heard—the ability for us to have a personal love relationship with our Savior, Jesus Christ! I am not saying that Mt. Sinai was not beneficial and does not remain beneficial for us all. It was at Sinai that God gave us the rules of conduct (the Law) that we may find peace with Him. But it is at Zion that we have learned to keep peace with God. It doesn't come from following rules. It comes from developing a relationship whereby we remain at peace with God.

But these very same rules taught in the law and given at Sinai have also inspired many of God's people to create division between man and man. This ought not to be. Give them some Zion. Give good tidings, despite differences. Preach good tidings from the precious feet of the preacher that have been prepared in advance to make peace. Keep peace and promote it among those at odds with one another.

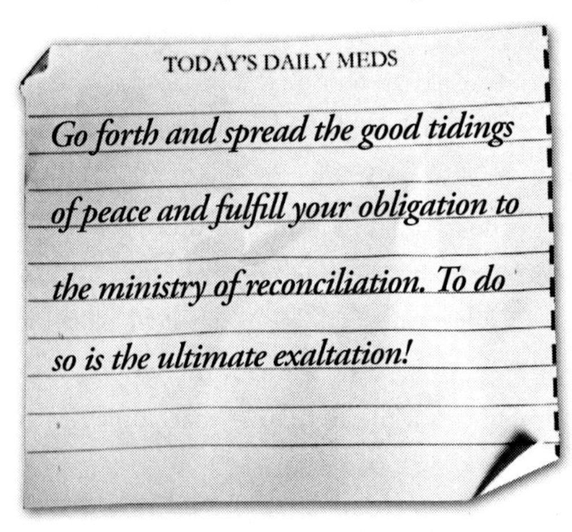

Jesus said, "Blessed are the peacemakers: for they shall be called the children of God" (Matthew 5:9). Nobody is happier than peacemakers.

Now that we have seen multiple examples from both the Old and New Testament alike, we must conclude one thing: Devils can only operate in environments of turmoil, but as our book title claims: with peace, there is release! With God's peace we have salvation from the turmoil of being lost and unjustified, as well as salvation from the turmoil of being miserably unsanctified. My friends, I exhort you to go forth and spread the good tidings of peace and fulfill your obligation to the ministry of reconciliation. To do so is the ultimate exaltation!

It proves we can be at peace with God and help others find peace with God as well. However, for our ministry of reconciliation to be effective, we must first make our peace with God. Then and only then can we reconcile others to Him.

And how, pray tell, do you suppose we bring others to be at peace with God? We can bring others to be a peace with God by our humble spirit, being at peace with others. And to be at peace with others, we must first be at peace within ourselves.

Our next chapter will focus on just that: finding peace with your fellow man and being at peace with one's self. Peace with God, peace with others and peace with self. It's God's design for mankind. And achieving this peace is going to be a war!

SEVEN

RU KEEPING PEACE?

The RUI Strongholds Study Course, which is the first book of the two-year discipleship program Gaining Remaining Fruit, defines *peace* as *to be free from worry in mind, spirit and body.* That is what peace *is*, but that is not what peace *does*. What does peace do? Having peace relaxes the soul of self. It is what puts our mind at ease, keeps our body from fear, and allows us to experience the power of His resurrection on our spirit.

You see, we as Christians are functioning trichotomies consisting of three parts: a spirit, soul and body. Our body is self-explanatory: it is simply our physical being. The soul is made up of our mind, will and emotions. And the inner man is our inherent spirit coupled with the Spirit of God that dwells within us as believers. (To learn more of this spiritual phenomenon, please read my book **Tall Law: When Trying Hard To Do Better Isn't Good Enough.)**

As trichotomies, our bodies are going to be under the influence of either our spirits or our souls. There is no other alternative. When the Bible talks about experiencing the power of the resurrection, it is referring to having our body empowered with His Spirit. This is commonly known as being led by the Spirit. We know that in order to be risen up with Christ, we must first die to self. But what takes place while we are buried with Christ in the tomb? Good old-fashioned, much-needed rest!

Keeping Peace with Self

Rest is simply another word for peace. So when we crucify our souls—comprising our minds, wills and emotions—and succeed in patiently waiting upon the power of His resurrection, we are at peace and rest with ourselves. Throughout the entire book of Acts—as well as in Romans 6, Hosea 6, Isaiah 26 and, especially, Philippians 3—we see that when our spirit is in control, our soul is permitted to be at rest. In other words, our minds, wills and emotions are at peace.

Consider this. Does the Bible say: Come unto Me all you who are weary and heavy laden, and I will give you work? No! God says, "I will give you rest" (Matthew 11:28). So we see that peace is having the soul at rest as a result of a resurrection of the Spirit. It is a supernatural by-product of the **d**eath, **b**urial and **r**esurrection of our Lord Jesus Christ—our very own DBR. (To learn more on how to experience your own DBR in difficult circumstances, please read my book **Today I Lay: Engaging the Power of His Resurrection).**

Conversely, worry is when our soul is not in a state of rest but, rather, in a state of *wrest.* Do not be distracted by the play on words here; this truly is the origin of worry. When our soul is at wrest, it is because we are being resistant to the spirit. When this occurs, our soul literally is wrestling with the spirit. But why, pray tell, would our souls wrestle with our spirits? The answer is simple. My friends, it is imperative that we realize that anything that brings our soul to a position of wrest, or unrest, is sin! It is sinful for our soul to be at any position other than rest, for the soul is to be in the tomb—and the spirit is to be alive!

With that in mind we must understand that when our soul is wresting, our spirit will never overtake its influence over the body. As a result of this, our soul will be grieved and resist the Spirit, and immediately everything we do will be done in our own power. When we engage in our own power, we can do nothing but have bold confidence in self. When this occurs, one of two events will ultimately unfold. God will either rip the cover off of our self-righteousness, thus precipitating anxiety, or we will soon find a complete void in confidence altogether and begin to fear. Either way, we worry!

"Don't worry; be happy"[1] is more easily sung than done. Worry is a sin of the mind, not of the will. After all, who *wants* to worry? This sin of our mind, however, most definitely affects our emotions. Stated more concisely, worry is a sin of the mind that creates fear in the will and agitation in the emotions. And what is agitation? It is defined by Webster as "a disturbance to the tranquility of the mind."

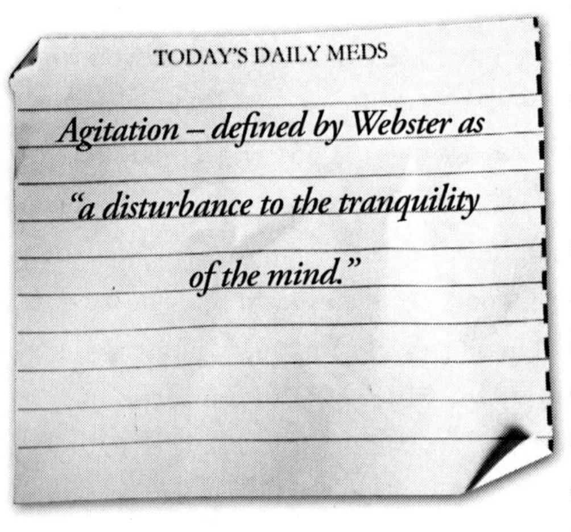

Without the power of Jesus' resurrection upon our lives, we cannot be Spirit-led. And, therefore, we are left with no choice but to be controlled by our soul. To illustrate what it is like to be anxious as a result of self-right "*soul* control," allow me to present to you an analogy.

Picture, if you will, a large raft afloat upon a sea. For our purposes, let us call it the sea of tranquility. As you look across the water, everything is calm, as smooth as glass. On our sea, visualize our raft floating peacefully along. Now for purposes of illustration, allow this sea of tranquility to represent our will, and the raft to represent our mind. Take it one step further and imagine that there is a large pink elephant sitting atop of the raft (our mind). So then the elephant represents what's on our mind; it is our problems. When things are heavy on our minds, they weigh us down, right?

Thus, on our sea of tranquility (our calm) we will have a heavily laden raft (a mind weighed down by our large problems). What is bound to happen next, my friends, is our elephant will decide to jump from the raft into the sea of tranquility. As a result of this disturbance, what happens to the water—the sea of tranquility—that represents our will? It becomes turbulent, and pretty soon, we've got our boat rocking violently. In other words, our problems make our will become fearful, and our meditations will become severely agitated. When this occurs, our emotions are put into a state of unrest, entirely absent of the peace that God intended for us to embrace.

My friends, this is what it is to be in soul-control! When our soul is in control, we allow something huge into our raft (mind), it will always have the potential to jump ship from our mind into our meditations, and the next thing you know everything is a mess! However, when we are Spirit-controlled, our seemingly huge problems can be released from our minds unto God. He carries the burden, not us.

That's right. Being led by the Spirit is to exchange the elephant for a grasshopper. Logic dictates that when a grasshopper (a small problem) upon our raft (mind) decides to jump into our sea of tranquility (our calm), it will create no significant disturbance. Therefore, our emotions are able to remain in a state of peace. Recognize that it is the size of our problems that determines the size of the eventual splash in our emotions. And the larger the splash we have, the greater our worry will be. Thus, there is a greater reduction of peace in our emotions.

Using this example, I encourage you to ask yourself whether your problems are more akin to an elephant, or are they more like a grasshopper? By inwardly assessing ourselves in this manner, we can get a good idea of how consistently we are empowered by His death, burial and resurrection. My friend, if we are at unrest as a result of overwhelming problems in our life, I can say with confidence that it is a result of a breakdown in the death, burial and resurrection (DBR) process. We are either not dying to self, or we are not restfully waiting in the tomb.

When we have a breakdown in our DBR process, worry, the anxiety and the full-fledged fear will inevitably occur. By seeing it this way, it becomes clear that worry is a sin of our mind. Now you may say what's the big deal? My worry isn't hurting anybody, is it? This is wrong! As our illustration shows, our worry will eventually disturb the peace of our emotions, causing us to act outside of God's will!

Worry increases stress and blood pressures. Worry can prompt a former addict to pick up a drink or drug. Worry can cause us to argue with a loved one or berate a fellow worker. Worry can lead to an automobile accident. Obviously, my friends, our worrying can and does hurt us and hurt others.

Furthermore, when we allow our wills to become fearful of our problems, it leaves us in a position of not knowing what to do. When we are scared, we become indecisive. But my friends, the Bible tells us that we should never *not* know what to do. For God promised, "I will instruct thee and teach thee in the way which thou shalt go: I will guide thee with mine eye" (Psalm 32:8). It says right there that God never intended for us to *not* know what to do. Sure, He may not give us guidance immediately when we want it, but He promises to never withhold His leadings from us any *later* than when we will need them.

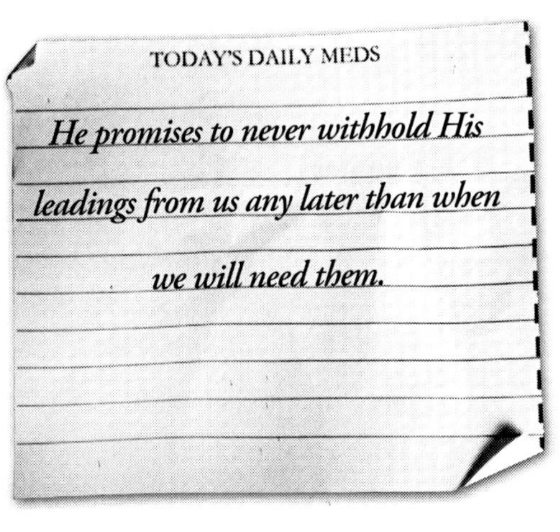

So we see that when we allow ourselves to get agitated and frustrated over situations and circumstances, we are no longer under the influence of the Spirit and therefore we cannot possibly receive good guidance. And this, my friends, only further exacerbates the problem.

If we fall into this cyclical trap, we are not only incapable of engaging in the ministry of reconciliation discussed in a previous chapter, but we are now in need of our own measure of reconciliation. Do you see how failing to be Spirit-controlled can render us entirely useless to God and others? Instead of reducing friction amongst others, we now create friction amongst others. This is not what Jesus intended for His Spiritual Brothers!

As we have seen, turmoil and unrest create a playground for Satan. When aging rocker Tom Petty sang, "Most things I worry about never happen anyway,"[2] he inadvertently identified one of the devil's greatest deceits. Studies have shown that more than 90 percent of the potential events we worry about never occur. Remember the acronym FEAR: False Evidence Appearing Real. The devil is a liar, and convincing us to worry over his lies is one of his most devastating weapons of mass destruction.

If we do not control what is on our minds by yielding to the Spirit of God by way of crucifying our souls' wrong thoughts, allowing ourselves to be at rest in the tomb and waiting for those proper thoughts to evolve, our problems will become unmanageable and wreak utter chaos in our lives and in the lives of those around us.

Peace Takes a Thrust of Trust

We now know that we can keep our problems from developing into elephants, but what specifically is betrothed to us by the Spirit that allows us to remain at peace? The answer is simple, my friends: trust—or more specifically—faith, which is a fruit of the Spirit (Galatians 5:22). We must gain and maintain an unfailing faith in God to be able to give our problems fully to Him. My friends, this is not something we can do in our own power. Rather, we must yield to the Spirit to express this fruit of faith.

Yet another terribly overlooked verse in Scripture that clearly shows us this truth is Isaiah 26:3, which says, "Thou wilt keep him in perfect peace, whose mind is stayed on thee: because he trusteth in thee." How do we stay in perfect peace? By keeping our minds stayed on God! The word *stayed* is synonymous with the word *abide*. Both words mean to *continue within a given place*. Isaiah is telling us that we will maintain *perfect* peace if we continually keep our minds within a given place.

What place is he referring to? In Christ! The world's philosophy will give you all sorts of methods to keep yourself at peace. Life insurance is supposed to give us peace of mind. Brokerage firms promise us financial peace (Hah!). Even some of our nuclear weapons have been called peacemakers.

> TODAY'S DAILY MEDS
>
> *Isaiah 26:3, "Thou wilt keep him in perfect peace, whose mind is stayed on thee: because he trusteth in thee."*
>
> *The word stayed is synonymous with the word abide. Both words mean to continue within a given place.*

However, the bottom line is that all of these prescriptions for peace are erroneous for the simple fact that we cannot keep ourselves at peace. No, my friends, we must instead look unto Jesus to provide us the peace that we need.

Now, this does not mean that we have to walk around saying Jesus, Jesus, Jesus! Although that would certainly help, what Isaiah is calling for is a consistent meditation upon the sufficiency of Christ in all turmoil. If we keep Jesus ever present at the forefront of our hearts, we will experience perfect peace! The Bible tells us, "All things work together for good" (Romans 8:28) but yet we consistently fail to trust in the Lord—and solace in this promise.

My friends, this is exactly what opens us up to spiritual battles! It is our inability to trust God through our difficult circumstances, lest our raft grasshoppers become unmanageable elephant hoppers! Often we think we are in the Spirit, but the moment something goes wrong, our once feasible grasshopper of a problem morphs into an insurmountable elephant! And to make matters worse, our elephant is no longer able to be supported upon our mind and thus takes a plunge into our sea of tranquility. Splashing and thrashing, we have an instant mess!

The good news is this will only happen, the Bible tells us, if we fail to keep our minds "stayed on thee." And why would we fail to keep our mind "stayed on thee"? Because of a lack of trust! Notice what the end of the verse says: "because he trusteth in thee." Before this phrase we see a colon, which indicates to us that the words explain a previous statement.

This verse is essentially saying that one who has perfect peace trusts fully in the Lord and therefore is able to keep his meditations consistently upon Him. Simplified further, God is saying that absent of trust, there can be no peace. Period. And not just trust in anybody, but trust in God!

Too often many of us put our trust into the wrong hands. Proverbs 25:19 states, "Confidence in an unfaithful man in time of trouble is like a broken tooth, and a foot out of joint." In case you have yet to realize it, let me just tell you that all people are unfaithful. No person can or should ever be your confidence. Solomon, the writer of this proverb, is likening a man's ability to uphold another in time of trouble to the ability of a dislocated foot to support the weight of man. Obviously, if you have a dislocated foot, you will not be able to stand on that foot. It is just as useless to place our trust in another person.

You may be saying to yourself: I would trust my life to my husband or my wife or whomever—they'd never let me down! This is good, but the simple truth is that no mortal can possibly provide the level of comfort and peace that almighty God intended for us to have. Furthermore, if you can find confidence in a *flawed* human, it should not be any problem for you to trust in a *perfect* God. After all, He is a God who has promised to be—and has never failed to be—the perfect Father. And what kind of father doesn't always have his children's best interests in mind? My friends, our confidence must always reside fully in the Lord if we are to have a perfect and consistent peace.

Keeping Peace with Others

We have seen that to have peace with God, we must be reconciled unto Him through Jesus Christ. We have also seen that to have peace with self, we must have a trust in the Lord that results in a mind that is stayed upon God and a Spirit-controlled soul. One final element remains before we may see the outcome of this beautiful equation: peace with others.

Before one can ever have peace with others, he must first have peace with God and self. This is an inescapable truth. We cannot expect to be at peace with our spouse if there is a war raging within ourselves. However, simply being at peace with God and self does not guarantee we will subsequently find peace with others. Oh no, my friends, there is one crucial factor we must add before we can enjoy peace with those among us.

Paul lays it out for us when he writes: "Finally, brethren, farewell. Be perfect, be of good comfort, be of one mind, live in peace; and the God of love and peace shall be with you" (II Corinthians 13:11). This verse neatly summarizes our entire discussion on peace and provides us with the answer of how to exactly experience the perfect peace of God.

Paul begins this verse by saying goodbye, but then he swings back around to revisit and encapsulate the purpose of his letter. He says for us to be perfect. Now perfect is a most confusing word that in this context simply means to be in a constant state of spiritual development.

To be in a state of spiritual growth indicates an adequate reconciliation with God; so he is telling us to be at peace with God and allow Him to mature us. He then says to be of good comfort, that is to say, allow the Comforter—the Holy Spirit—to be in control of our souls. This is Paul summarizing how we are to gain peace with ourselves, to be Spirit-led. We have previously discussed these two points, but it is the next point Paul makes that completes the solution to peace.

He goes on to say, "be of one mind." This is the key to finding peace with others! We know that Paul is addressing believers in this verse because his salutation is to the brethren. So what he is exhorting us to is a position of unity and agreement among those who follow Christ. He is indirectly calling for the cessation of all discord and division amongst the church. He is calling for a peace treaty among the brethren.

That is exactly what it takes to be at peace with others. We must not battle against each other, but instead against a very real and formidable enemy. We must not get caught up within our own body, for this will render the entire church ineffective. In short, to be at peace with others is to be of one mind with others.

The verse goes on to tell us that if we do these three things, we shall experience the love and peace that only God can provide. In order to achieve a perfect and consistent peace with God, self and others, we must:

Be in a perpetual state of spiritual growth, reconciled unto God (peace with God)

Be Spirit-controlled in our thoughts, words and deeds (peace with self)

Be of one mind with the brethren (peace with others)

If you do this, Paul promises, "the God of love and peace shall be with you." Amen.

Keeping the Peace of God

In a previous chapter, much was said about being reconciled unto God and thus being at peace with Him; but how do we maintain our peace with God? We have seen that if we lack peace with God, then we inevitably lack peace with ourselves and others. It is to this end that I wish to revisit this truth and expound a bit more on how to gain and maintain peace with our Lord and Savior.

The only way to keep peace with God is to allow Him to keep our minds. The word *keep* in this context means *protect*. Without God's protection over our minds, we will undoubtedly lose our peace with Him. God is the most important entity with Whom we ought to keep peace, for if we don't have peace with God, there will be no peace. Period! Take a look, if you will, at the following verses.

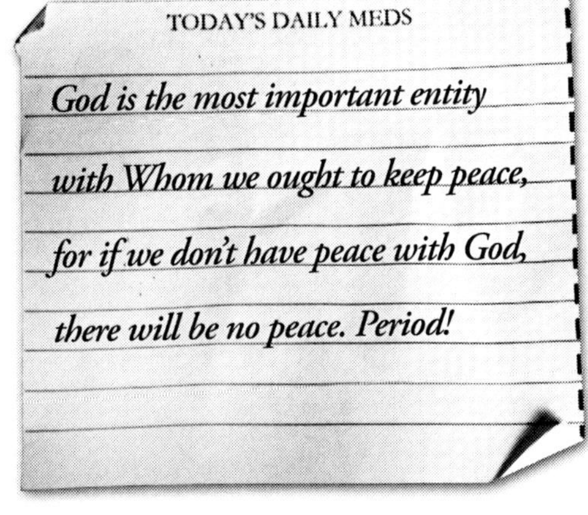

Philippians 4:6-7

"Be careful for nothing; but in every thing by prayer and supplication with thanksgiving let your requests be made known unto God. And the peace of God, which passeth all understanding, shall keep your hearts and minds through Christ Jesus."

When Paul tells us to "be careful for nothing" he is not telling us to go about our lives in a careless manner. Here the word *careful* means *anxious* or *worry*. So what he is actually saying is for us to not worry about anything! Now, generally speaking, how well do we collectively follow this Biblical mandate? Not very well. In today's society we have a health-care industry that is way too eager to dispense pills to take away people's anxiety. In our passage, Paul is telling the Philippians that there need not be such anxiety disorders if they will simply yield to a few steps.

As a side note, I was discussing anxiety disorders with our staff physician, Dr. George T. Crabb, D.O., who is an expert on the topic. We both concluded that we had never witnessed an individual with a genuine anxiety disorder who also had a satisfactory measure of peace with God. And because these folks lack peace with God, the ones we have counseled also cannot find peace with self and others either. Therefore, a full-blown anxiety disorder develops.

So the world's typical treatment for worry is some form of medication. But I'll be honest. If I was a doctor and somebody came to see me with an anxiety problem, I would write a prescription based upon their answers to the following questions:

1. Have you prayed?
2. Have you supplicated?
3. Have you given thanks to God?

Granted, I am being a bit facetious, but after all, this is the exact prescription that Dr. Paul writes. He essentially is saying to the Philippians: Okay, don't worry about anything anymore. All you have to do is pray to God (that's two-way communication), supplicate God (that's giving your burden to Him) and give Him thanks for the trial that you're enduring. If you do these things, Paul says, the peace of God shall keep your hearts and minds. Bingo! Goodbye anxiety!

Most of us are quick to pray to God when we are facing an adverse circumstance. You may have a big business meeting in five minutes or are due to deliver a speech soon. In these situations it is almost natural for Christians to say: Oh Lord, please help me nail this thing! Give me your power!

This is all well and good, but it is not true prayer. True prayer involves two-way conversation with God. We all are quick to talk to God, but we must pause and listen too! God is not a respecter of grocery-list prayers. And, remember, when God speaks back to you, take copious notes.

Second, Paul instructs us to supplicate the Lord. Again, this element of Christianity tends to come quite naturally to us. To *supplicate* means to *petition with earnestness and submission.* So it is clear that we are to ask God to shoulder the burdens that we would otherwise worry over. This is when we can pour out our grocery lists. The Lord already knows what our burdens are; He just wants us to ask Him for His help! After all, does He not say, "ask and ye shall receive"?

Now for the hard part—Paul says that we are to pray and supplicate with *thanksgiving.* We are to be thankful! Now sometimes it is easier than others to do this, but when we are in the midst of a trial, it is nearly impossible to be thankful—*nearly* impossible. It is only possible if we are walking in the Spirit. In our own power, we will inevitably fail to do so. We must recognize that God puts us into situations that will cause us to depend on Him. In doing so, we will be drawn closer to Him, and *this* is something for which we should be thankful! However, in our flesh, we will be absolutely blinded to this fact. He says to give thanks for everything.

Personally speaking, this is how I finally quit smoking. I started thanking God for my cigarettes. For months after I returned to church, I had prayed and supplicated to God for Him to take away my cigarette habit. After only experiencing marginal victory, I realized that I was not thanking God. And perhaps that was why I was not experiencing full victory.

So as a last-ditch effort, I began to thank God for each and every cigarette that I smoked. Pretty soon I got tired of thanking God for giving me an agent of sin. The conviction was unbearable. So I began to eventually smoke fewer cigarettes, and pretty soon I was taking fewer drags on each individual cigarette. Finally, one day I found myself utterly disgusted with the idea that I was thanking God for cigarettes—something that He was clearly telling me was against His will. That day I threw down the cigarettes and have yet to pick them up again!

When we find ourselves in a position in life where we have something that we are doing that we don't want to do—or know that we are not supposed to do—one of the best things we can do is give thanks to God for it. We are often faced with circumstances that we take to God and communicate with Him, trying to discern His will. At times He will allow our prayer to go unanswered. When this happens we are to supplicate to Him over our burden, literally begging Him to come through for us.

Again, at times God may allow our supplication to go unanswered. When this happens, all we can do is simply give thanks. The Bible says, "In every thing give thanks: for this is the will of God in Christ Jesus concerning you" (I Thessalonians 5:18). When we give thanks unto

God, it allows the power of Christ to rest upon us. How will this power manifest itself? By leaving us at peace. When people observe you in a state of peace amidst the most trying of times, it will blow their minds!

Moving on now, we see that Philippians 4:6-7 concludes, "let your request be made known unto God. And the peace of God, which passeth all understanding, shall keep your hearts and minds through Christ Jesus." Paul is very clear to say that it is the peace *of* God that will protect our hearts and minds.

Now remember, where does turmoil start? It starts in our minds and ends in our hearts. The heart is where we do our thinking, and our mind is where we store information; it acts as a hard drive, so to speak. So when our hard drive processes a thought into our heart, we begin to dwell on it. And if the said thought is negative, our dwelling can often cause us to forfeit our position of peace to a position of anxiety. All of this occurs because we allowed our brain to send a thought to our heart. Can you see now why we need our hearts and minds protected so badly?

Later in this book we will discuss the shield of faith that we must have to block the fiery darts that the enemy shoots at us. This is exactly what occurs when we embrace that faith. We are able to enjoy God's protection upon our hearts and minds.

At this point, you may be asking yourself: How exactly does God protect our hearts and minds? Well, first of all, He's God. He can do whatever He wants. But specifically, there is only one *way* for information to be taken in through our senses that would typically be negative to be transformed into positive. That *way* is when God protects us by supernaturally turning us from pessimists to optimists.

Have you ever noticed how two different people can have entirely different perceptions of a situation? How can this be? It is because

God is allowed to protect one of the minds from a tendency from looking at things from a critical, negative, pessimistic or competitive point of view. When we ask the Lord via prayer, supplication and thanksgiving to keep us from dwelling on negative things, more often than not, He will answer us.

I believe one of the reasons that God blessed me with my wife Lori is because He knew that I needed to have an optimist as a helpmate. By nature, I tend to be a pessimist, but through the years spent with Lori, she has taught me to be a more consistently positive thinker.

Granted, a large part of my role in the ministry is to be a watchman for many people. Part of that role is always looking down the road and trying to foresee potential problems. Because of this, I can tend to see things turning out negatively. For example, if I were to walk through our offices and notice that a garbage can had not been emptied in two weeks, my first reaction would always have been to reprove a staff member for their careless laziness. But nowadays, I am overtaken by my inner Optimist, making me realize that perhaps the garbage can hasn't been emptied because our staff is hard at work on more important things and just failed to notice or have yet to get to that duty.

Yet, my pessimistic tendencies can still create turmoil in no time at all. I have learned, however, through the years to reach out to God, as Paul instructs us, and over time I have seen a great level of victory in this area. Sometimes God uses people to help me in this area, as He has my wife. At other times, more stubborn times, God has responded to my prayer and supplication Himself.

Before I continue, I want to reiterate that the peace of God is a difficult subject to teach. As we previously discussed, the peace of God is something that "surpasses all understanding." Sometimes, we simply cannot attribute God's peace to any rational action or thought process.

While writing this chapter, my father passed away. Friends, I feared this occurrence for nearly my whole life. Because of this, I am completely astounded at the amount of peace I have experienced about the entire situation. It truly does surpass my understanding. I simply cannot explain it. I glory in the goodness of God. I cannot explain it because it surpasses understanding! To say I understand would be simple-minded pride.

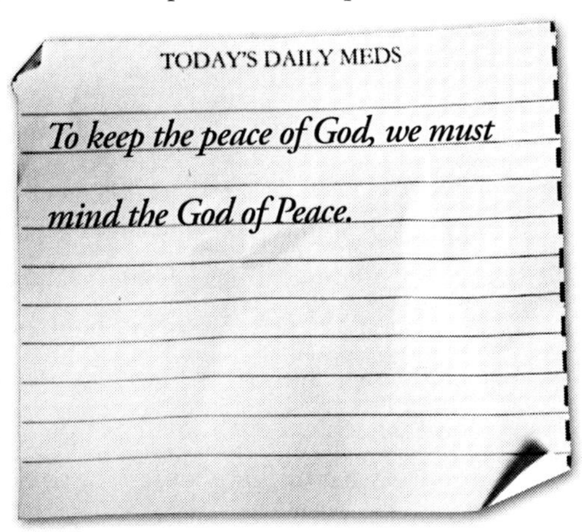

Keeping the God of Peace

To keep the peace of God, we must mind the God of Peace. The word *mind* means *to obey*. So if we want to keep God's peace, we must obey God. To teach this point, I am going to continue elucidating this portion of Scripture.

Philippians 4:8-9

"Finally, brethren, whatsoever things are true, whatsoever things are honest, whatsoever things are just, whatsoever things are pure, whatsoever things are lovely, whatsoever things are of good report; if there be any virtue, and if there be any praise, think on these things. Those things, which ye have both learned, and received, and heard, and seen in me, do: and the **God of peace** shall be with you."

Notice right after Paul teaches us that we should worry upon nothing and be granted the peace of God, he gives us a formula for proper thinking. This is yet more proof that it is our stinking thinking that leads us to all of our worries. Paul opens verse 8 using the word *finally*, as if to say: Here is what I have to tell you now that I've told you what I have told you in verses 6 and 7. He then lists beaucoup things we should think upon.

Notice also that he couples the positive element with its antithesis. He does this so that we may see from both angles what we should and should not think upon. He closes verse 8, saying, "if there be any praise, think on these things." *Praise* means *worth commending*. So he is telling us that if we are going to do anything with our lives that is worth commending, we must learn to think upon these positive things.

Now I tell you we are human beings, not human doings. But that doesn't mean we don't have something to do. We are not His workers; we are His workmanship. Workmanship is a manufactured product. So we are not, say, a bolt but we are a wrench. The wrench doesn't hold anything together, but the wrench does have a responsibility. We are not the nail; we are the hammer. The nail has the responsibility to hold things together, but we are the hammer.

God is going to use us in order to hold things together, but it's going to be the nail that holds things together. We are a manufactured product with a purpose. His purpose. And what is God through Paul telling us to do? Think right!

That's right! Think right. Now, folks, that is just about our only responsibility that I can discern from these passages of Scripture. We are supposed to control our thoughts. Now God is going to help us. Even though I am supposed to control my thoughts, God has promised that He will protect my heart. He'll protect my mind. He'll send people who will comfort me. He'll do these things, the Bible says, if I will cooperate.

There are those who, no matter what others say, no matter how God stimulates them toward optimism, are just dead-dog set on thinking negatively. They see it, they learn it, they receive it, they hear it, but they don't do it.

So the God of peace is not with them. Now the God of love, joy and longsuffering may be there. But the God of the third fruit, peace, and the God of the seventh fruit, faith, will be strangely absent. And then when they cry out, He says: Where is your faith? Why are you all worked up over this? And He calms it. But it doesn't have to get to that desperate of a situation.

If we exercise His faith instead of our faith, Galatians 2:20, Ephesians 13:9, and other parts of Scripture demonstrate that it's the faith of the fruit of the Spirit—and not our own human faith—that keeps our peace.

The only thing He asks us to do is think right. Now He'll give us all the help He can, but we are going to just have to be dead-dog set in our hearts that we are going to be optimists. We are going to trust that everything that looks bad is actually very, very good. That is how we may remain at peace with God, with others and with ourselves.

In our next chapter, we shall study our positioning for peace. We must position ourselves in order to be at peace with God and to overcome our enemy. We will learn MUCH about this formidable foe in this next chapter.

EIGHT

RU POSITIONED FOR PEACE

In our previous chapter, we concluded that in order to keep peace with God, we must let God *keep* our mind. We also saw that it is necessary to obey the God of Peace to keep peace with God. This is a position that we are going to have to take in life. The Bible promises us that if we obey God and think as He has taught us to think, the God of Peace shall be with us.

So we saw that peace has a God. It's our God! And when we are able to do these two things, He will be with us. And when the God of Peace is with us, we will also be granted access to His peace. In order to do this, we must be properly positioned. Now this peace is not found through a disposition of happiness, joy or excitement. Rather, it is found through a position.

Let's look at some lines from Scripture that confirm this truth.

John 16:33

"These things I have spoken unto you, that **in me** ye might have **peace. In the world** ye shall have **tribulation**: but be of good cheer; I have overcome the world."

Can you see it? Jesus is telling us that if we are positioned *in* Him, we can have peace! If you are positioned in the world, or in sin, you will have tribulation. As a matter of fact, peace is a by-product of our position in Him. Our disposition is determined by our position! In Him, there's peace. In the world, there's turmoil. It really is that simple. When we are safely positioned *in* Christ, He promises to protect our disposition, thus keeping us at peace.

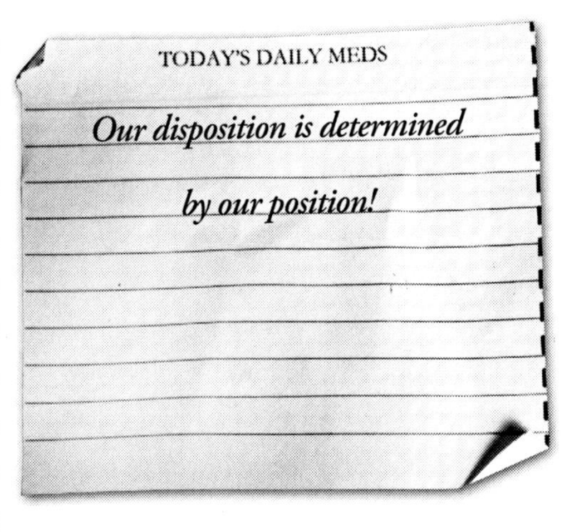

The following verse affirms this important spiritual principle.

Romans 8:1

"There is therefore now no condemnation to them who are in **Christ Jesus**, who walk not after the flesh, but after the Spirit."

The term *in Christ Jesus* is defined here when the apostle Paul refers to those "who walk not after the flesh, but after the Spirit." So how do we know when we are positioned In Jesus? Friends, if we are living the Spirit-filled life, walking according to the influence of the Spirit, and rejecting the lusts of the flesh, we can rest assured that we are *in* Christ Jesus.

Now we know that before we will ever do wrong, we first begin to think wrongly. When we obey God, meditationally speaking, we can be sure that we will remain in Him. Recognizing that it is wrong thinking that pulls us from our position in Christ, we can accurately say that it is our wrong thinking that will adversely impact our disposition. Thinking wrong thoughts causes us to get out of our position in Him, and therefore we are no longer under the influence of the God of Peace. As a result, turmoil begins to run rampant within our hearts (meditators) and eventually we will begin to do things improperly.

When faced with the turmoil that stems from stepping out of our position in Him, we inevitably will begin to attempt to do things in our own power, taking matters into our own hands. We set aside God's power in favor of our self-righteousness, and before long, the redundancy of doing so leads us to seek out various coping mechanisms. And, friends, just like that we fall back into the realm of unrighteousness. But I say to you now: This need not be!

The Bible is dogmatically clear that when we are positioned in Christ, we will be at peace. The following is a well-known verse that packs a powerful truth.

II Corinthians 5:17

"Therefore if any man be in Christ, he is a new creature: old things are passed away; behold, all things are become new."

Here the apostle Paul is telling us that all we have to do is position ourselves in Christ, and all those old things from our past that caused us a world of turmoil will become a distant memory. The hurt, the frustration, the dissension, the discouragement, and the all-out war that we once battled will be taken away as we find our disposition protected by our newfound position. If we abide in the God of Peace, we will surely enjoy the peace of God!

For more than 40 years, the Soviet Union pointed nuclear missiles at the United States. But the Soviets never launched any of those weapons of mass annihilation at us because we had thousands of nuclear missiles pointed right back at them. And so it is when we seek safety in the peace of God. The devil will still aim his weapons at us, but God will provide our nuclear umbrella, keeping us in perfect peace during our spiritual Cold War.

Here are more of God's words that show us how to attain a lasting peace in our lives.

Galatians 6:14-17

"But God forbid that I should glory, save in the cross of our Lord Jesus Christ, by whom the world is crucified unto me, and I unto the world. For in Christ Jesus neither circumcision availeth any thing, nor uncircumcision, but a new creature. And as many as walk according to this rule, **peace be** on them, and mercy, and upon the Israel of God. From henceforth **let no man trouble me:** for I bear in my body the marks of the Lord Jesus."

The word *glory* means *to make look good.* So what Paul is saying here is that we should never look good unless the glory that's coming from our lives stems from the cross that bore our Savior's body. He also is adding to what He taught in the aforementioned passage in II Corinthians. He is saying that when we are in Christ Jesus, it makes little difference what we are capable of in our own power, what our status is, or how well we are capable of walking according to rules.

These things matter not, for now we have become an entirely new creation in His grace. The apostle goes on to state that because he is a new creature and no longer has to walk according to the rules of circumcision that created so much turmoil, he now has peace upon him and is no longer troubled by mankind. He is declaring his very own personal peace.

From these verses and others, we are able to recognize that being in Christ is paramount to understanding how to have the God of Peace permeate our life with the peace of God. More than 170 times the Bible refers to abiding *in* Christ. Why, you ask, would such a simple truth be repeated so often? It is because our position *in* Christ is integral to essentially everything in the Christian life. For purposes of this book, however, it is sufficient to state that any wandering from a position *in* Christ will lead to turmoil in our lives each and every time. The Bible is clear in teaching that turmoil is a consequence of our disposition being negatively affected by a flawed position.

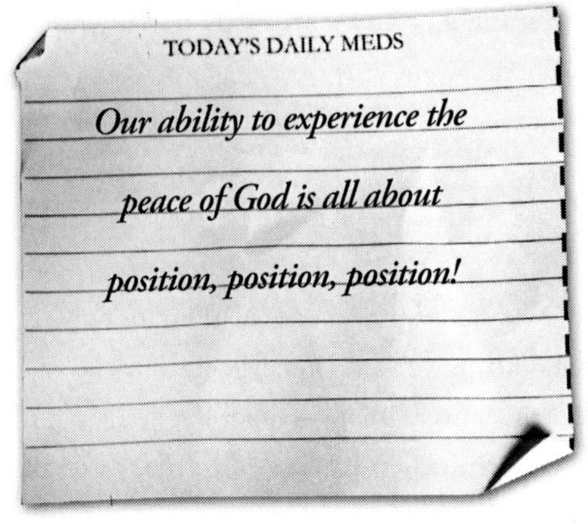

My friends, just as real estate is all about location, location, location, our ability to experience the peace of God is all about position, position, position! My friends, you decide: In Christ, you will have peace; in the sinful world, you will have turmoil. Pretty clear and simple, I would say!

We have seen that when we are in Christ, He protects our hearts and minds. Because of this protection resulting from our position in Christ, the God of Peace is with us. And because God is with us, His peace becomes ours.

Now it is important to know that we will not be spared tribulation as a result of our position in Christ. Oh no, my friends.

It is exactly the opposite. But our aforementioned verses prove to us that we will—if we remain in the proper position—be able to remain free of turmoil, thus remaining at peace.

Again, I stress that this does not mean that tribulation will be absent from our lives. My friends, Jesus Himself declared that in the world we will have tribulation. Like it or not, the world is the environment in which our bodies live. Our bodies make up one-third of our being; so naturally, our lives will be affected by the tribulations found in the world.

However, if our position is correct, we can overcome the tribulations of the world through Christ Jesus. It is imperative for us to understand at this point that when we position ourselves in Christ Jesus, we automatically declare war upon the enemies of God. The attacks don't decrease; they instead increase.

Here is an obscure verse that will help to explain exactly what Jesus is telling us in John 16:33.

Isaiah 45:6-7

"...I am the LORD, and there is none else. I form the light, and create darkness: I make peace, and create evil: I the LORD do all these things."

If we were to read over this quickly, it would more than likely cause us to question the sovereignty of God. We would certainly wonder what exactly He is saying that He has done and created. For surely God did not create evil or the darkness that so plagues our lives!

Yet, Isaiah 45:7 says He created darkness and He created evil. What gives? To understand this Scripture we must thoroughly study it.

What the prophet Isaiah is actually telling us is that when God formed the light, thus forming peace, the automatic by-product of this action was the creation of darkness, or evil. The Bible asserts that "...being justified by faith, we have peace with God through our Lord Jesus Christ:" (Romans 5:1). Now if we have peace with God, we can be sure that we are no longer at peace with the enemies of God. Paul goes on to explain this critically important point in the subsequent verses.

Romans 5:2-5

"By whom also we have access by faith into this grace wherein we stand, and rejoice in hope of the glory of God. And not only so, **but we glory in tribulations** also: knowing that tribulation worketh patience. And patience, experience; and experience, hope: And hope maketh not ashamed; because the love of God is shed abroad in our hearts by the Holy Ghost which is given unto us."

What the apostle is telling us is that we will inevitably have tribulation in our lives in spite of having peace with God. But, he says, the good news is this tribulation will bring glory to us and to God. If the peace that God gives us in the midst of tribulation makes Him look good, He is going to share that glory with us, thereby making *us* look good! Another benefit of this occurring, the Bible says, is that it will work patience, meaning that it will help us to develop the faith to wait on God.

And because we have patience we will gain experience, and this experience will bring us hope that will not make anybody ashamed, for it will cause the love of God to be shed abroad in our collective hearts. Wow! Can you see how God has taken what the devil attempts to destroy us with and uses it as a tool for the perfection of His saints?

Now going back to Isaiah 45:7, we see it says that God forms light and makes peace. The word *make* is synonymous with the word *form.*

To *make,* literally defined, means to *form* into a shape. So the Bible tells us that God formed light into a shape. And when He formed light, He likewise formed peace; they are supplementary in this context. But what, pray tell, does this actually mean? To find the answer we must look way back in Scripture to the very first dawn of day.

Genesis 1:1-5

"In the beginning God created the heaven and the earth. And the earth was without form, and void; and darkness was upon the face of the deep. And the Spirit of God moved upon the face of the waters. And God said, Let there be light: and there was light. And God saw the light, that it was good: and God *divided* the light from the darkness. And God called the light Day, and the darkness he called Night. And the evening and the morning were the first day."

Notice that verse 2 states: "darkness was upon the face of the deep." This indicates that darkness was present from the very beginning. Our passage then goes on to explain how God spoke light into existence: "And the Spirit of God moved upon the face of the waters. And God said, Let there be light: and there was light."

God *formed* the light out of the darkness. Next, we see that God saw the light and determined that it was good. He then divided the light from the darkness. The fact that God proclaims light to be good and then divides it from darkness, indicates that he saw darkness to be *not* good. More specifically, He chose to separate light from darkness because He saw darkness had the potential to be used for evil.

Now we see repeatedly in the Scriptures that anytime God creates something, the enemy seeks to take what is left over and use it for his advantage. Here we see that God created light, and the devil—the prince of darkness—consumed that which was left over. As soon as God separated the light from the darkness, the devil sought to conquer the darkness for his advancement.

The above passage marks the very first time we see God form something in the Bible. After all, it opens by saying, "In the beginning."
(And in baseball parlance, this was indeed a *big inning*.)

Recalling our verse in Isaiah, this is what it means when it says that God formed the light and created darkness. When God formed the light, the leftover element from that formation was darkness. Our verse also tells us that God made peace. And in doing so the devil was able to obtain the antithesis of peace: turmoil.

Remember that what is left over from God's formations becomes a *free* agent, so to speak, and the devil—like a demonic baseball GM—more often than not will *pick it up* to do whatever he so chooses with it. In this case, we see the devil *sign* darkness off eternity's *waiver wire* so that he can establish evil.

So we see that God did not create evil—as it would appear upon a cursory glance at this verse—as much as He created peace, thus instigating and allowing for the establishment of evil by the devil.

The word *create* literally means to *cause to exist*. The word *cause* means *to produce an effect*. Combining these definitions, we see that our passage actually is saying: When I made peace, I created, or produced an effect, that caused evil to exist. The devil then jumped onto the scene and claimed that evil to use upon the man whom God would later create. The Bible tells us that when this occurred, we instantly became enemies with evil, and rightfully so!

In essence, we became enemies with that which God allowed to be created as a result of what He had made. He made peace, thus precipitating evil. Why was the devil so quick to acquire evil and darkness? Because, as we know, it has always been the enemy's objective to gain preeminence over God.

To further elaborate on this point, let us look at the following passages.

Isaiah 14:12-16

"How art thou fallen from heaven, O Lucifer, son of the morning! how art thou cut down to the ground, which didst weaken the nations! For thou hast said in thine heart, I will ascend into heaven, I will exalt my throne above the stars of God: I will sit also upon the mount of the congregation, in the sides of the north: I will ascend above the heights of the clouds; I will be like the most High. Yet thou shalt be brought down to hell, to the sides of the pit. They that see thee shall narrowly look upon thee, and consider thee, saying, Is this the man that **made** the earth to tremble, that **did shake** kingdoms;"

The prophet Isaiah starts off by basically asking: How did you manage to get kicked out of heaven, Lucifer? He then goes on to answer his own question when he says: "For thou has said in thine heart… " When somebody says something in their heart, it means that they are thinking. Much like us, the devil got himself into trouble by thinking wrong thoughts! He had prideful, negative and competitive thoughts against God. The devil sought to exalt himself to a level at least "equal" to God and reign supreme.

This, of course, was not permitted by God. The passage continues: "yet thou shalt be brought down to hell, to the sides of the pit. They that see thee shall narrowly look upon thee…" We see here that God has cast the devil into hell, and all who see him will look upon him with hateful, squinted eyes.

Our selected passage concludes by explaining the thoughts of those who will look upon Satan in his shame. "…and (they) consider thee, saying, Is this the man that **made** the earth to tremble, that did **shake** kingdoms"? Observe carefully the verbiage here. You see, God made peace, and His making of peace created, or produced, an effect that caused evil as a by-product. And it was the devil who took this evil and used it to **make** the kingdoms of earth to tremble and shake.

So we see that the devil took the evil that was created as a result of what God had made—peace—and used it to instigate turmoil upon the earth. The turmoil that was instigated causes tribulations that effectively cause us to tremble to this day. As a matter of fact, if you study a commentary on this passage, it says that the word *evil* literally is the opposite of peace in this context. So when God made peace, guess what happened? It created war; therefore, anybody who makes peace with God immediately becomes an enemy of the devil.

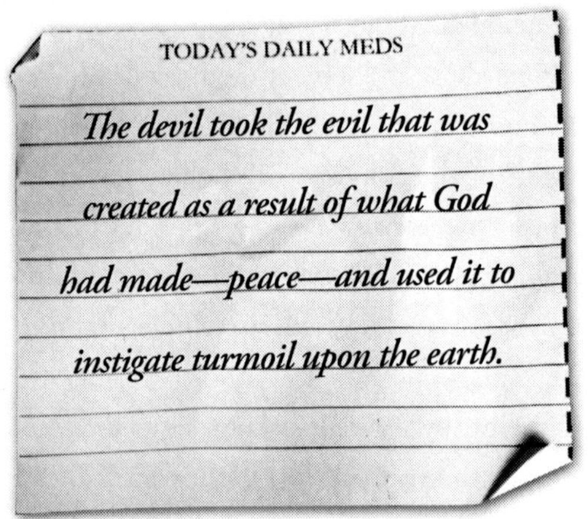

Leo Tolstoy's epic *War and Peace* chronicled the French invasion of Russia and consisted of 1,225 pages when it was first published in 1869.[1] But the world could not contain the number of large volumes of books that could be written about the wars that would follow in the 20th Century. According to historian Matthew White, there were 165 major wars resulting in the deaths of 180 million people, more casualties than in all of the wars of the previous 19 centuries.[2] That's how effective the devil is in making war. Of course, Jesus prophesied that in the last days wars shall rage with increasing abandon and indeed in the last 100 years they surely have.

Mark 13:5-7

"And Jesus answering them began to say, Take heed lest any *man* deceive you: For many shall come in my name, saying, I am *Christ*; and shall deceive many. And when ye shall hear of wars and rumors of wars, be ye not troubled: for *such things* must needs be; but the end *shall* not *be* yet."

The Bible tells us that the seeds of all wars were planted that fateful day in the garden.

Genesis 3:14-15

"And the LORD God said unto the serpent, Because thou hast done this, thou art cursed above all cattle, and above every beast of the field; upon thy belly shalt thou go, and dust shalt thou eat all the days of thy life: And I will put enmity between thee and the woman, and between thy seed and her seed; it shall bruise thy head, and thou shalt bruise his heel."

The serpent is indwelt by the devil, and this scripture describes what occurred after the devil tempted Adam and Eve in the garden. Notice the phraseology here. The author of Genesis, Moses, writes: "...between thy seed and her seed..." So we know then that everybody who is born into this world is going to be an enemy to the devil. "It will bruise thy head..."— meaning that the devil will seek to injure that which is producing the peace.

To clarify and summarize, we see that in the garden God had made peace (and thus peace with man), and evil was created (caused to exist) by virtue of being left over. The devil then took that evil to cause turmoil in the hearts and lives of Adam and Eve. This original occurrence of turmoil is what puts us at odds with God and at odds with the enemy, too.

From that day forward mankind had a choice: Either get the much-needed saving peace with God, or make peace with the devil. And this, my friends, has been the battle in each of our lives since that day. As a matter of fact, it is because of this very incident that evil exists! And all along man was unaware of this because he was at peace with God.

Notice what is stated a few verses later.

Genesis 3:22-24

"And the LORD God said, Behold, the man is become as one of us, **to know good and evil**: and now, lest he put forth his hand, and take also of the tree of life, and eat, and **live for ever**: Therefore the LORD God sent him forth from the garden of Eden, to till the ground from whence he was taken. So **he drove out** the man…"

We see here that Adam knew God. And this was all the good that he was ever going to need to know. After all, who needs to know any more good than God? There is nothing more 'good' than God, my friends. But, nevertheless, the Bible tells us that Adam also got to know evil. The devil came into the garden and tempted him to follow his leading, thereby introducing him—along with mankind—to evil.

Because man knew that which was good and that which was evil, God had no choice but to drive him from the garden. God was forced to drive him from the garden to save him from eating of the tree of life and thus living forever in a corrupt state. Had God not removed Adam from the garden, man would be forced to dwell forever with that which is evil.

So God drove Adam and Eve out of the garden. The word *drove* is the past tense of *drive*, which means *to urge forward by force*. Just as we would drive a nail into a two-by-four, God was forced to drive man from the garden. Although at a quick glance this appears to be an unmerciful act by God, it is actually quite the opposite. By forcing man out of the garden, God in his mercy was then able to make peace with him again.

As we previously saw, Romans 5:1 asserts that we are justified by faith and therefore have peace with God. But in order to have peace with God, we are going to have to accept the Lord Jesus Christ as well as the tribulation that comes in doing so.

The apostle Paul expounds upon this truth in the following lines.

Ephesians 2:13-15

"But now **in Christ Jesus** ye who sometimes were far off are **made nigh** by the blood of Christ. **For he is our peace**, who hath **made both one**, and hath broken down the middle wall of partition between us; **Having abolished in his flesh the enmity,** even the law of commandments contained in ordinances; for to make in himself of twain **one new man, so making peace**:"

So we see that it is Jesus who is our avenue to peace! Christ is the one who brings us to peace with God. This verse clearly tells us that Jesus is the only One capable of breaking down the partition that separates us from God. You see, there was this great partition—the holy of holies—that protected man from the holiness of God because of the evil that permeated our lives. But the Bible states that Jesus became our peace by ripping this veil in two. The battle is won. When two become one, the battle is won! It's done! Glory to the Son!

Now take a look at verse 15. Recall that *enmity* is the same word used back in Genesis 3 when we first experienced aught with God. Oh, my friends, can you see where this is going? The enmity between Adam and Eve and the devil that passed from his and her seed to our seed is the reason why everybody who has ever been born since then can now have peace with God through the Lord Jesus Christ! But, and this is a big but, obtaining this faith requires us to have faith. We must have faith in Him.

Now it is our faith *in* Christ that saves us, but it is the faith *of* Christ that changes us. In our next chapter we are going to talk about this faith in great detail. But for now, it is sufficient to know that the faith of Christ is what specifically grants us access to God. It is also this faith that allows us to overcome so many temptations that can lead to the vast amount of tribulations that we may face in our lives. When Adam and Eve failed to withstand their temptation in Genesis 3, it brought turmoil into their lives, and all peace they once had with God was forfeited.

Through the tribulations that they were allowed to endure, the first couple discovered that evil cannot coexist with peace. Because of their failure, they were driven out of the garden in a very unpleasant manner. But in driving them out, God mercifully formed an avenue of reconciliation for man, namely, the Lord Jesus Christ. And now, simply by our meager faith in Him, we can be granted access to peace with God. But it is by *His* faith that we are able to maintain our peace with God while living in this world of evil.

The world is a place of evil; there's no way around it. It was created when God made peace, and what was left over was taken over by the evil one. And Satan takes the evil and instigates turmoil in our lives. He does this because he understands that we become his enemy immediately after making peace with God. Yes, my friends, to find and refine this peace, we are going to need a heavy dose of faith. Not only the faith *in* Christ that saves us, but also the faith *of* Christ that changes us!

NINE

RU PENDING OR DEPENDING

In this study on battling spiritual warfare using a preparation of our meditation to maintain our peace, we are going to have to learn more about another fruit of the Spirit – the fruit of faith. We have spoken previously about this matter of faith and its importance in our spiritual warfare to maintain peace. In the following chapter, I wish to break down what faith is, and explain how we can use it in our day-to-day battles with the enemy. To do so, I will use an illustration from Scripture that points out the flaws in yielding to the wrong kind of faith.

In the apostle Paul's letter to the Galatians, we are introduced to a church that had previously been growing zealously in the grace of the Lord and had been subsequently doing great things for God. However, we see in this third chapter that this church began to stunt the grace that God had intended for them. Individually, and then collectively, the people of this great church began to cease submitting to what God was trying to accomplish through them. Hence, Paul opens this chapter with a bold admonition.

Galatians 3:1-3

"O foolish (ignorant) Galatians, who hath bewitched (charmed) you, that ye should not obey the truth, before whose eyes Jesus Christ hath been evidently set forth, crucified among you? This only would I learn of you, Received ye the Spirit by the works of the law, or by the hearing of faith? Are ye so foolish? Having begun in the Spirit, are ye now made perfect by the flesh?"

Paul is effectively calling this church ignorant for being charmed and fascinated into a position of disobedience to the "truth, before whose eyes Jesus Christ hath been evidently set forth, crucified among you..." He is reproving the Galatians for failing to submit to the work that Jesus is attempting to do through their church. He is essentially saying: Stop frustrating God's grace!

Verse 2 states, "This only would I learn of you..." This is Paul's unique way of saying: I have just one question for you. "...Received ye the Spirit by the works *of* the law, or by the hearing of faith?" He's asking: Did you get saved by doing good works (the law) or did you get saved by the hearing of faith (accepting Christ's free gifts)?

In verse 3, Paul pounds this point home, asking, "How can you be so foolish to have received the Spirit who is intended to equip you for good works through faith in Christ and then willfully turn away from that in favor of exercising your own power? The apostle writes these words in response to a church that had previously embraced God doing the work, only to exchange that blessing for the frustrating results of doing things in their own power.

Understand that it is necessary to study the context fully in order to comprehend why exactly Paul is leveling this blatant reproof. It is also important to know that the Bible as we know it today has been broken down into chapters and verses by man to make it easier for us to locate specific Scripture. It is for this reason that key truths that underlie this passage are actually in the previous verse, which is in the preceding chapter.

In Galatians 2:21, Paul writes: "I do not frustrate the grace of God…" This context indicates that what these folks at Galatia had done was so foolish that it was, in fact, frustrating God's grace.

There are many clichés in Christianity today, and one of the more prominent ones is the phrase the *grace of God.* Other clichés are the words *law, righteousness* and *faith.* These are all important words upon which our ministries rest. But if we fail to understand their true meaning, we can lose sight of what God intends to do not only through us, but for us and for others. Before I detail exactly what Paul is referring to when he says "the grace of God," allow me to first define another word: frustrate. To *frustrate* means *to stunt* or *bring to naught.*

In the Old Testament we see a covenant was made with God and the dispensation was thereof called "the age of the law." The law was when "man did something for God;" it's where man did all the work by himself. However, in the New Testament, we are introduced to the "age of grace." During this "age of grace," it is "Christ that does the work." It is accurate to say that during the age of the law, man did something for God; and during the age of grace, God does something for man. The Bible tells us that in the age of grace "sin shall not have dominion" or power over us (Romans 6:14). For in the age of grace we are no longer under tribute to the law, where it is necessary for man to do all the work; but, rather, we are under grace, where God seeks to do the work for us.

With that said, we know that when we see the phrase *the grace of God,* we recognize that the word *grace* is actually "God's work on our behalf;" it is what God wants to do through us. The Bible says, "For we are his workmanship, created in Christ Jesus unto good works, which God hath before ordained that we should walk in them" (Ephesians 2:10). Notice it does *not* say that we are His *workers,* but rather that we are His workmanship. The word *workmanship* is the Old English word for the modern English phrase *manufactured product.* So we ourselves are not to be manufacturers of His product, but instead be the product that is being manufactured! Knowing this, we can now see how the Galatians frustrated the grace of God by not allowing Him to work through them.

In the latter part of Galatians 2:21, Paul tells us "...for if righteousness come by the law, then Christ is dead in vain." The key word in this part of the verse is *righteousness.* There are two types of righteousness: one tied to justification, and the other tied to sanctification. When it comes to justification, all of our righteousness is like filthy rags (Isaiah 64:6). There is nothing that we ourselves can do to obtain justification. Remember that justification is freedom from the penalty of sin, that is, eternal damnation in hell. The second form of righteousness—sanctification—is different from justification. It is freedom from the *power* of sin. It is allowing Christ to live through our crucified or yielded soul for His purposes and glory.

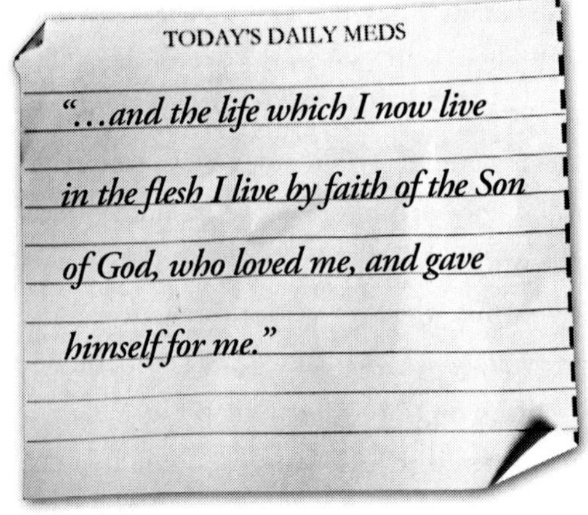

The righteousness linked to sanctification grants us the ability to triumph over sin and live a Christ-like life on earth. The Bible tells us in Titus 2:12 that "we should live soberly, **righteously**, and godly..." This verse clearly indicates that we have the ability to live righteously here on earth through Jesus Christ. It is absolutely impossible to live righteously in our own power—that is self-righteousness—but that is exactly what the Galatians were attempting. And this is why Paul emphatically said that they were foolishly frustrating the grace of God. Paul further supports his point by arguing that if we were in fact able to be righteous simply by following the law, then Jesus' sacrifice on the cross would have been for nothing.

So, how does this apply to us? You are probably wondering how you can avoid falling into the same trap as the Galatians. The key to this conundrum lies in one simple term: faith. To best explain this all-important truth, we need to look back at one more verse in our passage. A verse that has forever changed my life.

Galatians 2:20

"I am crucified with Christ: nevertheless I live; yet not I, but Christ liveth in me: and the life which I now live in the flesh **I live by the faith of the Son of God**, who loved me, and gave himself for me."

Paul says, "I am crucified with Christ…" What does this mean? It means that he willfully dies to self. In other words, he forsakes his own desires that he may clear the way for more effective, supernatural power. He next states, "nevertheless I live…" Wait a minute! How can he die but yet be alive? Let's hear his explanation: "…yet not I, but Christ liveth in me…" Ah, there's the answer! Paul has died, but Christ within him continues to live through him as Paul rises up alongside of Him. What an amazing truth! And therein lies the key to the Spirit-filled life.

But how, pray tell, do we achieve this? The latter half of Galatians 2:20 provides us with the answer. It says, "…and the life which I now live in the flesh I live **by faith of the Son of God**, who loved me, and gave himself for me."

Do you see it? Do you see where Paul tells us *how* he is able to live the crucified Christian life? He does it by the faith *of* the Son of God. It is not by "a faith *in* Christ," but rather it is "THE faith *of* Christ." He is not saying that we are to have faith in Christ in order to live the crucified life, but rather he is saying that we are to have Christ's faith. Post-conversion, our faith will simply not get the job done. We can't maintain our peace in our faith; we will only maintain peace in His faith!

My friend, again, there is great theology in the prepositions of the New Testament! The word *of* is yet another preposition that carries a vast amount of truth. Dissected and defined, *of* means *belonging to*. So Paul is actually saying: I'm dead, but I've come back to life. It's not me who has come back to life, but rather it's Christ who lives in me. So the life that I now live is by a faith that doesn't belong to me, but rather a faith that belongs to Him. And if I stop yielding to that faith and start yielding to the meager faith that saved me, then I'm going to stunt the grace of God and **become a** foolish person that tries to do the work of God in my own power!

My friends, our faith is necessary to get saved. But once God saves us, He doesn't want us to rely upon our information-dependent faith anymore. Oh no, sir! He died so that we may obtain *His* faith.

Before I got saved I knew how to love people, but my measure of love was nowhere near the measure of love that I now can express by yielding to the fruit-of-the-Spirit love! The love of God is illustrated this way: "Give and it shall be given unto you; good measure, pressed down, and shaken together, and running over, shall men give unto your bosom" (Luke 6:38). That's a demonstration of God's overflowing love.

Again, we reiterate what we have learned in past chapters: It is likewise with all nine fruits of the Spirit. We can experience some joy apart from the influence of the Holy Spirit, but our human joy does not even compare to the supernatural joy that we get when we embrace the joy of Christ. I had some peace before Christ, but it is the fruit of the Spirit peace—which He now grants me—that I am learning to maintain. Our human peace is always fleeting. His peace passes understanding! Likewise, my friends, upon conversion we are afforded the opportunity to exchange our limited faith for the seventh fruit of the Spirit, His limitless faith. Remember, *our* faith is simply knowledge-based, and has no real amount of power to it. But Christ's faith only needs a mustard-seed measure in order to move mountains!

Unfortunately, there are a great many people raised in Christian circles who live their entire lives by their own faith, rather than by His faith. And this is why this point must be stressed to such a great degree. We have already seen that we will be absolutely vulnerable to the turmoil of the enemy if we lack an adequate amount of faith, or confidence, in Christ to be our deliverer. It is all too typical for Christians to be up and down, up and down, allowing God to begin good works and then stunting them from full fruition. My friends, this is not what God intended for us His saints. Living by our own faith yields not the abundant Christian life, but sadly, produces a redundant Christian life.

Through the years of serving in the ministry of Reformers Unanimous, I have observed a remarkable phenomenon. It is often typical for a newly converted former addict to be able to yield to God's faith with more regularity than people who have been "churched" their whole lives. The reason for this is that those who have grown up in strong Christian environments more often than not have a great degree of good character instilled into them. Good character, in and of itself, is certainly not a bad thing. It's actually quite the contrary. However, when one possesses strong character, he can easily slip into relying upon his own self-righteous faith rather than yielding to the Holy Spirit and His fruits.

On the other hand, the ex-addict is typically lacking the measure of character necessary to be able to "perform" as a Christian when walking in his own power. When the erstwhile addict with little or no character is not walking in the Spirit, it becomes painfully apparent because he has very limited self-righteousness. Granted, this can be both a blessing and a curse. Yes, the converted addict tends to experience God's fruits more than many churched people due to the simple fact that this is his only option if he wishes to maintain his testimony.

However, when the new Christian who lacks character walks outside of the Spirit, he will quickly fall into unrighteousness and, thus, a deeper and more egregious level of sin. You see, those who lack good character have a very limited propensity for self-righteousness. It simply is not within their grasp.

But what exactly is self-righteousness? It is Christian lingo for *doing good in your own power.* The Bible clearly teaches that God prefers even unrighteousness over self-righteousness. Note what our Lord Himself said: "So then because thou art lukewarm, and neither cold nor hot, I will spue thee out of my mouth" (Revelation 3:16). Self-righteousness is the result of rejecting the faith of Jesus in favor of our own character and personal measure of faith in facts and assumptions.

Now, the word *faith* is the Old English word for the modern English word *dependence*, or *confidence.* If I were to say I have faith in a chair but then fully support my weight upon a rail as I gently sit down, you would say: "No Steve, you don't have faith in that chair!" Now if I were to let go of the rail and gently sit down in the chair, you would say: "Well, it looks like you have a little more faith in the chair now." Lastly, if I were to simply plop down into the chair and then lift my legs off the ground, thus allowing the chair to fully support my entire weight, then you could say: "Ah, there you go! Now you have faith in the chair!"

It is only when we fully depend upon someone or something that we can say that we have complete faith in that entity. This is the faith that the Bible calls us to have, and as Christians we have all the faith we will ever need; we have the faith of the Lord Jesus Christ. However, when the disciples said, "increase our faith," they were not referring to a quantity of faith but, rather, the duration of faith. They were requesting assistance in order to increase the duration whereby they yielded to His faith rather than their own faith.

Let's take a look at another verse that teaches us more about this word *of* and how it is connected to the word *faith* in Jesus Christ. It is no different than the love of God, or the joy of the Lord, or the peace of God we so desperately need to maintain in difficult circumstance. To keep the peace of God, we are going to need the faith of God.

Galatians 3:22

"But the scripture hath concluded all under sin, that the promise **by faith of Jesus Christ** might be **given to them that believe**."

Now, if you were to study the context surrounding this verse, it would be clear that Paul is not referring to the penalty of sin, but instead he is speaking of the power that sin holds over us. Paul is pointing out here that there is no reason why we as believers should be held hostage to the power of sin. He says that if we will simply embrace the promise that Jesus Christ has given us, we need not be under the power of sin. How do we do this? "...by faith OF Jesus Christ..." Again, we see that the faith *of* Christ is not a faith that saves us. It's THE faith that changes us! To those of us who are believers, we—and only we—have access to this faith, this faith *of* Christ.

To further distinguish the difference between our faith and the faith of Christ, read ahead.

Galatians 3:24-25

"Wherefore the law was our schoolmaster to bring us unto Christ, that we might be justified by faith. But after that faith is come, we are no longer under a schoolmaster."

When we are yet to come to Christ, we can do nothing but follow a law in attempting to remain at peace with God or to keep ourselves at peace with others. This is why Paul refers to the law as being our schoolmaster prior to coming to Christ. However, once we obtain *our* own measure of faith in Christ's propitiation payment for our sin in order to justify us, we are then granted a new faith—His faith—and we are no longer subject to the old schoolmaster and our pathetic information-dependent faith. Rather, we are now governed by grace through the faith *of* Jesus Christ. This is what it means to transition from rules to relationship.

Take my six-year-old son, Chance, for example. My wife Lori and I are always reminding him that it is a rule to make his bed each morning. Most days, he will submit to this rule and make his bed before beginning his day. However, if Chance follows the pattern of my other older children, he will eventually begin to make his bed willfully every day. Why? Because he hopes he will make the transition from rules to relationship. Sooner or later, Chance will realize that because he loves me and has a relationship with me, he ought to make his bed because he wishes to please me.

This, my friends, is exactly what occurs to us as we exchange our meager faith for His miraculous faith. We begin to transition from dogmatic rules to dynamic relationship, from law to grace. And as we have seen, this can only be accomplished by incorporating into our meditations the faith *of* Jesus Christ, which is not dependent upon perception but on promises!

I want to be clear that justification is simply obtained only through our faith in Christ. No amount of good works or law-abiding behavior can save us from the penalty of our sin. However, the point is that it is *our* faith that saves us, and once we come to a saving faith, we are then gifted the faith *of* Christ that sanctifies us. The tragedy that so often occurs is that Christians tend to cling to their own limited faith even after being granted access to His faith, thus foregoing any real benefits of our sanctification. And this, my friend, does not lead to any true and lasting sin-defeating power. It is this error that leaves us serving who Paul calls the "schoolmaster" even after we have been saved.

In another of the apostle Paul's epistles, we see yet more language that differentiates between the faith that justifies (our faith *in* Christ) and the faith that sanctifies (the faith *of* Christ).

Romans 3:20-22

"Therefore by the deeds of the law there shall no flesh be justified in his sight: for by the law is the knowledge of sin. But now the righteousness of God without the law is manifested, being witnessed by the law and the prophets; Even the righteousness of God which is by **faith of Jesus Christ unto all and upon all them that believe**: for there is no difference:"

When Paul writes that "by the deeds of the law there shall no flesh be justified in his sight: for by the law is the knowledge of sin... " he is stating the fact that nobody is able to live a sinless life and adhere to the law in its entirety. He goes on to say: "the righteousness of God without the law is manifested...by faith *of* Jesus Christ unto all and upon all them that believe..."

Now, recall that the word *righteousness* in this verse, like the last verse we studied, means *the ability to live right.* So we see here that Paul is telling us the only way we can live right is by expressing the faith *of* Jesus Christ. Furthermore, Paul is very clear to state that the faith *of* Jesus Christ is available unto "all them that believe..." Again, we see that it is *our* faith that brings us to believe *in* Christ, and it is the faith *of* Christ that allows us to live righteous, or live right. In short, what Paul is telling us is that if you believe with a faith that saves you, you receive the faith that changes you! Granted, this faith must be nurtured within our nature, but we absolutely are granted it upon salvation.

Perhaps the simplest statement that Paul makes to teach this truth is found elsewhere in this epistle.

Romans 5:1-2

"Therefore being justified by faith, we have peace with God through our Lord Jesus Christ: **by whom <u>also</u>** we have access **by faith** into this grace wherein we stand, and rejoice in hope of the glory of God."

Again, we see here we are justified by faith—our faith—to a position of peace with God by believing in our Lord Jesus Christ. It brings us the peace we need with God in order to live at peace with others. Next, Paul goes on to say that through Jesus, we also have access to a new kind of faith that will propel us into the realm of grace. He says "by whom also..." This phrase indicates that we now have something added to our faith because of a faith in Someone else. He is saying that we now have Christ's access to grace. Remember, grace is when God does the work for us. So by having faith *in* Christ, we receive the faith of Christ that opens the door to His grace. Pretty cool stuff!

Students often ask me: "Steve, why do I keep falling all the time?" After studying this passage, I would now point them to this piece of Scripture. Notice Paul goes on to state in verse 2 "*...wherein we stand...*" The word *wherein* simply means *in where*. So we can see then that if we want to remain standing––thus avoiding falls––we must remain in Christ's grace. Only by having the faith *of* Christ can we reside where His grace is.

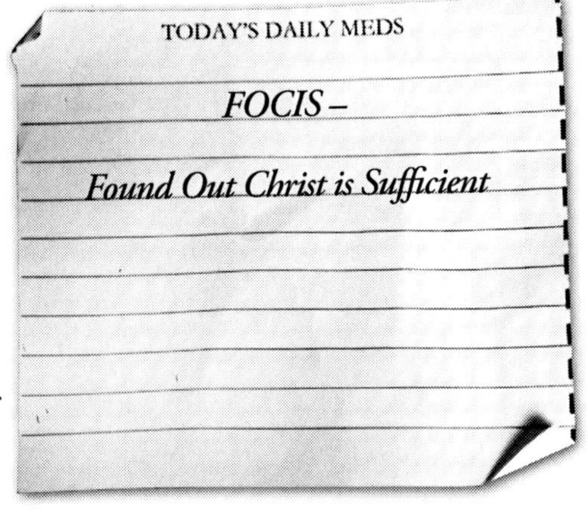

This truth is deep yet simple. If we are able to live in God's grace, we will stand—not fall—and rejoice in the glory of God! My friends, that is exactly the kind of life I wish to live, and I am sure you do, too. All we have to do is exercise the faith *of* Christ that will lead us to His grace. To have the faith of Christ is to be *in* Christ, and the quickest way to fall is to get out from this position.

Jesus tells us a total of 25 times in the Scriptures to abide in Him. He does not say to reside (come and go) in Him, but to abide in Him. He wants us to stay there. We are to stay fixed *in* Jesus. We are to focus on Him alone. A helpful acrostic to remember is FOCIS, which stands for: Found Out Christ Is Sufficient.

Now, He wouldn't have told us to abide in Him if it were impossible to wander from Him. But granted, when we are saved, Jesus comes to live in our hearts, and this is something that we cannot lose no matter what.

However, it is possible to wander from our position *in* Christ. Can't you just feel yourself pulling away from Him sometimes? I know I sure can. This is why the apostle Paul tells us 76 times to remain *in* Christ. If you count all the times Paul says "in Christ," "through Christ," "in Him" and "through Him," it adds up to 174 times! Obviously, my friends, Paul sought to place great importance upon our positioning. We will discuss this more in a later chapter.

All of these positions are based on transitioning out from under our faith and turning instead to His faith. With our faith we can do good, but it's all in our own power and not pleasing to the Lord. We can try harder to do better, but we will never experience the fruit God has for us until we let go of our own faith and yield to the faith of Christ. This will be a requirement to maintain our peace in the midst of a spiritual attack from the enemy.

To abide in Him, we must keep our eyes fixed on Jesus. Even in 1865, hymn writer Frances R. Havergal understood this concept as she penned these words:

Like a river glorious **is God's perfect peace,**
Over all victorious, in its bright increase;
Perfect, yet it floweth fuller every day,
Perfect, yet it groweth deeper all the way.

Refrain:
Stayed upon Jehovah, hearts are fully blest
Finding, as He promised, perfect peace and rest.

Hidden in the hollow of His blessed hand,
Never foe can follow, never traitor stand;
Not a surge of worry, not a shade of care,

Not a blast of hurry touch the spirit there.
Every joy or trial falleth from above,
Traced upon our dial by the Sun of Love;
We may trust Him fully all for us to do;
They who trust Him wholly find Him wholly true.

Romans 5:3-5

"And not only [so], but we glory in tribulations also: knowing that tribulation worketh patience; And patience, experience; and experience, hope: And hope maketh not ashamed; because the love of God is shed abroad in our hearts by the Holy Ghost which is given unto us."

The word *glory* means *to make look good.* Now, how many of us truly look good in the midst of tribulations? Paul is telling us right here that it is possible and that we should, in fact, glory through our trials. Why do we so often fail to do so? Because, we are rejecting our indwelling fruit of the Spirit, and most importantly, His faith. The latter part of verse 5 states "because the love of God is shed abroad in our hearts by the Holy Ghost which is given unto us." This is the reason, Paul says, that we are able to look good through tribulations. It starts with the first fruit of the Spirit: love, then progresses to joy, then to peace, and so on all the way down to temperance.

But this fruitful life is not possible, my friends, if we operate in our own power. When we operate in our own power, we frustrate our God who wishes to see us look good through life's adverse circumstances. For when we look good, it is a direct reflection upon His power over our lives. He wants to use us as a territory for His glory!

After being named Most Valuable Player of Super Bowl XXXIV,

St. Louis Rams quarterback Kurt Warner had a chance to glorify himself before a global television audience of about 2 billion people. Instead, the record-setting Warner said: "I have to give praise and glory to my Lord and Savior up above. Thank you, Jesus."[1] Now that's making God look good! So what do ya' say? Let's not frustrate Him, friends! Let's make God look good, and in the process, make ourselves look good, too! This territory of God's glory will grant us a release and promote the gospel of peace.

I wish to observe one final passage to further detail this truth about two distinct faiths. Take a look at what Paul writes in the following verses.

Romans 1:16-17

"For I am not ashamed of the gospel of Christ: for it is the power of God unto salvation to every one that believeth; to the Jew first, and also to the Greek. For **therein** is the righteousness of God revealed **from faith to faith**: as it is written, **The just shall live by faith."**

Just as there are two separate and distinct faiths, there are also two elements of sin—the penalty of sin and the power of sin. One faith—our faith—gets us out from underneath the penalty of sin; this is justification. The other faith, His faith, gets us out from underneath the power of sin; this is sanctification. Paul says everyone who believeth, or exercises their own faith, is given the power of God that extends salvation. He then goes on to say, "therein is the righteousness of God revealed from faith to faith… " The word *therein* simply means *in there*. So when we are saved by God, we are granted the ability to be in there—in Christ—and thereby living by His righteousness.

Paul says this is revealed from "faith to faith." This is God's way of saying that righteousness is found by transitioning from our faith to the faith of Christ. He closes this truth by saying, "...The just shall live by faith." The only way to live justly—to be right with God—is by living by faith. And it is not our faith that will do this, my friends; it is His faith!

Perhaps the finest overall example of the transition from our faith to the faith of Christ can be observed in Romans 6-8. In Romans 6, we see that the age of the law, when it was necessary for man to do all the work by obeying rules, was eliminated. In Romans 8, we see the inception of the age of grace, when God does the work for man.

This leaves Chapter 7, where we see that Paul is very frustrated as he strives to make the transition from the law to grace. My friends, this is the battle that we will engage in for the rest of our lives! We must constantly check ourselves to see if we are living by the law (rules) or by grace (relationship). We see in Romans 7 that Paul is seeking not to be a performer (self-righteous), but rather a conformer (to His righteousness).

By conforming to the image of Christ, we may make the transition from Romans 6 Christians to Romans 8 Christians. Now, how do we become able to do this, you ask? The only way is by developing a dynamic love relationship with Jesus Christ. It will be in the early hours of the day that Jesus will reveal to you whether or not you are living by your own faith, or by His faith. Personally speaking, I quite often find myself convicted over things the Lord shows me where I blew it by choosing my own meager faith over His magnificent faith. I can then take this conviction and get right with God, thus learning from my mistake and drawing closer to Him. This, my friends, is the *only* way to master the embracing of His righteousness!

John Owen, bracketed with Jonathan Edwards as one of the

weightiest Puritan theologians of all time, once said: "See in the meantime that your faith brings forth obedience, and God in due time will cause it to bring forth peace." Our job is to exercise our faith to save us, and His faith—which is demonstrated by our obedience—to change us. It is that obedient faith of the Lord Jesus Christ will bring forth a lasting peace in every pressure of life.

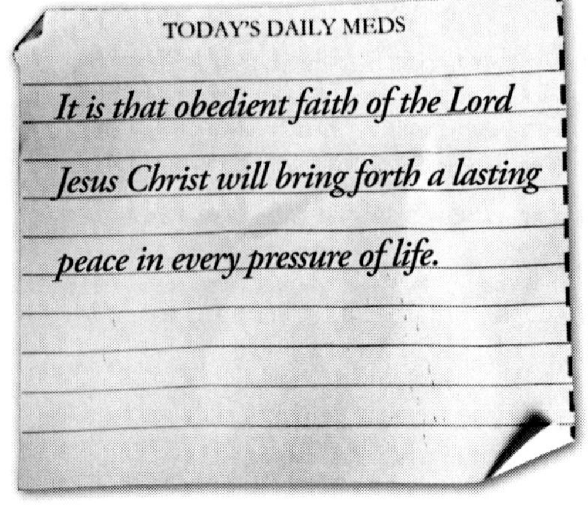

Finally, let's take a look at Paul's writings in the book of Philippians. This letter was written later in his life, and I believe that he had a stronger grasp upon many issues at this stage. The first 10 verses of Chapter 3 eloquently illustrate what it is to live by the faith of Christ and therefore embrace His righteousness. Please take the time to study this important passage, and then I will break it down piece by piece.

Philippians 3:1-10

"Finally, my brethren, **rejoice in the Lord**. To write the same things to you, to me indeed is not grievous, but for you it is safe. Beware of dogs, beware of evil workers, beware of the concision. For we are the circumcision, **which worship God in the spirit**, and **rejoice in Christ Jesus**, and have **no confidence in the flesh**. Though I might also have confidence in the flesh. If any other man thinketh that he hath whereof he might trust in the flesh, I more: Circumcised the eighth day, of the stock of Israel, [of] the tribe of Benjamin, an Hebrew of the Hebrews; as touching the law, a Pharisee; Concerning zeal, persecuting the church; touching the righteousness which is in the law, blameless. But what things were gain to me, those I counted loss for Christ. Yea doubtless, and I count all things [but] loss for the excellency of the knowledge of Christ Jesus my Lord: for whom I have suffered the loss of all things, and do count them [but] dung, that I may win Christ, And be found **in him**, not having **mine own righteousness**, which is **of the law**, but that which is through the **faith of Christ**, the righteousness which is **of God by faith**: That I may know him, and the power of his resurrection, and the fellowship of his sufferings, being made conformable unto his death;"

In this passage, Paul is delivering a eulogy of sorts. He begins verse 1 by saying, "Finally, my brethren, rejoice in the Lord…" Rejoice is a joy that repeats itself. "To write the same things to you, to me indeed is not grievous, but for you it is safe." What he is saying here is that he has, for the most part, gotten to the point where he only preaches one message. He states that this fact is not troublesome to him, and it is safe, or beneficial, for those to whom he is speaking.

When broken down, all preaching can be put into two primary categories: salvation messages and relationship messages. Friend, if you're saved today, you have undoubtedly heard and have gotten the point of the former. And since Paul is speaking to the brethren––saved people at Philippi—he is obviously saying that he now is content with repeatedly teaching truths concerning our relationship with Christ.

In verse 2, Paul goes on to say: "Beware of dogs, beware of evil workers, beware of the concision." Here he is giving us three epitaphs defining the *Judeizers.* The Judeizers were those who taught that salvation came via faith plus circumcision. And this of course is nothing more than vain symbolism. Can you see how this applies to today, my friends? We see this type of symbolism throughout many so-called Christian circles, and it is weakening Christianity at a rapid pace. Too often we see Christians who seek to express their faith by following rules on the outside rather than embracing a relationship with Christ on the inside. This is what Paul is referring to when he cautions us to beware. Be aware of those who are pretenders.

Paul elucidates this point in verse 3: "For we are the circumcision, which worship God in the spirit, and rejoice in Christ Jesus, and have no confidence in the flesh." He is clear to say that we (meaning himself and the Philippian brethren) worship in the Spirit, not the soul via our mind, will and emotions. Our devotion and interaction with God, he is saying, is on a personal, spiritual level that has nothing to do with purposeful outward shows of symbolism. And because of this type of worship, Paul says, he rejoices—experiences repeating joy—in Christ and what He is able to do through him.

He then states that such a relationship leaves him with no reason to seek confidence—or faith—in flesh, or self. It is important to note that the apostle is not referring to wicked flesh here. It is obvious that we cannot please God by worshiping Him with wicked flesh. But where many Christians err is when they attempt to worship God with good flesh. God is not impressed with any kind of worship done in our own power. Period.

Let's pause to further develop this point. We have discussed how we are a trichotomy made up of a body, soul and spirit. We recognize that when we are doing good in our own power, it is still the soul that is in control, and this is what we call self-righteousness. The world would refer to this as character. Granted, good character is valuable and it plays a vital role in a Christian's life, but what we must strive to obtain is Spirit-control.

Spirit-control is just that: our bodies being under the influence of the Spirit; and this is the avenue to living the true Christian life. Going back to character, allow me to reiterate that good character is, indeed, an important attribute of a Christian. We want everyone to have good character, especially our children. But good character is no substitute for good Christianity. If our character dominates us, we will tend to take an attitude that says, "Well, I can do this. I've got willpower!"

Strictly speaking, willpower is part of the soul, and we don't need soul-control to excel at the Christian life. No, my friends, we must instead train ourselves to be willing to throw out our willpower and be willing to submit to God's power!

It is to this end that Paul writes verses 4-6: "Though I might also have confidence in the flesh. If any other man thinketh that he hath whereof he might trust in the flesh, I more: Circumcised the eighth day, of the stock of Israel, of the tribe of Benjamin, an Hebrew of the Hebrews; as touching the law, a Pharisee; Concerning zeal, persecuting the church; touching the righteousness which is in the law, blameless."

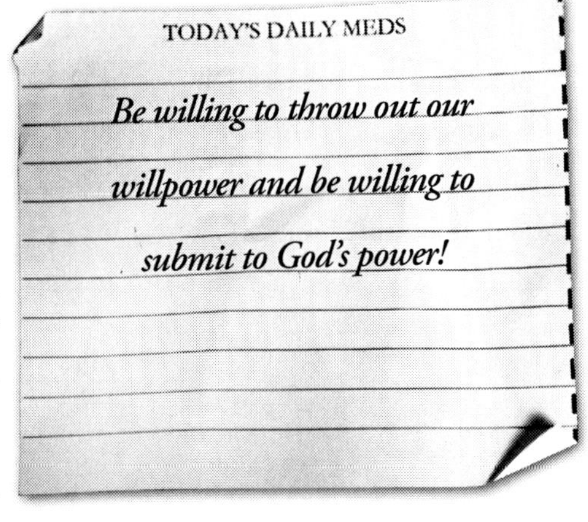

Paul is making a point to the Philippians by proving that if there is anybody worthy of having confidence in their own flesh, or in themselves, it would be him. But he tells us that he counts it all for loss, meaning that he considers it not when it comes time to draw power from God. How amazing it is that Paul, a blameless Pharisee who had himself written the rules, drew no strength from himself. He instead yielded to the Spirit and counted his own credentials "all but loss." In today's world, this would be tantamount to a graduate of Harvard Law School omitting his education from his résumé.

Paul puts it this it like this in verses 7-8: "But what things were gain to me, those I counted loss for Christ. Yea doubtless, and I count all things but loss for the excellency of the knowledge of Christ Jesus my Lord: for whom I have suffered the loss of all things, and do count them but dung, that I may win Christ." Simplified to its most basic meaning, Paul is telling us that all things are of no value when compared to the value of a personal love relationship with Jesus Christ. It is the personal relationship that precipitates the pure meditations that will clean up our hearts and thus our behaviors.

A love relationship with Christ gives us those coveted Philippians 4:8 thoughts of optimism and purges the negative, critical, pessimistic and competitive thoughts that can so easily destroy our peace, and eventually, our lives. I have heard it taught that one must change their thoughts in order to develop a dynamic relationship with God. My friends, this is works-based sanctification and simply not true! When we develop a relationship with the Lord, it is then that He will begin to change our thoughts!

And this is the sole reason that Paul considers anything that hinders his personal relationship with God to be but dung. He knows the intrinsic value of having an undefiled avenue of communication with our Savior. Paul goes on to explain the outcome of the personal relationship of which he is speaking. He says in verses 9-10: "And be found in him, not having mine own righteousness (which is self-righteousness), which is of the law (based on rules), but that which is through the faith *of* Christ, the righteousness which is of God by faith: That I may know him, and the power of his resurrection, and the fellowship of his sufferings, being made conformable unto his death;" The key phrase in verse 9 is "found in Him."

Paul is teaching us that it is our position *in* Christ that allows us to utilize and yield to His righteousness. He is saying that he desires not to have any measure of righteousness that comes from self through obedience to rules, but rather he desires the righteousness of Christ that can only be obtained—here's our key phrase again—through the faith *of* Christ. Why does he desire this so desperately? It is because he understands that to have the faith of Christ is the only true way that he "...may know him, and the power of his resurrection, and the fellowship of his sufferings..." And there it is my friends. The only way to know God, to experience the power of His resurrection, to understand the fellowship of His tomb, and to experience blessed Calvary is to yield to the faith of Christ.

So we see that two simple prepositions in our English language comprise the platform upon which preparation of our peace is dependent: *of* and *in*. The faith *of* Christ, and our position *in* Christ. It takes a *relationship* to take *ownership* of these two prepositions. And that's a good proposition. A proposition from a preposition that will provide our preparation with the meditation we need to portray peace in every situation.

TEN

RU WINKING OR THINKING?

A lot of people think that when they first begin to experience peace in their lives, that in order to maintain that peace, they must learn to overlook the mistakes of others. The Bible calls this *winking* at sin. Too often we make the mistake of winking at the sins of those who become closest to us in an effort to maintain peace. This futile effort may not cause division between us and the offending party but it will eventually cause us to lose our peace with ourselves!

When we begin to feel the turmoil and difficulty caused by the problems of others in our lives, we often mistakenly feel we need to give them a free pass, lest the negative dwelling upon their behavior eventually overcomes us. My friends, this is not the way God wants us to battle against sin! He does not want us to maintain our peace by raising our tolerance for wickedness.

Rather than winking at sin and setting ourselves up to embrace discouraging behaviors, He wants us to point our thoughts toward

Him. He wants us *thinking* on Him instead of *winking* at sin! Now God thinks about us unceasingly, and He wants us to think on Him in a like manner. You see, the truth is that when we prepare for the turmoil that we can safely assume is sure to come into our lives by thinking primarily upon Him in anticipation of negative situations, we will establish the spiritual momentum we need to maintain a heart of peace through the most dire of these circumstances.

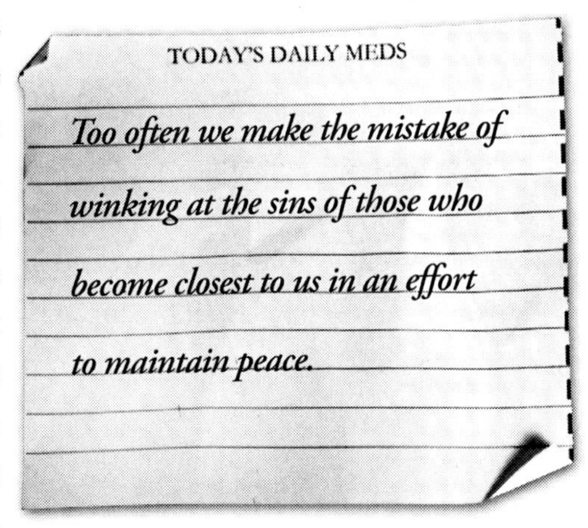

Now, this does not mean that others' sin will not bother us or have an emotional effect on us. Oh no, sin in the lives of those we love surely will affect us. However, when we at first begin to feel the agitation as a result of another's transgression, our meditations should be able to quickly recognize our peace has been compromised, and we can subsequently cast down those negative thoughts. Instead of dwelling on the wrongs that have been done, we will be able to maintain a mindset on Him. We cannot let the enemy occupy territory in our hearts. We must think on Him and thus experience the sweet peace that He has reserved for us.

Just this past week as I was headed to the office for an RU staff meeting, I found myself thrown into a world of potential strife. As I was driving, I received a call informing me that a significant amount of money that had been committed to our ministry would not arrive when expected, if at all. Given our current financial position, this was very distressing news, to say the least. The caller told me that the funds had been delayed for up to a year, and even worse yet, they may be forgone altogether.

Now prior to receiving this call, I was literally singing praises to the Lord, dwelling on the truth that I intended to share with my staff in just a few minutes. After receiving the call, I was stunned! I began to become anxious and my heart began to race. But then I recognized that I had 50 staff people waiting for me to encourage them.

It was my responsibility to prepare them for our national conference! It was at this point that I was at a crossroads. I could downplay our financial condition and completely overlook this bad news, but I knew this would inevitably put us in a more difficult position. Or, I could return my thinking back to Him, and recognize that God is in charge of our ministry's finances. He promised, after all, to supply all our needs "according to his riches" (Philippians 4:19). God does not require anybody to cooperate with Him for me to receive any benefit I need financially, personally or professionally.

So sure enough, by recognizing myself beginning to experience turmoil and forfeiting my tranquility, I was able to recover and maintain the peace of God! How was this done? By advance preparations of my meditations in advance of my situations, that's how! Glory to God, the devil declared war but I declared peace. *That* battle was won because I and His Spirit were one! Because God empowered me to do this, we were blessed to have a strong staff meeting. The staff was moved by what was discussed, and as I returned to the office, I realized I had just undergone and overcome spiritual oppression.

I was faced with an opportunity to continue to think on Him, or to get all worked up and anxious over an uncontrollable situation. Or worse yet, I could have chosen to blow off the bad news and act as if nothing had happened. Instead I was eventually able to focus on it and determine effective strategies to ensure liquidity.

To do nothing in a crisis, by the way, is *not* trusting Christ. That's negligence. Negligence has never won ONE battle, much less a war. More often than not, God wants us to take action one way or another. You will not find the phrase "let go and let God" in the Bible. However, trusting Christ is an acknowledgement in our hearts that though we are concerned, we completely trust our heavenly Father to do what is best for us and to respond quickly and submissively to the prompted responses of those meditations. We must know our circumstances are in His hands, and thus keep our thoughts stayed on Him because we *know* that He is thinking about our well-being.

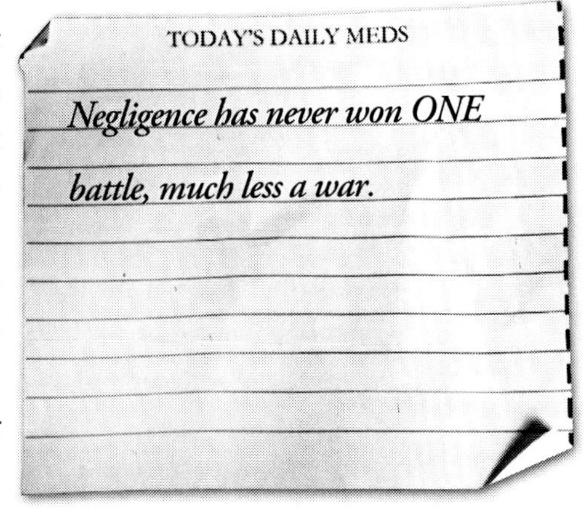

The Bible states, "For I know the thoughts that **I think toward you**, saith the LORD, thoughts of peace, and not of evil, to give you an expected end" (Jeremiah 29:11). We see by this verse that God does indeed think of us. And better still, He thinks of us with thoughts of peace rather than the evil our behavior would typically warrant! He never thinks evil of us!

My friends, we can be sure that if God is thinking on us, He's certainly got our back, too. In our last chapter we learned that when God made peace, evil was created as a leftover by-product. We also learned that Lucifer took that evil and used it to rock and shake the foundations of the world. Since that time, turmoil and war have been embedded elements here on earth. It is important to know that God does not take into account the remnants of His creation when He thinks upon us; evil is a forgotten and never--used entity when God considers His saints.

Instead, God sees us in the peace that He formed for a reason. He views us this way so that He may, the prophet Jeremiah goes on to say, "bring us to an expected end. "You see, my friends, God has an expected end for each of us, and it does not require the cooperation of anybody to see that it comes to pass.

Therefore, the evil that plagues our lives in this world is essentially moot. When we sin, or when others' sin comes into our lives, the turmoil that is precipitated—believe it or not—has no distracting effect on His expected end for us. Unless, of course, God permitted that circumstance to enter our lives, resulting in the turmoil necessary to RE-guide us toward His expected end. And friends, when you arrive at your expected end, the verse continues, "then shall ye call upon the Lord, and ye shall go and pray unto me, and I will hearken unto you" (Jeremiah 29:12).

The word *upon* is a preposition that is rarely used in our mother tongue today. According to the Webster's 1828 dictionary, it is a word that *notes approach*. So Jeremiah is saying it is when we come to our expected end that we approach the Lord. The passage continues, "And ye shall seek me, and find [me], when ye shall search for me with all your heart" (v. 13).

But what is this all saying? It is simply saying that we cannot alter

God's plan, and therefore it is pointless to fight it or allow turmoil to come into our lives as a result of it. Rather, we should allow God to take us to our expected end while maintaining a spirit of peace. And when we do this, we can find God standing behind each and every circumstance that has manifested itself in our lives.

You see, the devil's primary objective is to use people, places and things to instigate us to evil—to cause turmoil in our lives that will limit God's power upon us. In other words, his goal is all-out war against the brethren. The Bible tells us that we ought to be blameless sons of God without rebuke amongst a crooked and perverse nation among whom we shine as lights in the world (Philippians 2:15).

The devil seeks to destroy our testimonies to the world so that the world, in turn, will view our God with contempt. As we have previously discussed, one of Satan's best-used tactics is to create turmoil in our lives by way of those whom we love.

With that said, we must expect that we will be faced with sin in others' lives, and know the devil wants us to do one of two things in response to it. He either wants us to wink at it, that is to say, ignore it; or he wants us to be pulled out from our position in Christ that gives us the peace of God. When he is successful in getting us to do one of these two things, then he has effectively done the antithesis of glorifying God. He makes God look bad and us, too!

So knowing what the devil wants us to do, what do you think God would have us do in such adverse circumstances? He wants us to look directly at the sin, not wink at it, consider it and then seek the Lord's face by saying: Lord, I need Your heart, I need Your peace, and I need You to keep me at peace with You and those who are making these mistakes.

So we see that we cannot gain God's influential peace if we are

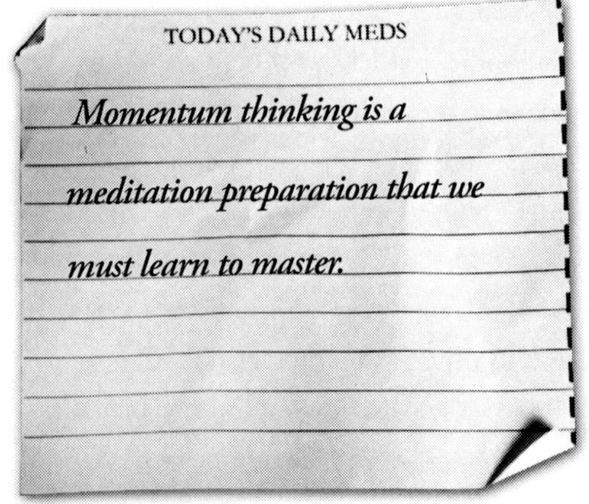

winking at sin. No, my friends, sin winked at will only fester upon our hearts, and the devil will use it to place all sorts of condemnation and turmoil into our meditations. The only way to avoid winking at sin or reacting fleshly toward it is to make prior preparation for it by constantly thinking on Him. I call this momentum thinking.

Momentum thinking is a meditation preparation that we must learn to master. For purposes of this book, let's call this particular meditation *operation preparation*. Allow me to give you a little bit of background here. An operation is a movement. So it can be said that when something is moving, it is in operation. In the military, this word is most often used to describe military strategy.

Typically, when we hear about a military operation, it is referring to the mass movement of a number of soldiers and/or war materials. Recall, if you will, January 1991 when we observed with awe as Operation Desert Storm was played out right in front of our eyes on our television screens. Now, Operation Desert Storm was most assuredly a complex military maneuver with extensive tactics and strategy. But let us now examine a few operations that are more easily conceptualized, allowing us to draw comparisons to spiritual warfare.

Head-On Warfare

Let us begin by looking at perhaps the most basic of all military operations: the head-on operation. Until the advent of modern warfare around the beginning of the 20th century, head-on operational warfare was the primary mode of battle. This type of warfare is exactly what its name suggests: head-on, face-to-face combat.

Now when an army is implementing direct warfare, it needs primarily one thing to be successful—superior numbers over the enemy. The more overwhelming a force's numbers compared to its adversary, the easier the battle will inevitably be won. An interesting statistic to note is that of all military conflicts throughout history, fewer than 4 percent were won by inferior numbers of forces.

It should also be noted that each of these occasions in which the smaller army reigned supreme happens to be documented in the Holy Bible. And by studying these against-all-odds battles, it is clear that the hand of Jehovah supernaturally ensured each victory. The battle tactic of Gideon is perhaps the greatest of these examples.

Now nowhere in the Scriptures do we see the Lord suggesting that we go head-on against the enemy, save for a few clearly inspired instances. It is likewise that God does not desire for us to take on the devil directly. My friends, the enemy and his vast array of delegated forces would love for us to challenge them head-on, for they know that they can crush us that way!

This is a fundamental truth: Don't seek evil. The Bible instructs us in Proverbs 3:7 to "depart from evil," remember? However, when we do find ourselves inadvertently squared off with the enemy as a result of him seeking us, we must keep the aforementioned principle in mind: strength comes in numbers!

In military jargon, this is what is known as *concentrated forces.*

My friends, we all have the forces capable of overcoming the enemy and his wiles. God plus one comprises a majority. The question is: Are our forces concentrated enough to withstand the attack? We must circle the wagons, so to speak, and then, and only then, engage the enemy. Until we have sufficiently concentrated our forces, it is best to retreat, allowing for time to regroup.

You probably recall the famous Battle of Gettysburg from the Civil War. Historians refer to this great battle as the turning point of this most tragic of American conflicts. It was at Gettysburg that the Union Army finally put a stop to the Confederate onslaught. The manner in which this occurred, however, is not quite as well known.

Allow me to give you a brief history lesson. In the days leading up to the battle at Gettysburg, the South's commanding general, Robert E. Lee, had planned a surprise attack upon the Union Army, which was camped in this natural amphitheater-like terrain. In preparation for this attack, Gen. Lee had banded together a massive force of infantry that would presumably be able to overwhelm the considerably smaller Northern army camped unaware in Gettysburg.

Before the Confederate attack commenced, the Union caught wind of the South's operations and scrambled to make preparation. The Union general, Ulysses S. Grant, scurried to call to assembly myriad brigades scattered throughout the northeastern United States. You see, Grant's army was widely dispersed because he knew not where the Confederate Army would seek to attack until the very last hour, so to speak. For this reason he had his regiments spread out to protect a number of key areas that could possibly be attacked.

To abbreviate this crash course in history, allow me to breeze through many of the details. Suffice it to say that Lee and his men did indeed attack Gettysburg at a time when they held a tremendous numerical advantage against the North. Grant, however, knowing his army stood little chance due to his numerical disadvantage, had his army retreat into the ridges that surrounded Gettysburg.

Grant attempted to hold off the attack, stalling it for as long as possible to allow time for reinforcements to arrive at Gettysburg. This tactic proved to be successful when a large amount of union soldiers poured into Gettysburg and gave the Union forces an eventual numbers' advantage.

And consistent with history, the army that held numerical superiority proved to be triumphant in this case as well. Though he was almost too late, Gen. Grant did succeed in effectively *concentrating* his forces and allowing for a stop to the advancing Confederate Army in their head-on tactic.

Basic warfare principle dictates that that if an opponent were to outnumber you 3:1, after the first round of engagement, the undermanned army would be lucky to emerge with 9:1 odds of surviving. And it does not take a mathematician to see that at these odds, an entity cannot remain standing for long.

Just as we see this in physical warfare, so it is also in spiritual warfare. When the devil's brigades outnumber us, we stand not a chance to stand! Friends, do not tarry in calling in the reinforcements!

How do we do this? We must train ourselves, like Gen. Grant, to call in the reinforcements in times of weakness. We must concentrate our forces to be able to withstand the attacks of the enemy. To do this we can enlist everybody and anybody we know to stand beside us in the midst of battle. Too often we allow our pride to keep us from reaching out to the reinforcements that God has placed into our lives.

My friend, transparency is an all-important survival skill. If we are hurting and don't tell anyone in our infantry, we'll soon be a dead man, just another fallen soldier rendered ineffective for God. You see, in straight-ahead warfare, it's not who has the most guns, but rather who has got the most guns now. We must not be shy to cry out to our brethren. "Iron sharpeneth iron..." (Proverbs 27:17).

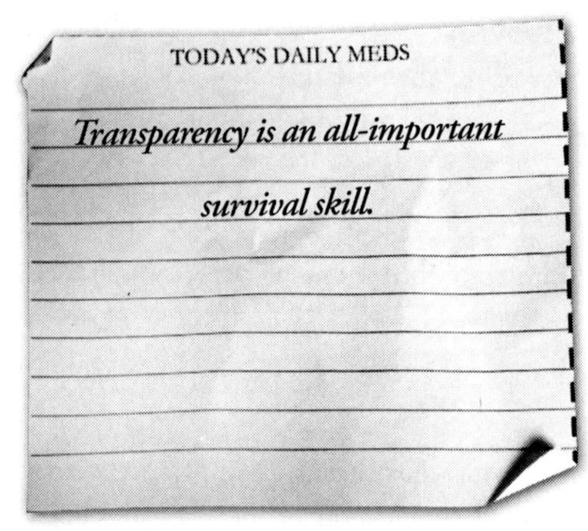

If we allow our pride to keep us from concentrating our forces, we are playing right into the devil's hand. This is exactly how he wants us to oppose him: alone! He knows that we are weak when left to ourselves. This is why, friends, it is so important to concentrate a force of believers to oppose the enemy's attacks against our lives.

Granted, we should never purposefully engage the enemy in head-on warfare. Rather, we should fight in a unique way that we will see momentarily. In the meantime, when we find ourselves defending against a frontal assault initiated by Satan, we must be entirely transparent with those whom we know. We must tell them we are struggling and let them know we need them to stand with us.

As I mentioned, the Bible tells us that we can resist the devil or we can flee the devil, but Scripture never encourages us to take Satan head-on. Now sometimes we find ourselves in this position and must go into hyper-defense mode as detailed above, but what is our standard operation of offensive procedure?

Well, the devil is supernatural and we are natural. He is "cunning, baffling and powerful," to borrow Bill Wilson's famous phrase. We cannot, in and of ourselves, outnumber Satan. With that being the case, offensive warfare against this formidable enemy calls for a better battle technique than direct warfare. We can be sure, however, that someday the devil is going to face a foe that outnumbers him.

The Bible says that at the return of Christ, we will see one seriously bloody battle. Furthermore, it tells us that at the end of this mother of all battles, the triumphant victor will be Jesus Christ! After all, remember that the Bible says that the angels outnumber demons by a ratio of 3:1. The Scriptures tell us that only one-third of the angels actually fell from heaven, thus leaving us two-thirds for the heavenly host! With these odds, we know that we have the advantage. Praise God we are on the winning side!

Take a look, if you will, at the following details of the upcoming war to end all wars.

Revelation 12:7-10

"And there was war in heaven: Michael and his angels fought against the dragon; and the dragon fought and his angels, And prevailed not; neither was their place found any more in heaven. And the great dragon was cast out, that old serpent, called the Devil, and Satan, which deceiveth the whole world: he was cast out into the earth, and his angels were cast out with him. And I heard a loud voice saying in heaven, Now is come salvation, and strength, and the kingdom of our God, and the power of his Christ: for the accuser of our brethren is cast down, which accused them before our God day and night."

In this stunning piece of Scripture, we see that Michael and his angels, the two-thirds force, fought a battle against the dragon and his contingent of angels, the one-third force. The verses above indicate that our enemy, dubbed the dragon here, plays the role of a merciless accuser of us to God. However, because of the triumph of good over evil, we are granted salvation, strength and the power of God.

Imagine being placed on trial for murder and facing the death penalty. The devil is the prosecuting attorney, but your public defender is the Lord Jesus Christ. And the judge, almighty God, is the Father of your attorney. Talk about nepotism! My friend, you cannot lose this case with Jesus as your defense.

In the coming revelation, the angels of God will able to overcome the enemy and his forces by way of two things: the blood of the Lamb, and the word of their testimonies. Oh, my friends, can you see how important our testimonies are! When our testimonies stay strong and pure, and we are able to exhibit peace and stability amidst an attack, we are able to glorify God and advance His kingdom to vast territories!

It is for this reason that the devil seeks to bring us to turmoil through his seemingly endless list of schemes that precipitate demonic oppression. The enemy knows how damaging our failure to remain at peace through tribulation can be to those whom he seeks to overpower. When we ourselves are willing to stay strong and committed to not allowing the accuser of the brethren to find something wrong with us, it glorifies God in a most profound way. And friends, the devil despises this, hence, his ceaseless efforts to bring us to shame.

So we see the eternal importance in the saints of God being able to display peace amidst turmoil. We must be able to remain at peace with God, with ourselves and with others through the most trying of circumstances. However, we cannot seek to do this by simply winking at sin, for this gives the devil a very different, albeit just as damaging, victory.

It is most imperative that we handle the sin and turmoil that others bring into our lives in an appropriate manner. Friends, our actions speak volumes as a testimony to the power of our God, and rest assured, others are watching what we are doing! It is clearly laid out for us in the Bible that when we maintain our testimony by keeping our mind on our **ONE,** the battle will surely be **WON**! Better yet, with the testimony of **ONE,** the battle has already been **WON**! Praise God!

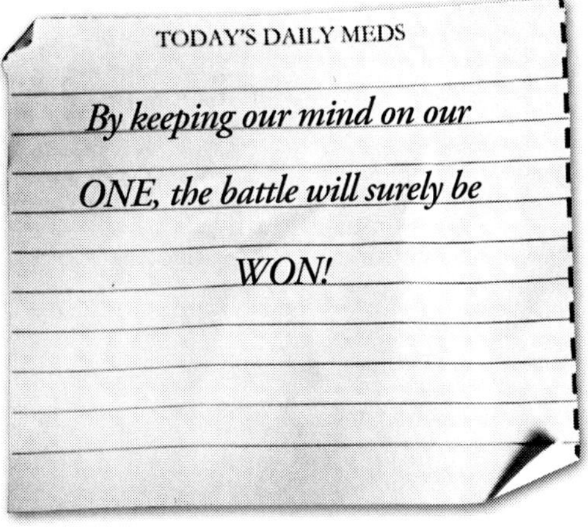

Guerilla Warfare

The second type of warfare, which is a much wiser type of embattlement for those of us who are beleaguered believers, is what military strategists refer to as guerilla warfare. Without a doubt, guerilla warfare is the greatest of strategies that we can employ until the King of Kings and the Lord of Lords returns.

Simply explained, guerilla warfare is a small force cleverly engaging a larger, more formidable force. Guerilla warfare consists of a tightly condensed fighting unit occupying a small segment of landscape—small enough so it can be defended—and engaging the enemy in repetitive yet random attacks. In this kind of warfare, the fighting unit never exposes itself, never taunts the enemy, and goes offensive only when the enemy is weak or ill prepared.

The objective of guerilla warfare is to systematically damage the enemy's ranks in a small but crucial manner. The impact is often felt more psychologically than in actual damages or casualties that may occur.

According to Wikipedia, the online information giant, guerilla warfare is defined as "an unconventional form of combat in which a small group of combatants uses mobile tactics in the form of ambushes and raids to oppose a larger and less mobile formed army." In Spanish, *guerilla* means *little war.* The term was coined during the British and French Peninsula war in the early 1800s.

This type of warfare targets vulnerable objectives that lie behind enemy lines, and is always executed in a covert and swift manner. The guerilla force is generally comprised of a small but ardent body of soldiers—like God's people—who are seeking to oppose a much-larger, more-established fighting body. In earthly warfare, the larger force is usually a state military. More often than not, the success of any guerilla force is dependent upon the support it maintains from the local population or parts thereof.

Notice that the guerilla force is small, comparatively speaking, and its success depends on the support of the surrounding community. With that said, can you see the parallel that a militia-like guerilla force draws to our local, New Testament churches? Each of our churches, if actively engaged in God's work, acts as an individual guerilla force.

As individual, spiritual-fighting units, our churches seek to gain the support of the local population and engage in combat against the armies of the world. Our churches' various ministries are but different methods of attack to go behind enemy lines and strike a blow against the world and reclaim for Christ what the world has consumed.

As previously noted, the impact that a guerilla force has in warfare is evidenced more in its underlying psychological or political implications. Take for example the guerilla tactics used by the colonists during the American Revolution. As British taxation and interference increasingly choked the freedom of the 13 colonies, groups of patriotic men formed small fighting units to oppose the oppression of the English military.

In the early stages of the revolution, a majority of colonists remained loyal to the king of England. However, as individual guerilla forces began to strike against the oppressive British military, a change began to occur. Because the guerilla attacks angered the seemingly all-powerful British army, they began to retaliate back with over-eager tactics that often were considered brutal and cruel.

Although the patriotic guerillas suffered many casualties as a result of the British army's retaliation, a bigger more-important agenda was being advanced. You see, the colonists who had originally sided with the British loyalists began to take notice of the increasingly oppressive and brutal tactics being performed by the king's army. They saw the overly aggressive retaliation being executed by the British soldiers and began to resent their presence in the New World.

These once-loyal colonists then began to shift their ideology and eventually most of them came to side with the patriots seeking independence. So while the original patriots did not do a significant amount of tangible physical damage to the British war machine, the political damage that was rendered was certainly worth the sacrificed lives.

As previously noted, a guerilla force gains formidability as it gains support with the local population. So, in the case of the American Revolution, we saw that as more loyalists began to become patriots, the stronger the colonial militia became. This situation perpetuated itself until eventually a very legitimate fighting body materialized with a great majority of support of the local civilians.

In the end, the patriots won the Revolutionary War because they succeeded in creating such a headache for the British that it was neither viable nor profitable for them to maintain imperialism in colonial America. Rather than continuing to be frustrated with the colonies' revolting behavior, the British opted to withdraw from the land and, thus, a new nation was born.

My friends, this is the very model by which Christ intended for His church to operate. Rather than taking on our enemy directly and suffering enormous casualties, our churches should engage in guerilla tactics to seek victories against Satan and his principality—the world.

Our small fighting units, churches, can use covert tactics—Bible studies, bus ministries, Christian schools, door-to-door soul winning—to reclaim what the devil's army has taken from God. Each soul won on a doorstep and brought into the church to be discipled is a blow to the enemy's ranks.

The possibilities are endless and only limited by the faith of God's saints. As a church becomes increasingly effective in its guerilla tactics, it will see the support of the locals begin to increase. Why? Because even the world can recognize when a church ministry begins to influence a community in a positive way. The effects are self-perpetuating because ministries become more effective as they gain the surrounding population's support.

A great example of this can be seen in our local Reformers Unanimous jail ministry in Rockford, Illinois. Through the years our housing ministry has endeavored to minister to those who would be otherwise incarcerated. This program started small, but today it is funded by the county and has had a great impact upon our local court system.

You see, it started with one individual being reached by a staff member incorporating guerilla-like tactics. This man went into a courtroom and beseeched a judge to give custody of an individual to the RU Men's School of Discipleship. The judge, on a whim, decided to exercise his discretion in this case and agreed to allow the man to go to the men's home in lieu of going to jail. The transformation of this man was remarkable and well documented in the local media.

As a result, support was established in the community for the RU program as a viable alternative to incarceration. Year after year, more and more support has been garnered as an increasing amount of men and women have been sent from the judiciary system to our program, with consistently impressive results. Today, Winnebago County boasts a very successful alternative-sentencing program that uses RU as its fulcrum. And that, my friends, is how God intends for us to engage in guerilla warfare!

Many men and women who would have otherwise been caught in the revolving door that has plagued our correctional system are now enjoying a free life in the grace of Jesus Christ. Why? Simply because a church ministry used God's intended strategy of guerilla warfare to reach out and steal a soldier from the enemy. The same men that once sold crack to our teenagers are now helping their own teenagers sell candy bars for church fundraisers! Praise be to God!

A more personal example dear to my heart is a man named Dan. Dan grew up in my neighborhood and is a year younger than I am. I went to Christian school, and Dan attended public school; so we did not see much of each other, except in the summers. I remember looking forward to summertime when I was younger just because I knew I would get to play with Dan. Eventually, however, I lost touch with my friend. All I had heard of him were rumors that he had gotten tangled up in a severe heroin addiction. By all rights my friendship with Dan had become a distant childhood memory.

In the spring of 2007, it came to my attention via a crime-stoppers poster that Dan was wanted on a warrant for drug charges. Granted, it had been more than 20 years since I last had any interaction with my childhood friend. Later that week, I saw a news report that he had been picked up in a police bust and was now in jail awaiting trial. I didn't think much of this and put it in the back of my head—at least I tried to, anyway. Well, after wrestling with continued promptings of the Holy Spirit to do something for Dan, I decided to send a staff member to the courthouse on the day of Dan's preliminary hearing, just to encourage Dan on my behalf. Two hours later, Dan came strolling into my office and gave me a gigantic bear hug. I was unsure of what to think at that point, but was anxious to help my old friend. Dan was granted a scholarship to attend our men's school of discipleship.

To make a long story short, Dan just got married last week to a godly Christian woman whom he met in church and is now an active, vibrant church member doing great things for God. I cannot tell you, friends, how incredibly rewarding it is to reclaim a soldier for the cause of Christ. Ultimately, I recognize that God does all the work in these types of situations, but one thing remains clear—God needs guerillas! Why, pray-tell, go head-on and be crushed with frustration and defeat when we can cleverly attack the gates of hell by way of guerilla tactics? This has become a fundamental principle by which we minister here at Reformers Unanimous, and it is one that we will not soon abandon!

Flanking Warfare

As far as I am concerned, the most effective strategy for warfare is *flanking*. In flanking warfare you hold your lines in the front center, and then you bring battalions of soldiers in from the flank, or the sides, to attack your enemy. While you are defending your fort in the front, occupying the enemy's attention, forces then sweep around to engage the enemy from multiple sides.

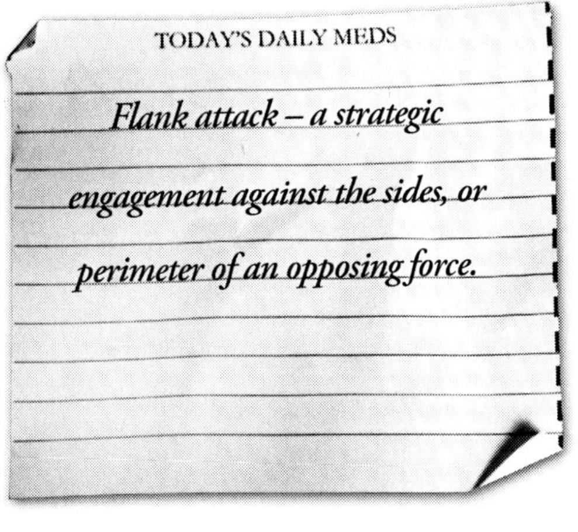

As the rolling of the flank—or attack on the outskirts of the enemy lines—begins to gain headway, the interior of the line must reposition to flank, thus making the center of the line the weak point. When the attacking army senses this occurring, the commander will order a full-scale charge into the center of the line that generally results in the retreating of the enemy. When this takes place, it is absolutely imperative for the attacking force to pursue with vigor and capture or kill as many enemy soldiers as possible.

Wikipedia defines a flank attack as "a strategic engagement

against the sides, or perimeter of an opposing force." If a flanking maneuver is successful, the "flanked" army is surrounded from two or more directions, thereby significantly reducing its maneuverability and ability to defend itself. A force that is outflanking its enemy typically gains a psychological advantage because the opposing force is caught off guard by it.

One of the biggest drawbacks to flanking warfare is that it can create potential friendly-fire hazards. As friendly forces enclose upon an enemy position from opposing directions, it is imperative that care be taken to establish fields of fire and that troop movements remain within the pre-established areas of engagement. If a flanking force fails to do this, friendly-fire casualties can tragically occur.

In church work, we like to put people on the front lines with instructions to hold the fort, for we know that Jesus is eventually returning. And then we use creative strategies to flank the enemy from the sides. Such strategies might include food banks, addictions programs, divorce-resolution ministries and innumerable others. These ministries attack our enemy—the prince of this world—and catch him off guard. As the devil is focusing on the front lines of church work, trying to defend against our pulpit and other core ministries, he is left vulnerable to the various flanking ministries that our churches may employ.

This is how I envision the work of Reformers Unanimous. As the enemy advances against our churches and its primary ministries, programs such as RU are left in a tremendously advantageous position to sneak around the enemy's radar, so to speak, and deliver a hefty blow for the kingdom of God.

In RU, this blow is often made in the form of reclaimed lives. These lives that were once enslaved by addiction were brought to the

Lord, and He set them free. In sports, a team will often sign a player whose skills have been diminished by injury. These players are often called reclamation projects. On God's team, we are all reclamation projects in need of rehabilitation from sin.

We at RU are essentially engaging in a form of espionage to convince the enemy's very own soldiers to defect to the side of righteousness. So as each one of us seeks to minister to an addicted individual, we are in fact engaging behind enemy lines in an effort to diminish the ranks of the devil. James Bond ain't got nothing on us, my friends!

The most important thing that we Christians can do to make us effective in flanking warfare is to prepare for it. And how do we prepare for it, you ask? We prepare simply by preparing our meditations with the Gospel of Peace.

Just as an army must prepare in advance to set up an effective flanking maneuver, we church members must prepare as well. An army does not simply go into a head-to-head battle and all of a sudden decide to attempt a flanking maneuver. No! The commanding officers will pre-plan the flanking tactic well in advance and have the soldiers properly briefed to execute it accordingly. Can you see the parallel here my friends? Effective worldly warfare requires advance preparation, and so does spiritual warfare!

We cannot send out our church members to flank the enemy behind his very own lines and expect them to not face resistance. Oh no, my friends. The devil will re-allocate his forces in a hurry to defend his flanks. He does not want to lose one single soldier to God's army. So how do we prepare ourselves as Christian soldiers seeking to engage in flanking warfare? We do all the things that we have previously discussed throughout this book that will enable us to keep peace with God, with ourselves and with others. Having a sufficient amount of peace in our lives is a necessity before we can ever become effective spiritual soldiers.

In our individual lives, our head-on maneuvers include activities like prayer, our Bible reading, our daily walk with God, and the moral standards that we maintain. But when it comes to flanking maneuvers, it is going to require a meditation preparation to allow us to remain at peace as we sneak in the devil's "side door." We must recognize that the key ingredient to success is to mobilize Operation Meditation Preparation prior to ever doing any work on the ground.

The Bible tells us that before we engage in battle with the enemy, we are going to have to prepare. When God tells us to prepare using the Gospel of Peace, He wants us to recognize that our flanking maneuvers may not actually be carried out by us specifically.

Ponies Are for Phonies

The Bible states, "The horse [is] prepared against the day of battle: but safety [is] of the LORD" (Proverbs 21:31). Dissected and defined, the word *horse* is referring to a method of attack. It says here that this method of attack is prepared—or made ready—for a specified time of battle. Solomon, the proverb's author, asserts that safety—or freedom from danger—comes from the Lord. He is effectively saying that we make ready our methods for a scheduled encounter with the enemy. However, true freedom from danger comes from a self-existent Lord.

In Biblical times, oxen labored with a plow and a cart, donkeys and camels carried back loads, and mules were used for human transport. But great war horses were deployed to support the weight of an armored soldier. A sturdy suit of armor in those days would weigh approximately 70 pounds, so war horses were bred to be able to consistently carry more than 300 pounds. The horses were also shod with nailed footwear that would puncture enemies that lay in their path. Needless to say, the horse was a very potent and formidable weapon.

The Bible teaches us that no matter how powerful a horse may be in battle, it is ineffective absent of the safety of the Lord. My friends, **ponies are for phonies!** God's word tells us: "An horse is a vain thing for safety: neither shall he deliver any by his great strength" (Psalm 33:17). What the psalmist is saying here is that though a horse may *have* great strength, it is unable to *deliver* great strength.

Furthermore, the Bible tells us in Psalm 147:10, "He delighteth not in the strength of the horse: he taketh not pleasure in the legs of a man." What he is saying here is that a horse's strength, or the ability of man, gives God no pleasure. In the eyes of the Lord, neither the horse nor the man is expected to be an integral force in the battle.

King David wrote: "Now know I that the LORD saveth his anointed; he will hear him from his holy heaven with the saving strength of his right hand. Some trust in chariots, and some in horses: but we will remember the name of the LORD our God. They are brought down and fallen: but we are risen, and stand upright" (Psalm 33:17).

Why are we risen and stand upright? It is because, David says, we don't trust in chariots or horses or other vain things. We understand that it is the power of the Lord that matters. It's not the training of the equestrian; it's our training that is in question. The Book of Exodus explains this.

Exodus: 14:8-10; 13-14; 21-24; 28-30

"And the LORD hardened the heart of Pharaoh king of Egypt, and he pursued after the children of Israel: and the children of Israel went out with an high hand. But the Egyptians pursued after them, all the horses and chariots of Pharaoh and his horsemen, and his army…And…the children of Israel lifted up their eyes…and they were sore afraid: and the children of Israel cried out unto the LORD. And Moses said unto the people. Fear ye not, stand still, and see the salvation of the LORD, which he will shew to you to day: for the Egyptians whom ye have seen to day, ye shall see them again no more for ever. The LORD shall fight for you…And the Egyptians shall know that He is the LORD, when He has gotten Himself honour upon Pharaoh, upon his chariots, and upon his horsemen. And Moses stretched out his hand over the sea; and the LORD caused the sea to go back by a strong east wind all that night, and made the sea dry land, and the waters were divided. And the children of Israel went into the midst of the sea upon the dry ground: and the waters were a wall unto them on their right hand, and on their left And the Egyptians pursued…even all pharaoh's horses, his chariots, and his horsemen. And it came to pass, that in the morning watch the LORD troubled the host of the Egyptians…so that the Egyptians said, Let us flee from the face of Israel; for the LORD fighteth for them… And the LORD said unto Moses, Stretch out thine hand over the sea, that the waters may come again upon the Egyptians, upon their chariots, and upon their horsemen. And the waters returned, and covered the chariots, and the horsemen, and all the host of Pharaoh that came into the sea after them; there remained not so much as one of them. But the children of Israel walked upon dry land in the midst of the sea; and the waters were a wall unto them on their right hand, and on their left. Thus the LORD saved Israel that day out of the hand of the Egyptians; and Israel saw the Egyptians dead upon the sea shore."

Notice that this historic passage mentions chariots, horsemen and the waters coming up over the Egyptians; but it doesn't say anything about the horses that drowned. Why do you suppose this is? It is because God cares little about horses, but He holds man in the highest regard. God never intended His children to plan methods by which to win wars. He confirms this truth in another early book of the Bible.

Deuteronomy 17:15-16

"Thou shalt in any wise set him king over thee, whom the LORD thy God shall choose: one from among thy brethren shalt thou set king over thee: thou mayest not set a stranger over thee, which is not thy brother. But he shall not multiply horses to himself, nor cause the people to return to Egypt, to the end that he should multiply horses: forasmuch as the LORD hath said unto you, Ye shall henceforth return no more that way."

Here we see God saying that in the midst of a battle: I don't want you to multiply horses. Nor do I want you to return to Egypt, the where place you once were. You see, horses were generally furnished as instruments of war. As a result of this, God prohibited the Israelites from multiplying them for three reasons:

1. Lest there should be such commerce with Egypt.

2. Lest the people might depend on a well-appointed cavalry as a means of security, and thus cease from trusting in the strength and protection of God.

3. That they might not be tempted to extend their dominion by

means of cavalry, and get scattered among the surrounding idolatrous nations, and thus cease, in process of time, to be that distinct and separate people which God intended they should be, and without which the prophecies relative to the Messiah could not be known to have their full accomplishment. (Taken from Clark Commentary.)

The Bible further states, "Woe to them that go down to Egypt for help; and stay on horses, and trust in chariots, because they are many; and in horsemen, because they are very strong; but they look not unto the Holy One of Israel, neither seek the LORD" (Isaiah 31:1).

Essentially, what this passage is telling us is that God does not want the children of Israel to trust in chariots or horsemen because by doing so, they will forego trusting in the Holy One. God wants us to recognize that the battle is His! It's not the horse, of course, but rather it's the Lord's, of course!

It is to this end that God intends for His children to prepare their meditations to win wars. He does not want us to prepare in any other manner other than by applying the peace that can only be found through Him. Remember, the battle belongs to the Lord, and we are the Lord's horse. And that, my friends, is where we have been going wrong!

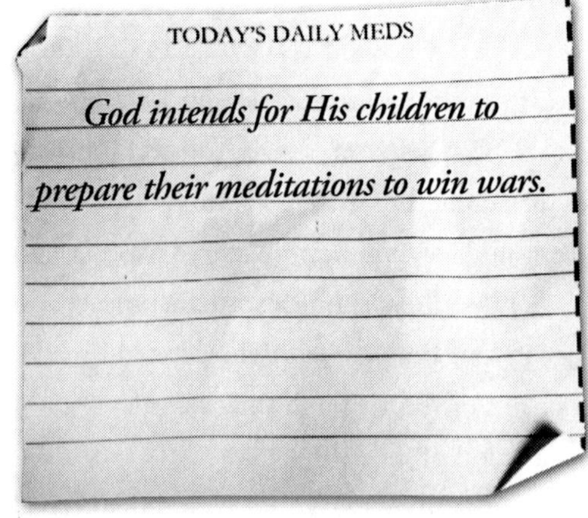

Our problem is not the Equestrian; it's the training that is in question. You see, when we start acting as if we must go to battle ourselves, we are fully outnumbered in this head-on combat. We must realize that our job is meditation preparation, and recognize that we are the horse!

When we know that we are going to battle, and upon our backside will ride the Lord Jesus Christ, only then will we win this spiritual war. Don't you see that He's got our back? All we have to do is take Him to where our enemy is, and our enemy will be taken over.

ELEVEN

RU GIVING PLACE?

As we learned in our last chapter, there are many different ways to fight an enemy. We looked primarily at ways in which we may counterattack against our archenemy: the prince of darkness. Indeed, it is important for us to strategize offensive measures for the perpetual warfare in which we are engaged, but it is equally important for us to understand how to defend ourselves when we are under demonic attack.

In the opening chapter of this book, we saw that one of the enemy's primary tools of destruction is tempting us into turmoil and tribulation. We discussed how Satan's goal is to tempt us to trust in ourselves or in external, erroneous information so that we may lose our confidence in the faith of Christ. The devil knows that once our heart becomes focused on our own faith, we will become discouraged and forfeit valuable place to him.

The Bible tells us in Ephesians 4:27 to "neither give place to the devil." You see, when we allow ourselves to keep wrong thoughts on our hearts, we will inevitably surrender precious real estate to the devil, and he will use this to try to destroy us. We learned in our chapter on war tactics that battles are almost always fought to gain territory. The phrase Paul uses to annunciate this forfeiture is to *give place*. The word *place* is the old English translation of the Greek word *topos*, which literally means topography or territory.

It is important to realize that the devil may not build anything on the territory we render him right away. Oh no, the Angel of Light is more cunning than that. He knows that if he moves too quickly, he will alarm us to the fact he is constructing strongholds in our lives. More often than not, the devil will patiently wait until we have allowed him to reside within our minds—the conceded territory—for a period of time so that he may silently construct infrastructure in our thought processes that he will later use to devour us.

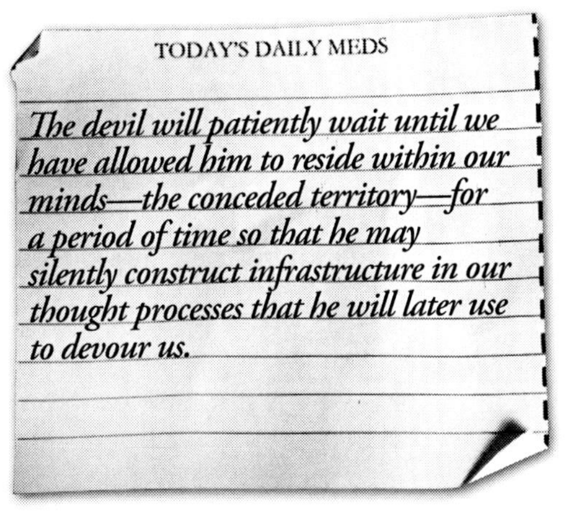

So we see that it is absolutely imperative that we are diligent in our guard and not allow the enemy to capture any territory in our minds. Again, one of the primary ways the devil will seek to advance upon us is through temptation. If his tactic of temptation is successful, we will be faced with an onslaught of turmoil that will likely interrupt our peace and overwhelm our meditations. My friends, Jesus clearly tells us that He does not want this to occur. Let us take a look at a portion of Scripture that demonstrates this truth.

John 14:25-27

"These things have I spoken unto you, being yet present with you. But the Comforter, which is the Holy Ghost, whom the Father will send in my name, he shall teach you all things, and bring all things to your remembrance, whatsoever I have said unto you. **Peace I leave with you, my peace I give unto you**: not as the world giveth, give I unto you. **Let not your heart be troubled, neither let it be afraid."**

We see here that one of the Comforter's—the Holy Spirit's—primary jobs is to bring things to our remembrance. It must be noted, however, that if the Spirit is to bring something to our remembrance, it must first have been something that we previously had known. In other words, we cannot remember something that has never been a part of our memory!

Knowing this, it is clear that God intends for us to prepare for turmoil by spending quality time in His Word and committing the knowledge therein to memory. When we do this, God promises us, the Comforter will enable us to remain at peace in the midst of difficult circumstances and not fall victim to temptation and its resulting turmoil.

Like the godfather of every evil, the devil is trying to make us an offer we can't refuse. As we begin to draw this book to a close, we will learn how to refuse a number of things. We will see how to refuse the turmoil that troubles our heart, how to refuse the adversity that makes us afraid, and how to refuse that which would allow the enemy to capture valuable territory within our minds. However, before we can go any further into our study on spiritual warfare, it is necessary to recap and expand upon some of the truths that we have touched on thus far.

Recall that in our first chapter, we discussed how God uses the devil's temptation as an examination for our self-evaluation. Our discussion on James 1:1-12 showcased the apostle teaching his brethren that we should consider it enjoyable when we fall into various temptations because when our faith is put on trial, it works patience that leads to endurance. And it is ultimately this endurance that will allow us to remain standing through the tumult of adversity.

James went on to say that if any of us lacks wisdom—that's the leading of the Holy Spirit in today's age of grace—then we should simply ask God for more of His Spirit. But he says not to just ask flippantly, but rather to "ask in faith." He is not referring to *our* faith here; he is talking about the faith of God! Why? Because God's faith is unwavering. You see, our faith, absent of the supplementary power of His faith, is very sporadic, ebbing and flowing like the waves of an ocean. God wants our faith to be consistent and strong. Our faith is not strong if it is simply based on information instead of a personal relation.

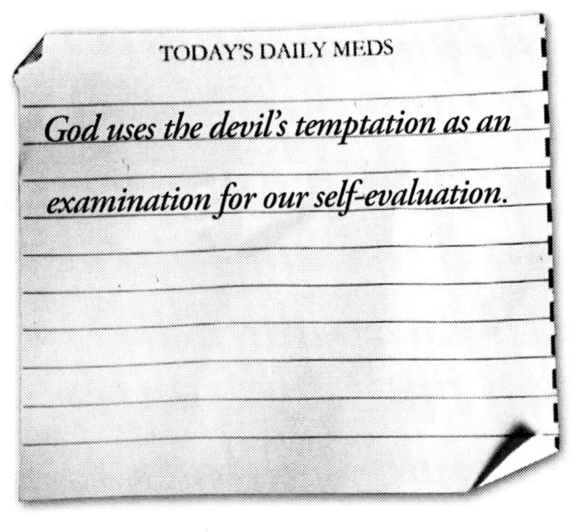

So we saw that for us to have unwavering faith, we must yield to the faith of Christ and reject our natural inclination to embrace our own faith. The Bible says that the person who is yielding to his own faith is a double-minded man who is unstable in all his ways. The reason he is double-minded is that he yields to his faith at times and to God's faith at other times. There is no consistency on which to build a solid foundation of faith.

Not only is the two faith, two-faced man unstable, the Bible goes on to say, this man should not think that he will receive anything from the Lord (James 1:7). Why do you suppose this is, my friends? It is because he is double-minded and he cannot keep his focus on two things at once. God demands that we focus only on Him—with no exceptions! He wants our heart, by faith, to trust only in Him. The double-minded man is essentially giving place to the devil by denouncing the truth that is the faith of Jesus Christ. So I ask you now: RU giving place to the devil?

Take a look at the following passage.

Ephesians 3:16-17

"That he would grant you, according to the riches of his glory, to be strengthened with might by his Spirit in the inner man; That Christ may dwell in your hearts by faith…."

We see that it is the faith of Christ that keeps the placement of Christ within our hearts (our meditations). The bifurcated man cannot attain this blessing in any capacity because his mind is prone to waver from his own faith to Christ's faith and back again at any given time. Because the duplicitous person cannot embrace the faith of Jesus, he or she is left vulnerable to temptation. The term *man*, as in double-minded *man*, is gender-neutral—meaning it refers to women as well.

Let's reiterate one of our key verses: "But every man is tempted, when he is drawn away of his own lust, and enticed" (James 1:14). The word *drawn* means *to be attracted to,* and when James uses the phrase *own lust,* he is literally referring to our very-own designer desires. These are our personally crafted besetting sins.

They are the sins that forged themselves into our lives through our environment and upbringing, causing us to continuously stumble. Designer desires can be as diverse as smoking crack cocaine to eating too many Krispy Kreme doughnuts. Whatever our designer desires may be, we can rest assured the devil is aware of them and will seek to use them to draw us away from God's way!

Though God and the devil are surely aware of our designer desires, it is not uncommon for us to be ignorant of them. Often, we will not realize that we carry a propensity for such things as critical attitudes or harsh judgments. Our designer desires could be myriad things to which we are not privy! Sometimes, we may even erroneously consider our besetting designer desires to be strengths.

So it is that when we are drawn toward our designer desires, we are being tempted by the enemy. Temptation is nothing more than oppression that causes us to be enticed. Now, the word *oppression* is the Old English word for the modern English phrase *outside pressure.* And the word *enticed* literally means *instigated to evil.* So we see that when some form of outside pressure comes into our life and instigates us to evil—toward our designer desires—we can conclude that we are being tempted.

At this point, we have not sinned. It is not until the thought is conceived that we cross the line. Crossing lines of sin is a slippery slope that can lead to death. The apostle Judas exemplifies the tragic trajectory of sin. Judas started out as a thief, stealing from the apostle's treasury (John 12:6). Then he simply had a conversation with the chief priests about how much money he could make by turning in Our Lord (Matthew 26:14-16). Then he committed the horrific deed, betraying the Son of God (John 18:2-5). And, finally, the guilt-stricken betrayer committed suicide (Matthew 27:5). The aggregate wages of Judas' sin were indeed death.

The devil will try to set this same death trap for us by placing outside pressure on us to pull down wrong thoughts from our minds and lead us to dwell, or meditate, upon them in our hearts. And it is at this point, my friends, that we have given place to the devil and committed sin. We conceive the wicked imagination in our minds and pass them on down to our hearts. The word *conceived* literally means *to frame in the mind.*

So we see that as soon as we allow the wrong thought to be framed in our mind and then travel the 18 inches or so from our head to our heart, we commit sin—regardless of whether or not we act upon that thought.

A VCR operates similarly to this process of framing wrong thoughts in our minds and passing them down into our hearts to be dwelled upon. We take the bad thought and we hit STOP, PLAY, REWIND. STOP, PLAY, REWIND. STOP, PLAY, REWIND. This takes place over and over again, until we inevitably begin to experience turmoil in our lives.

At this point sin has already occurred, and the devil has struck somewhat of a victory. However, we now have the chance to kick into high damage-control mode. When lust is conceived, or our designer desires are framed in our mind, we can do one of two things. We can either choose to meditate upon the wrong thoughts, thereby precipitating wrong action, or we can choose to endure the temptation. When we choose to go forward with our conceived lusts, the Bible tells us, this brings forth death (Romans 6:23).

More often than not, this verse is referring to a spiritual defeat of sorts, but this death can certainly manifest itself in a premature physical demise as well. Remember, as Principle No. 10 of RUI teaches, the consequences for our sin are inevitable, incalculable and entirely up to God.

"Do not err, my beloved brethren," the Bible implores in James 1:16. To not err is to not stray from His way. We can choose to do this and forgo the death that is promised as a result of putting our wicked imaginations into actions. It would be nice if we could opt for the 1 Corinthians 10:13 model at this point. This verse assures us that "with the temptation," God will "make a way to escape." For sure, this simultaneous way of escape is always granted to us and is the easiest way to avoid allowing the devil to gain a complete victory via his tool of temptation. Again, the escape comes *with* the temptation. Why? Because it's His simultaneous examination!

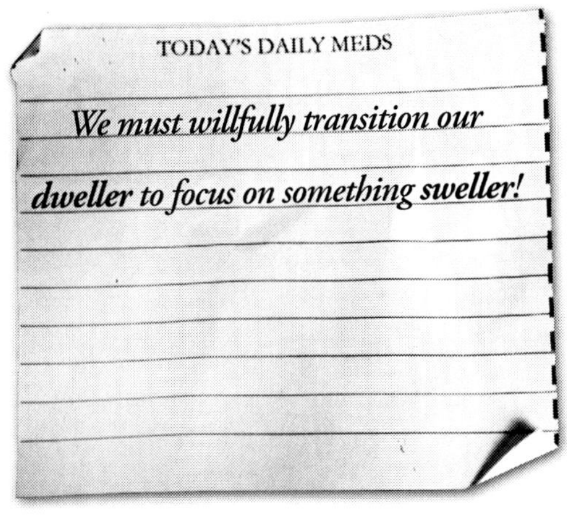

However, we will often miss the way of escape or fail to see one altogether. What do we do at this point? Well, going back to James 1:12, we see that the apostle says that the man who endures temptation shall receive the crown of life. Yes, my friends, it is possible to endure, or ride out, the temptations that are placed before us. The only way we can do this is to keep our hearts and minds completely stayed on Jesus. We must willfully transition our *dweller* to focus on something *sweller*! The Bible tells us that we, like the devil, have tools to use in environments of turmoil. While the devil's tools are designed to exacerbate turmoil, ours are designed to diminish it.

Another critical passage explains God's tool of spiritual examination.

2 Corinthians 10:3-4

"For though we walk in the flesh, we do not war after the flesh: for the weapons of our warfare are not carnal, but mighty through God to the pulling down of strongholds."

We know that we wrestle not against flesh and blood, but instead we war against principalities. Therefore, no carnal—or worldly—weapon will suffice. We need the weapons of God. Now, our passage says that our weapon is mighty enough to pull down strongholds that we cannot otherwise get rid of on our own. What, pray tell, is this technique that is said to be so powerful? God's response to the devil's temptation is to help us turn it into a self-examination!

The examination comes when we realize the outside pressure has become too much for us to handle, thus causing us to look inward and discern whether or not Christ is dwelling within our hearts. Is He anywhere near our hearts in this situation? Have I yielded to His faith or have I failed and relied upon my own measly faith? These are the questions that God intends for us to ask ourselves through a temptation examination.

It is safe to say that each and every time we succumb to one of Satan's temptations, and we in turn conduct an honest self-examination, God will always show us where we have erred. And again, the Scripture tells us that this mighty technique will effectively reclaim place and pull down our strongholds.

A stronghold is exactly what it sounds like. It is a besetting sin that the enemy places into our life that has a hold on us that is very strong. In order to create a stronghold, the devil must first win territory in our minds. When he does this, he builds encampments that will morph in time into strongholds. Once he has successfully planted a stronghold in our lives, no carnal weapon is going to be able to remove it. But, praise God, He grants us a weapon that is mighty enough to tear down these strongholds that paralyze our lives.

There are two techniques that God uses by way of examination to pull down our strongholds, and they are revealed in His word.

2 Corinthians 10:5

"Casting down imaginations, and every high thing that exalteth itself against the knowledge of God, and bringing into captivity every thought to the obedience of Christ."

The phrase *knowledge of God* literally means *a personal relationship with Jesus Christ.* The term *casting down* means to *throw away.* And as we have already learned, the word *imaginations* simply means *stored images*. Wow! I don't know about you, friend, but I certainly have an overabundance of stored images with which to reckon. Not all need to be cast out, but we must take time to discern which stored images are possibly standing between God and us.

So, the first method to pull down strongholds that Paul teaches us is essentially to throw away anything—physical or psychological—that exalts itself against the knowledge of Jesus Christ. Or, in other words, get rid of the things that hinder your relationship with God. Throw them out! When we find ourselves with wicked thoughts framed into our minds, our peace is in jeopardy! Be sure that God provides us with the ability—the tool—to cast them out and return our thoughts to Him.

We need not allow such thoughts to create chaos in our minds and precipitate turmoil. Simply take the time to discern whether or not the thoughts you are considering will ultimately harm your walk with God, and if they do, get rid of them like hot potatoes. Toss them away as far as you can. In football vernacular, throw the bomb!

Casting out wrong thoughts is only half the battle. At Reformers Unanimous, we teach the doctrine of replacement. It is not sufficient to simply rid yourself of evil and allow a void to exist. Rather, we must replace the space to save face! That's right. We must insert God-honoring thoughts in place of the evil thoughts we have.

I have heard a lot of people say: "Garbage in, garbage out; garbage in, garbage out." My friends, this may work for computers but not for processing the worldly things that poison our minds. The actual formula for this process is: Garbage in, garbage on and garbage out. That is to say garbage enters our minds via our senses; it then gets framed in our minds and passed down onto our heart's meditations. Finally, because it is overflowing with garbage, the heart spews out fleshly words or dirty deeds.

So, again, trash comes into our minds, rests on our hearts, and goes out through our mouths or bodies. Remember the Bible tells us that out of the abundance of the heart, the mouth speaks (Matthew 12:34). Thus, we can conclude that when garbage begins to collect upon our hearts, it will eventually be manifested in an ugly display of flesh. We are giving place to the garbage man.

Just as trash is processed in this manner, so are quality things. This is the second principle upon which is based the proper technique for pulling down strongholds. Second Corinthians 10:5 continues, "and bringing into captivity every thought to the obedience of Christ." Herein is the scriptural basis for the doctrine of replacement. The word *captivity* literally means the *state of being a prisoner.*

So we see that we are first to cast down the bad thoughts, and then we are to take into captivity the good thoughts. Simplified, it's the replacement doctrine. Casting down bad thoughts without replacing them by captivating good thoughts is like casting down a basketball. It's going to bounce right back. That thought will control your heart again and captivate your emotions once more. The game changer is when we roll it away and pick up a different ball. New Game!

Now, consider this: Why would Paul think it necessary to tell us to cast down negative thinking and to take hostage positive thinking? I would think that it is fairly self-explanatory. It's just like the venerable song goes: "Accentuate the positive, eliminate the negative." We know we need to limit the negative and increase the positive, right? We are reminded repeatedly in Scripture to think heavenly thoughts. Why then do we mentally dwell in hell? My friends, this is the age-old battle of the mind in which we will forever engage.

Our sinful nature inclines us to think on the negative, critical, pessimistic and competitive things of our souls rather than on the positive, Spirit-led things of God. It must come down to a conscious choice to embrace Spirit-filled, Philippians 4:8 thoughts. Why do we fail to do this?

Take a look back at the first part of 1 Corinthians 10:13. "There hath no temptation taken you but such as is common to man." Paul is saying that none of us is faced with anything that is not experienced by other men; or in other words, we all experience the same amount of temptation. We must be careful here to note that as we mature in the faith, the devil will certainly heighten the level of intensity of his temptations. But regardless, the types of temptation are common—or the same—for everybody.

Now, when we consider that all people are experiencing similar levels of temptations, we must take note of what God, through Paul, said previously in verse 12: "Wherefore let him that thinketh he standeth take heed lest he fall." He is telling us: BUYER BEWARE! Before the apostle even begins his discussion on temptation, he is careful to say that it is our nature to fallaciously believe that we can stand on our own throughout it.

Recall the story of Peter emptied by the first fire. He was told by the Lord Jesus Christ that he would come to disappoint Him by denying Him. And how did Peter respond to Jesus telling him this? He boldly proclaimed that he would follow Jesus even unto death.

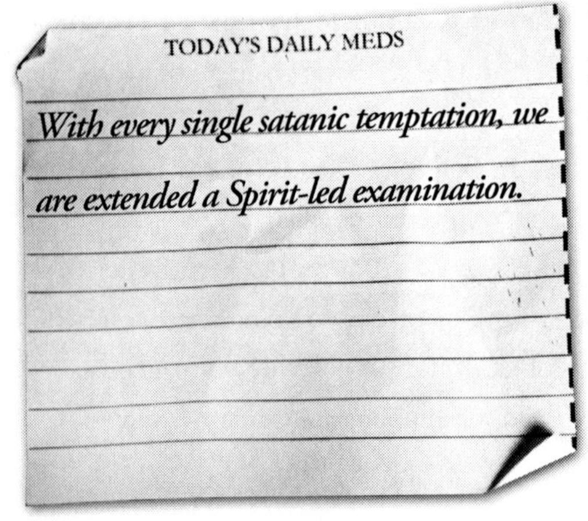

Oh, Peter, how wrong you were! As it turned out, Peter wouldn't even follow Him to the crucifixion, let alone unto His death. As a result, Peter was humbled and emptied. You see, this disciple in his blinding pride thought that he would be able to stand against the oppression of the devil. And this is the exact mistake that Paul cautions us to avoid.

So we see that with every single satanic temptation, we are extended a Spirit-led examination. We have two choices: pass the exam or fail. I encourage you to ask yourself: RU applying yourself towards God's examinations, or are RU repeatedly giving place to the devil?

Remember, the penalty for failing is not summer school, my friends, but death! If we choose to pass, however, we see that we have two techniques that comprise the doctrine of replacement that will help us to keep our mind on Him, thus granting us His faith. And once we obtain the faith of Christ, we can patiently endure any temptation and, as the Bible promises, receive the crown of life! Praise God!

Now in the midst of such persistent temptation, the goal is to endure until we are given His Supernatural way of escape. But in our next chapter, I shall warn you: if you *resist*, it will *persist*!

TWELVE

RU RESISTING OR REFOCUSING?

Through our previous discussions, we have seen that it is imperative that we not resist the examinations that come with temptations. We discussed in detail the importance and implications of allowing ourselves to be examined through our trials, and we concluded that we should not resist this.

There is something, however, that we should resist. Obviously, we should strive to resist the devil. Now the key here is not actually resisting the devil per se, but rather resisting the wrong thinking he seeks to place into our hearts. Furthermore, when I say that we are to resist these bad thoughts, it is important to note that there is just one way to accomplish this, and that is to cast them down.

If we try to simply resist, or willfully try to not allow them to come into our heads, we will inevitably fail. When we take that approach, our focus actually becomes more intensely placed upon evil things. Wrong thoughts will come into our minds. The only effective measure of protection against damaging thoughts is to cast them out at once. **If you resist, they will persist!**

My friends, do not seek to resist wrong thinking; instead seek to cast down the bad thoughts as soon as they come across your mind. This is the only way to overcome bad thinking. ***We don't need to resist*; we need to *refocus*.**

When we refocus ourselves toward pure thoughts, we will inevitably draw our minds away from thoughts of evil. Again, we can see the doctrine of replacement. If we simply resist bad thoughts but do not *refocus* ourselves to good thoughts, our minds will be left with a void that will eventually be filled with that wickedness or worse. But if we refocus our thoughts, thus replacing the bad with good, we will move our minds completely away from where the devil would have them to be.

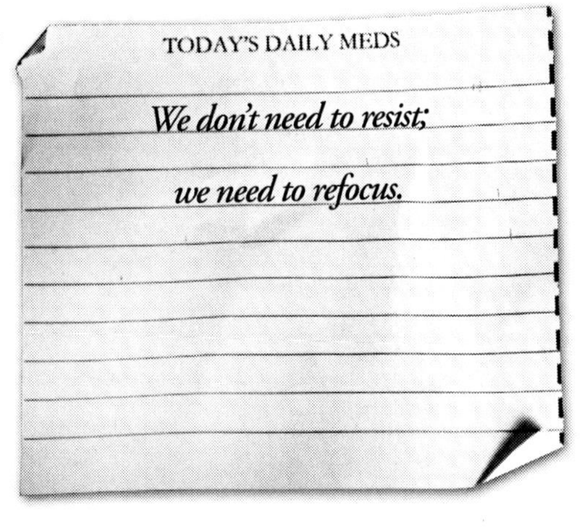

This is exactly what the Scriptures intend for us to do through temptations of examinations. When something bad happens in our life and we get frustrated or discouraged, God wants us to take a look at exactly why we are feeling that way. Why are we discouraged? Why are we frustrated? He wants us to shift our focus away from the evil circumstance and place it back on Him, so that He may reveal Himself for our perfecting.

You see, God has promised us that all things work together for good (Romans 8:28) and He has assured us that He will never leave nor forsake us (Hebrews 13:5). He has promised so many great things that it would be impossible to list them all. However, these promises are what God wants us to focus on, not the adverse circumstances that leave us discouraged!

The world's psychology model will often tell those who are depressed or anxious to simply stop thinking upon those things that make them feel that way. My friend, this is wrong! Say, for example, that a wife is depressed because her husband left her. If I were to advise her to stop thinking about her husband, what do you think she will do? By trying not to think on her husband, she will be doing exactly that!

It's like trying to *not* think about that pink elephant thrashing for survival in our sea of tranquility. (Remember him?) Herein lies the key for those of us who struggle with negative, critical, pessimistic and competitive thoughts. We simply must willingly and willfully think on something else—something healthy and pure—and forsake any mental ongoing effort to overcome the negative.

In 1970, Vice President Spiro T. Agnew famously labeled the news media as "nattering nabobs of negativism." Of course, the news by definition is negative. When things are going well, it is not newsworthy. But despite the decidedly negative world that we live in, we are commanded by God to be optimists.

Recall in Philippians 4:8 that Paul gives us a list of things on which we should think. He says that if anything valuable is to come as a result of our lives, then we must think on these things. All of these things are positive, God-honoring, thought triggers. When we refocus our minds, thinking on positive things, the negative that once consumed our minds will grow strangely dim.

As I have stated previously, I am not promoting the power of positive thinking here. Rather, I am simply pointing out the dangers of negative thinking. You see, negative thinking is nothing but an avenue of weakness that the devil will use to travel into our minds, thus infiltrating our hearts.

Allow me to reiterate that we cannot avoid the dangers of negative thinking by seeking to resist such thoughts. No sir! The only way to avoid negativity is to engage in a complete refocusing of the mind toward that which is positive. Jesus Himself said so.

Matthew 6:22-23

"The light of the body is the eye: if therefore **thine eye be single**, thy whole body shall be **full of light**. But if thine **eye be evil**, thy whole body shall be **full of darkness**. If therefore **the light** that is **in thee** be **darkness**, how **great** is that darkness."

Our Lord is saying that our eyes illuminate our bodies because we focus with our eyes. Now, the word *single* as it is used here means *completely focused.* So we see that if our eyes are focused on light—or things and thoughts that God used to shape peace after making light—our whole bodies will be illuminated. To have one's entire body illuminated means to bring to a state of complete peace.

Jesus goes on to say in verse 23 that the opposite is true, too. If our eyes are focused on evil, our bodies shall be placed in darkness—a state of turmoil. Remember that darkness was the remnant of light. Now the latter half of this verse can be a bit confusing. What He is saying here is that the light that we have within us is still somewhat evil.

We know this is true because we, in and of ourselves, can do no good thing. So what Jesus is saying is that if the light we possess is actually bad, then imagine how bad the darkness we choose to possess would be. In other words, He is saying: Hey, your good is not even good. I would hate to see how bad your bad is!

My friends, what a pathetic position it is to be focused on darkness. We see that we are inevitably drawn into darkness by our evil imaginations. This is a result of our attempting to resist thinking upon such things rather than casting them out of our minds. To illustrate the ramifications of such a fallacious approach to our examinations, I want to point out a particular place in Scripture. We are introduced to a group that many people think are the unsaved apostates.

Allow me to just say that they very well may be unsaved apostates, but I would like to take a different viewpoint of them for the purposes of this book. My perception of this chapter is that these people are not only saved, but they have also willfully or unknowingly rejected the benefits of their sanctification.

These people trusted Christ as their Savior, thus being granted justification—freedom from the penalty of sin—but they allowed themselves to capture wrong imaginations instead of casting them down. And it is because of this that they have rejected their sanctification, or freedom from the power of sin. The Scriptures indicate repeatedly that these people would continuously reject that which is right in favor of that which is wrong; and as is typical, this process always began in their hearts. Let's see what the apostle Paul says to these people.

Romans 1:16-19

"For **I am not ashamed** of the gospel of Christ: for it is the **power of God** unto salvation to every one that believeth; to the Jew first, and also to the Greek. For therein is the righteousness of God revealed from **faith to faith**: as it is written, The just shall live by faith. For the wrath of God is revealed from heaven against all ungodliness and unrighteousness of men, **who hold the truth** in unrighteousness, Because that which **may be known of God** is manifest **in them**; for God hath **shewed it** unto them."

Paul tells them that he is not ashamed of the Gospel because he knows that some are obviously just that—ashamed! Now, it is important to note that this does not mean that these folks did not accept the gospel; it simply means that they were afraid to show that they had accepted the gospel.

He continues in the latter half of verse 16, saying that the power of God comes on us at salvation for not only freedom from the penalty of sin, but also to free us from the power of sin. So we know that we—and most likely these Romans—have been granted the power to overcome death and hell as well as attain a new triumphant life over sin.

Paul goes on to state "it is written, The just shall live by faith." The word *therein* means exactly that—*in there*. So Paul is saying that these people have accepted the power of Christ and they've transitioned from their faith which brought them justification to His faith that provides us our sanctification. He further asserts that the just shall live by faith, not their own faith, but the new faith required to enjoy the benefits of salvation that is acquired through Christ. And this is how Christians should live their lives.

Notice that Paul also says that the wrath of God is revealed against those who hold the truth, against those who hold Jesus in unrighteousness. In other words, these are people who are saved and they possess Jesus in their Spirit, but nevertheless they live unrighteously. This could be the result of one or two factors: they either could be the unknowing victims of not being adequately discipled, or they could be those who willfully chose to walk away from God in rebellion.

Note that when Paul says "that which may be known of God," he is referring to the Holy Spirit. So what this verse actually tells us is that these people possessed the Holy Spirit because God showed it to them upon their conversion. Knowing this, we can deduce from our earlier studies that they also possess the illumination that accompanies the Holy Spirit. This verse gives me even greater cause to believe that these people are, indeed, saved. However, they have never come to enjoy the benefits of sanctification.

Skipping ahead to verse 21, Paul writes, "Because that, when they knew God, they glorified him not as God, neither were thankful; but became vain in their imaginations, and their foolish heart was darkened." The phrase *knew God* means *to have intimacy with God.* Knowing God, in this context, does not refer to knowing information about Him, but instead having an intimate relationship with Him. This verse tells us that these people did not glorify God; they did not make God look good, nor were they thankful for God.

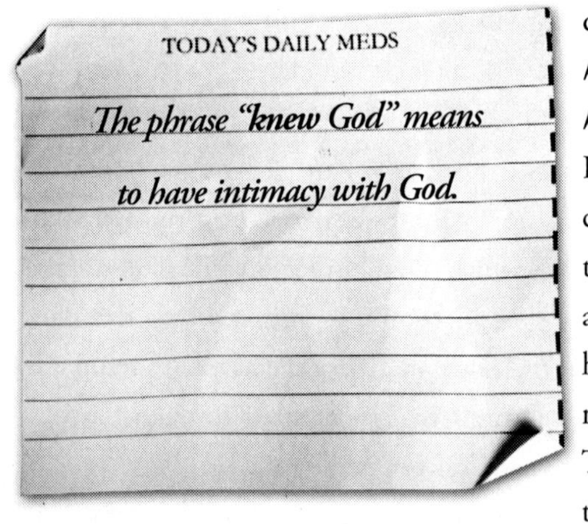

Can I ask you a question? If these people were unsaved, why ***would*** they have anything to be thankful to God for? The fact that

Paul notes that the Romans here were unthankful is a clear indication to me that these were saved but sad Christians; for we know that only God's people, who have received the generosity of the Lord Jesus Christ, have something for which they ought to be thankful.

Moreover, Paul says, they have become vain in their imaginations, meaning that the stored images in their minds that they choose to recall have become disastrous. So according to Paul, the progression of their demise goes like this: They knew God, meaning they were intimate with God, but nevertheless they refused to glorify God. They didn't glorify God because they were ungrateful, and because they were ungrateful, they were critical. Their critical nature gave way to a negative attitude that precipitated the dwelling upon the negative films of their wicked stored images (home movies).

So at this point we can deduce that their meditations are entirely useless to God. And we know that before we ever do anything, we think it. If your meditations are useless, your actions are going to be useless as well. As a result of all of this, Paul concludes, their foolish hearts were darkened.

The word *darkened* literally means *deprived of illumination, or light.* What this essentially means is that God **ceased** to reveal Himself to them and therefore they ceased to grow. And friends, in the Christian life, if you are not progressing forward, you will inevitably slide backwards.

Our passage indicates that these Romans became fools. The word *became* means to *pass from one state to another.* Now, it is important to recognize that one cannot pass from the state of being simple to the state of being a fool. One must be wise to begin with if he is to regress to the state of a fool. Knowing this, the Romans must have followed this progression: they went from simple to wise upon conversion, and then from wise to foolish in their backsliding.

Now, a fool is "somebody who knows right but chooses wrong". We see that these people professed themselves to be spirit-led and wise. But they passed from that state to being fools; they knew right but nonetheless chose wrong. Why do you suspect this occurred? It is because their hearts had ceased to receive the illumination from God so they dwelt on the imaginations of their mind.

As a result, their imaginations became even more wicked and devoid due to the regular recall of detrimental stored images. These stored images yielded vanity in thought and deed, leaving them apathetically unthankful and focused upon their own glory. Ha! It cost them their intimacy with God. The Bible then tells us these type of rebellious "believers" went from this apathetic self righteousness to abominable unrighteousness in no time at all! This is NOT *apostasy*, my friends, this is *hypocrisy*!

Let's read more about these once-wise people who **became** foolish.

Romans 1:23-25

"And changed the glory of the uncorruptible God into an image made like to corruptible man, and to birds, and fourfooted beasts, and creeping things. Wherefore God also gave them up to uncleanness through the lusts of their own hearts, to dishonour their own bodies between themselves: Who changed the truth of God into a lie, and worshipped and served the creature more than the Creator, who is blessed for ever. Amen."

My friends, what a sad state we find ourselves in when we refuse to conquer through casting down our stored images. Romans chapter 1 is a warning to those who get saved and then fall away. Whether this occurs unknowingly due to a lack of discipleship, or whether it is a conscious choice made out rebellion, it matters not.

I can see no other meaning behind Paul's assertions about these people. They are clearly indicative of a group who was saved and then fell grossly away from the Lord. We know that once we are saved, we are always saved. So, of course, these people did not lose their salvation, but they turned down the free gift of sanctification benefits.

Before God in heaven would ever allow His children to regress back to the point of acting as if they were unsaved, He would most certainly administer a hefty amount of chastening. Imagine that you have a son who is experiencing great turmoil in his life. You, as the father, would of course be heavily involved. Furthermore, if your son was doing wrong, you would most likely chasten him in some form or fashion in hopes of returning him to his former position of peace with God.

Well, God does likewise to his kids, as the Bible notes.

Hebrews 12:5-6

"And ye have forgotten the exhortation which speaketh unto you as unto children, My son, despise not thou the chastening of the Lord, nor faint when thou art rebuked of him: For whom the Lord loveth he chasteneth, and scourgeth every son whom he receivith."

Now the author of Hebrews is in dispute, although many scholars believe that it resonates with the writing of Paul. Nevertheless, like all Scripture, Hebrews is written with divine authority.

Inspired by the Holy Spirit, the author says that he wants to remind of us something as well as encourage us. In addition, he views his readers as spiritual children and will teach them accordingly.

Then the writer gets to the point; he says don't resent it when God chastens—or corrects—us.

You see, just as we must correct our children for their misbehavior, God also must correct us for ours. So we are not to despise God for chastening us, for we know that He does it out of love and for our own benefit.

He refers specifically to "whom he receiveth." Through the author, God seems to be saying: Listen, pal, I don't want you to be upset about this. I am only punishing you because I love you and want to exhort you back into a right relationship with Me.

Now jump ahead, if you will, to verse 11: "Now no chastening for the present seemeth to be joyous, but grievous: nevertheless afterward it yieldeth the **peaceable** fruit of righteousness unto them which are exercised thereby."

Here, he makes no attempt to hide the fact that we will always find chastening to be grievous at first. When we are chastened, he says, it produces no joy, but rather pain. He goes on to say, however, that afterwards it produces the fruit of righteousness.

Now, the next phrase is: "...unto them which are exercised thereby." The word *exercised* literally means *trained.* So he is saying essentially that God is going to put us on a training program. The training program is going to consist of examinations that when failed, will levy submission to temptation. And when we submit to these temptations, we will then be chastened by the hand of the Lord.

However, if we choose to reject the chastening of the Lord, or if we have exhausted God's longsuffering by insisting upon our sin, then eventually God will give us over to our vain imaginations. In essence, he says that absent of chastening, we will become a complete waste to God as a believer.

Now, my friends, our passage also indicates one other profound benefit of being chastened of the Lord. It tells us that the fruit yielded by doing so is *peaceable*. By embracing God's chastening and allowing it to teach us will afford us a peace that, as the Bible says, surpasses all understanding.

Allow me to discuss for a moment God's righteousness in our daily lives. We will see that our yielding to the righteousness of God will all produce peace in our lives. Let's begin by looking at another confirmatory passage.

Psalm 85:8-10

"I will hear what God the LORD will speak: for he will speak **peace** unto his people, and to his saints: but let them not turn again to folly. Surely his salvation is nigh them that fear him; that glory may dwell in our land. Mercy and truth are met together; **righteousness** and **peace** have kissed each other."

My friends, if you are listening to God talk, you are listening to a God that is speaking peace. He doesn't talk turmoil, he doesn't talk worry, he doesn't talk divisively or spread discord, and he doesn't ever talk war toward His offspring. He talks peace to His saints, but He says to those to whom he's speaking peace: let them not turn again to folly.

Folly means weakness of the mind. So he says: I will hear what God the Lord will speak, for He will speak peace unto the people. He goes on to say that mercy (that's not getting what one deserves) and truth (that which is strongly held to be right) are met together. The balance of mercy and truth are found in all environments of peace. And likewise, we see that righteousness and peace are so close that they "kiss."

The psalmist is telling us that God speaks peace, and peace produces righteousness. And of course, righteousness brings along the fruit of the Spirit—love, joy, longsuffering, gentleness, goodness, faith, temperance and, you guessed it—PEACE!

This is not the only passage in which God tells us that righteousness and peace come together.

Isaiah 32:17

"And the **work of righteousness** shall be **peace**; and the **effect of righteousness quietness** and **assurance** for ever."

Now, the word *work* is the Old English word for the modern English word *effort.* The efforts of righteousness shall be peace and the effect of righteousness shall be quietness and assurance forever.

Furthermore, can you guess what the effort of righteousness produces in the end? That's right—peace! The word *shall* means under *obligation.* So peace is obligated when we put forth the effort to live a righteous life by crucifying our flesh, denying our affections and lusts, embracing the Spirit-filled life, and cooperating with the Spirit by remaining holy. And the effect of righteousness is the quietness and assurance that forever comes from that peace.

To further understand this important Biblical concept, let's look back to one of our favorite epistles.

James 3:13-18

"Who is a wise man and endued with knowledge among you? Let him shew out of a good conversation his works with meekness of wisdom. But if you have envying and strife in your hearts, glory not, and lie not against the truth. This wisdom descendeth not from above, but is earthly, sensual, devilish. For where envying and strife is, there is confusion and every evil work. But the wisdom that is from above is first pure, then **peaceable**, gentle, and easy to be entreated, full of mercy and good fruits, without partiality, and without **hypocrisy**. And the **fruit of righteousness** is sown in **peace** of them that **make peace**."

A meek man does not cause friction. And the wise are led by the Spirit. So meekness here refers to one of the fruits of the Spirit. Then he gives a list of being bitter, envious, and holding strife in our hearts. He says; don't let that be in your heart! Why? He says that this type of wisdom does not come from above!

Where there be envy and strife, there is confusion. God is not the author of confusion, but the author of peace (I Corinthians 13:43). But James says that when you have this envy and strife, it is earthly and sensual and devilish. Not only that, but it brings confusion and every evil work! However, he continues, the wisdom that's from above is first pure, then peaceable.

That word peaceable means that your mind is free of agitation. First pure, he says, and then peaceable. Gentle and easy to be entreated, full of mercy and good fruits without partiality, and without hypocrisy, which means faking another's personality.

So, he says: Hey, get this! The wisdom that comes from above is not only pure, but the mind of that wisdom is free of agitation. It's gentle, it's easy to be solicited, it's full of mercy, it has lots of good fruit, it doesn't favor another party, and it doesn't fake another personality. And that, my friends, is what comes from above.

Then he says that the fruit of righteousness is sewn in peace. From who? From them that make peace.

Let's take a glance at a corresponding verse from the Old Testament.

Isaiah 48:17-18

"Thus saith the LORD thy Redeemer. The Holy One of Israel, I am the Lord thy God which teaches thee to profit, which leadeth thee by the way that thou shouldest go. O that thou hadst hearkened my commandments! Then had the **peace been as a river** and thy **righteousness as the waves of the sea**:"

He's saying: I will teach you how to profit. I am the Lord who will lead you where to go. I will give you direction. So listen and obey! If you had listened to me in the first place, you would have peace.

Returning to Romans, we learn more about how to attain peace in our lives.

Romans 14:13-19

"Let us not therefore judge one another anymore: but judge this rather, that no man put a stumblingblock or an occasion to fall in his brother's way. I know, and am persuaded by the Lord Jesus, that there is nothing unclean of itself: but to him that esteemeth any thing to be unclean, to him it is unclean. But if thy brother be grieved with thy meat, **now** walkest thou not charitably. Destroy not him with thy meat, for whom Christ died. Let not then your good be evil spoken of: For the kingdom of God is not meat and drink: but **righteousness, and peace, and joy in the Holy Ghost**. For he that in these things serveth Christ is acceptable to God, and approved of men. Let us therefore follow after the things which make for peace, and things wherewith one may edify another."

First, it says here that we should not be judging people. We especially should not be judging those who eat meat. Then, it's as if Paul is saying: Hey, you're doing well, but don't speak evil. For the kingdom of God is not meat and drink, but righteousness and peace and joy in the Holy Ghost. Why are these things listed beside each other so often? It is because righteousness produces peace, and peace gives us the ability to remain righteous in our life.

He adds: You know what? Don't fight over meat and all of that, but rather do whatever it takes to build people up and to create peace!

These are but a few examples where we see righteousness tied to peace. Throughout the Scriptures there are multiples more and I encourage you to sit down and make a study out of finding them!

Most of what we have discussed would appear to be common sense; however, it obviously is not, for so many of us still insist on focusing on negative things. Summarizing, one of the most damaging effects of a negative focus is when we choose to continuously recall adverse things that have happened to us in the past. Many a drink or drug has been consumed by those who dwelled on the painful past. The No. 1 cause of suicide is people not getting past their past.

We recall these unfortunate occasions, and then respond to them as if we do in fact wrestle against flesh and blood. When we stubbornly insist upon dwelling upon such things, it will inevitably blanket any light that we may have had in complete darkness. And we have seen that when our bodies are in complete darkness, they are in a state of turmoil.

When we are in turmoil, peace is not possible. But in our final chapter, we will see that peace can indeed become a permanent reality in the lives of those who will but refocus from that which they simply cannot resist.

T H I R T E E N

RU STILL STRUGGLING?

This is our final chapter and, as it should be, it will also be our longest chapter. Please ensure you are prepared to focus on what remains to be read in this study. Peace brings release, but peace, if not protected, will be *fleeting* and in the battle you will be *retreating.*

So, in our last segment of this book on preparing for peace, I want to give you **three reasons** why we are struggling to maintain peace in the midst of tough circumstances. It is also my goal to help you understand the reasons, as I have come to understand them, for why ***life*** seems to

TODAY'S DAILY MEDS

Peace brings release, but peace, if not protected, will be fleeting and in the battle you will be retreating

be so ***rife*** with ***strife***!

The Bible tells us that strife comes from pride. There's no way around it, for the Scriptures tell us in Proverbs 13:10, that "only by pride cometh contention..."

Those of us who have struggled with addiction have a special spiritual kinship with the apostle James. I am told the early membership of Alcoholics Anonymous were so influenced with the apostle's epistle that they called themselves the "James Club". I once read that the early, more Christ-centered, meetings would read the entire letter at every one of their meetings. A.A. historian Dick B. writes: "In fact the whole original A.A. process...involved several of the surrender, prayer, confession, forgiveness, and healing suggestions found in the Book of James."[1]

And so it is appropriate that we turn again to this insightful disciple, who was part of the Lord's inner circle, to ascertain Biblical truths.

James 4:1-2

"From whence come **wars** and **fightings among you**? come they not hence, even of **your lusts** that **war in your members**? Ye lust, and have not: ye kill, and desire to have, and cannot obtain: ye fight and war, yet ye have not, because ye ask not."

What causes us to be engaged in fighting battles among one another? James tells us that the battles come from our lusts. Now recall from chapter one that lusts are simply our designer desires that we have formed throughout the course of our lives. He goes on to say that these lusts **war** in our members. *Members* is the Old English word for the modern English phrase *body parts.* So we see here that our lusts will manifest themselves through our body parts. How does this occur, you ask? Well, let us take a look…

The desires in our bodies stimulate our minds, and our minds then begin to dwell on them in our hearts. It is the dwelling upon these desires that influences our will. The will, doing what wills do, then stimulates our emotions to bring forth a desire. Once this occurs, we will inevitably engage in wrong behaviors. We will then feel temporary, abnormal satisfaction and then "crash" back to a subnormal emotional state. Do you see the cycle? I once it said, regarding our emotions, that we should pray, "Dear fragile, fickle, feeble, ferocious friend of mine. Lord, mount this filly high and ride her till I die!"

So for what *should* we be asking God? Once again, the Holy Spirit revealed the answer to James.

James 1:5-8

"If any of you **lack wisdom**, let him **ask of God**, that giveth to all men liberally, and upbraideth not; and it shall be given him. But let him **ask in faith**, nothing wavering. For he that wavereth is like a wave of the sea driven with the wind and tossed. For let not that man think that he shall receive any thing of the Lord. A **double minded man is unstable** in all his ways."

So, we see that we are to ask God for wisdom—the wisdom of the Holy Spirit! As we have seen, we must make our requests to God through faith in Him, and it is this point that is stressed by James in this verse. It is important for us to recognize that wavering faith is *our* faith, and our faith is insufficient in the eyes of God. He demands that we yield to His faith! More often than not, it is our wavering faith that keeps us from doing anything for, or getting anything from, the Lord.

Taking this a little deeper, go to back to James 4:2, where he tells us: "Ye lust, and have not: ye kill, and desire to have, and cannot obtain: ye fight and war, yet ye have not, because ye ask not." He is saying that we do not have our desires met because we either do not ask God properly, or we fail to ask Him at all.

James then goes on to state, "Ye ask, and receive not, because ye ask amiss, that ye may consume it upon your lusts" (James 4:3). What this actually means is that we often do not have our requests granted because God knows we intend to use them to fulfill our lusts. And as we have previously discussed, God does not bless a double-minded man because he is unstable in all his ways.

Essentially, we see that the reason we have fighting and wars is because we have desires that we try to satisfy in our own power, rather than asking God for the wisdom to overcome them, or simply letting Him take care of them Himself. Friends, when we trust in self, we are entering into a form of friendship with the world that will ultimately fail us every time!

James continues in verse 4, "Ye adulterers and adulteresses, know ye not that the friendship of the world is enmity with God? whosoever therefore will be a friend of the world is the enemy of God." The term *enmity* is the key word here. It's the same word Genesis used to indicate the division between mankind and Satan that was forged amidst the turmoil in the garden. Here, James is saying that we are bypassing a love relationship with *Christ* for a love relationship with the *world*, and this relationship with our lusts and the world will most definitely cause us to be at ought with God! And that is why we have wars and battle with each other; they are a by-product of our being fully consumed by our efforts to do, be, and have everything we want and to obtain it in our own power.

Because we frequently fail by our resorting to self-empowerment, we create a kinship with the world that puts us squarely within its system of management. Also, when we are entrapped in the world's management system, we are no longer going to look to God and ask for the wisdom of the Ghost that we might experience the most!

My friends, know we not that when we reside in the world, God becomes terribly envious? You might say, "How can God become envious? That's a sin!"

Look, He's God and He can do whatever He wants, plus, His envy is for our ultimate perfection. In the very next verse in our study, James 4:5 actually asks, "Do ye think that the scripture saith in vain, The spirit that dwelleth in us lusteth to envy?"

May I remind you at this point that lusts are actually formed in our members, or our body parts? With that being said, we can deduce that it is the Spirit Who becomes frustrated with our soul's desire to satisfy our body rather than to satisfy His promptings which causes Him to lust with envy. And once this lust is conceived, we are told, it causes instant enmity with God.

But, praise God, the Bible tells us that our Lord has yet more grace for us in this situation. Our next verse tells us, "But he giveth more grace. Wherefore he saith, God **resisteth the proud**, but **giveth grace** unto the **humble**" (James 4:6). You see, it is pride that causes us to do things in our own power, and doing things in our own power is what causes us to struggle! Likewise, this is also what causes other people the struggles which bring turmoil into our lives. Often, people looking for relief from their stressors will bring us their turmoil for two reasons: Either they want us to fix their unrest, or they are frustrated and want somebody else to feel their pain.

Of course, all of this is a humanistic way of dealing with our own unsatisfied desires. God says He'll resist the proud and give more grace to the humble. We learned earlier that grace is when God does the work on our behalf. So, basically, if we humble ourselves, God will come alive through us and do the work that creates victorious Christian living. Our next two verses of this study are definitely worth noting:

James 4:7-8

"Submit yourselves therefore to God. Resist the devil, and he will flee from you. Draw nigh to God, and he will draw nigh to you. Cleanse your hands, ye sinners; and purify your hearts, ye double minded."

Now our discussion on this chapter should seem familiar to you in a peculiar way. That is because James 4:1-8 has a direct correlation to James 1:1-8, which is a chapter we have previously exposited. In James 1, recall that he said we should rejoice when faced with temptations. We are also instructed to ask God in faith, without wavering (using His faith, not ours) to make us single-minded and completely focused on Him. When we do this, James 1 tells us we will create patience within our lives that allows us to endure and overcome temptation. And this process is what we referred to as an examination, for God uses this to reveal to us exactly where we are at in our spiritual walk.

However, in James 4:1-8, he begins by saying that this view of an examination temptation as depicted in James 1 will not be a reality for those who are at war. In fact, James 4 tells us that we will inevitably and regularly experience wars and fighting as a result of these lusts that reside within our bodies. When this happens, James says, we begin to live in our own power and as a result, our soul-controlled lusts begin to overrule the wishes of the Spirit. Also, James tells us that striving in our own power is direct evidence of having one foot in the world and being what he calls "double-minded."

He tells us also that when we are duplicitous, we strike a friendship with the world that immediately makes God an enemy toward us. Obviously, my friends, when we become enemies with God, we will be struggling! God will no longer empower us to do anything, nor will He give us anything! Our lives will become void of any supernatural influence.

So what do we do when this happens? James says that we must, as sinners, cleanse our hands and purify our hearts. The first step in doing this is submitting fully to God. Submitting to God should start with a dialogue between you and Him somewhere along the lines of this: "God, I want to be at peace. I don't want turmoil in my life anymore. Help me to resist the devil when he tries to bring unrest into my life. Help me to reject the **thoughts** that the enemy will use to stir up my lusts."

The Bible says those thoughts, along with the devil who seeks to instill those thoughts in us, will flee from us when we draw nigh to God, and He subsequently draws nigh unto us. So, when we submit ourselves to Him, we are empowered to resist the stimulation within our body and avoid the tendency of dwelling on selfish thoughts. As a result of this, the devil flees and we can stop fighting and start drawing nearer to God. Because we are no longer consumed with every *thing* in our life, we can begin to develop an intimate relationship with God.

To begin this building process, James tells us to cleanse our hands. Cleansing our hands is a figurative illustration for purifying what we do because, my friends, we *are* our hearts. Recall that the Bible says as a man "thinketh in his heart, so is he" (Proverbs 23:7), and "out of the abundance of the heart, the mouth speaketh" (Matthew 12:34). We know that all sin begins in the heart. Cleaning up the things upon which we think will place us in position to cleanse our actions. James tells us that by purifying our hearts, we can clean the sin that permeates our hands (lives).

But why are our hearts in need of purifying? The answer is because upon conversion, man becomes double-minded. Only saved people can be double-minded because we are the only humans with two natures. When we receive Christ we should become spiritually and singly minded, but we tend to keep one foot in the world, James says. Said differently, our hearts have two thought processes. In fact, the apostle says this earlier himself. "Out of the same mouth proceedeth blessing and cursing. My brethren, these things ought not so to be" (James 3:10).

My friends, we are the type of people that will satisfy our every indulgence and then turn around and praise God for all the great things that He has given us. And we will make a public display of our sacrifice for Christ, then complain that we don't have the things we need, and worse yet, wonder why God is not blessing us. Do you see it now? These, my brethren, are the primary reasons we struggle! These are the main reasons we are at war! We are double minded.

Even though we are a weak people, we still have a lot of pride. Many of us prefer to pray for easier lives. Phillip Brooks, the 19th century preacher and author of the Christmas Hymn *O Little Town of Bethlehem* said, "Do not pray for easier lives; pray for stronger people." You see, when we become stronger people *in* Christ Jesus, we are willing to say **no** – no matter the desires of all the worldly vices, wishes, and wants. We become willing to sacrifice these things that once tripped us up so effectively.

It takes a strong spiritual grounding to say "no" to the flesh. That's why so many were unable to join the "Just say no to drugs" campaign of former first lady Nancy Reagan. It has been said that it doesn't take a strong person to satisfy his needs; it takes a strong person to *sacrifice* his needs. And, my friends, when we learn to do this, God will begin to purify our hearts, and we'll begin to change the way we think.

Upon this transformation, we will evolve from a pessimist who sees *difficulty in every opportunity* into an optimist who sees *opportunity in every difficulty*! This is how we turn our obstacles into opportunities, our adversities into advantage, and our stumbling blocks into stepping stones. We've got to change the way we look at things. Period.

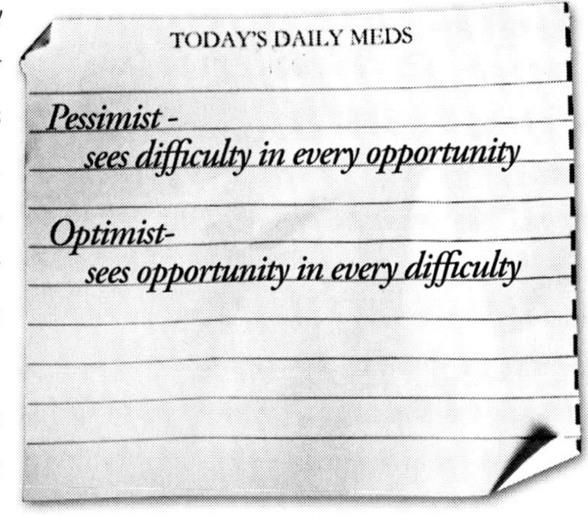

Purpose #1 for Strife: For You To Promote Peace

Why is it so important that we carry a positive viewpoint? We must recognize that our job on earth is to *be* strong in the Lord that we might help others *become* strong in the Lord. This includes all types of people. Those who want help, those who don't want help, and even those who don't know they need help! We even need to help those who want to help others, as they sometimes need help too!

Allow me to further explain what I mean here. **One of the primary reasons God in heaven allows turmoil into our life is to restore those struggling.** The Bible instructs us in Hebrews 12:14 to "Follow peace with all men, and holiness, without which no man shall see the Lord:" When God says to follow peace with all men, He is expressing a desire for us to bring peace unto people with issues and problems. So we see one of the principle purposes of strife in our life is to allow us to minister to those who are struggling.

Ministry is a tool the devil intends to use to destroy our peace, while God, conversely, intends to use our ministry to develop our peace. The Bible tells us in Matthew 5:9, "Blessed are the peacemakers for they shall be called the children of God. " Wow! That's even better than winning the Nobel Peace Prize!

Some of God's choicest Christians are those who promote peace. My friends, when we promote peace to the people—especially the lost—we are showing the lost that we are indeed God's children. Our testimonies are so very important in our work for Christ! John reminds us of this in Revelation 12:11, "...they overcame him by the blood of the Lamb, and by the word of their testimony."

When people bring us *their* turmoil it is God's design for us, and for our peace, to reduce the *stress* of their *unrest.* Those who come to us seeking refuge from their war most often do whatever we ask because they are in desperate need of assistance! Their turmoil is overwhelming them, but to us their turmoil may seem miniscule. Their problems often will seem simple compared to the problems we typically carry. And this, my friends, is why it is so important that we support our weaker brethren through their struggles.

Just the other day I came home from the office after a stressful day in which God had allowed me to supernaturally maintain my peace. To His glory, I refrained from becoming overwhelmed all day long. So on this peaceful day, just as I got home and put down my briefcase, my children rushed me for hugs and kisses.

Then, in typical fashion, they all dispersed just as quickly as they came upon me—except for my youngest son, Chance. He looked up at me with a big tear nearly spilling from his eye and said, "Dad, will you help me get this knot out of my shoe; I wanna go out and play."

My son needed my help and, of course, I was going to give it to him. So I began working on this knot and, boy, it was a doozey! After about three or four minutes of working on it, I became very frustrated. Just then, I abruptly took the shoe off my son's foot and tossed it over toward my wife Lori, saying, "You've got fingernails; you get it out!"

As I turned back around and glanced at Chance, I could see that he was startled. He thought he was in trouble! I thought to myself, "Way to go, Steve. You just interrupted your little boy's peace!" He was sitting there counting on his dad to help him out and, instead, all I did was catch him off guard with my abruptness. I, who was supposed to be the peace-maker, failed to maintain peace myself! I was immediately convicted for what I had done. I realized quickly that I should have called Lori over to help bring peace to *my* turmoil and my son would have learned a valuable lesson about overcoming adversity using teamwork. Lesson learned – not by him, but by me!

You see, to my son the problem with the knot was everything; but to me it should have been nothing. However, it became something to me because I allowed myself to lose my peace. But this should not usually be the case as a weaker vessel brings a burden to a stronger vessel. In most instances, the burdens of many troubled individuals are not of a challenging nature to those who are seasoned in warfare.

Our job as veteran Christians is to help those with struggles that are not nearly as unmanageable to us as they seem to be to them. It should be noted, however, that when we turn somebody's turmoil into peace, they are going to want it more often and they will come to need it more often, and likewise request it more often. As a result, they will return more often as they will too soon require our help. When we find ourselves in this situation, we must carefully teach the dependent brother or sister how to maintain peace on his own. 2 Timothy 2:2 says, "And the things that thou hast heard of me among many witnesses, the same commit thou to faithful men, who shall be able to teach others also." So as Paul suggests, we must take it as a responsibility to not just relieve others of their unrest, but also to teach them *how to* find rest.

Continuing on the thought from Hebrews 12:14 mentioned earlier, "Follow peace with all men and holiness, without which, no man shall see the Lord." When we become peacemakers, it becomes clear that we are God's children. The Lord, however, will not be glorified in our life if we are not following peace and holiness. Even if you are spreading peace, if you are doing it absent of holiness, it does not glorify the Lord, for you are simply using worldly tactics. This is why, my friends, we have seen most peace treaties broken throughout history.

The very next verse tells us, "Looking diligently lest any man fail of the grace of God; lest any root of bitterness springing up trouble you, and thereby many be defiled;" (Hebrews 12:15). God is telling us that if we don't follow peace and live holy lives, we are going to have nothing but bitterness and turmoil and trouble. My friend, do you think you can be troubled and maintain peace? No! Trouble is what destroys peace!

All of these things come, Paul says, because the grace of God is overlooked. When we fail to look diligently for God's grace, we will inevitably wind up in trouble. If we don't follow peace, we are sure to have inner personal conflict.

Now take a look at another verse that confirms this truth:

I Thessalonians 5:23

"And the very **God of peace** sanctify you **wholly;** and I pray God your whole **spirit** and **soul** and **body** be preserved blameless unto the coming of our Lord Jesus Christ."

The word *wholly* means *all three parts of our being.* And the word *sanctify* means to *set apart from.* So, Paul is saying the peace of God will set apart all three parts of our trichotomy (spirit, soul, and body). Until Jesus comes back, He wants all parts of our being to be sanctified and remain fully at peace. How do we do this? By avoiding everybody that brings turmoil into our lives? No! Instead, he tells us at the beginning of this dissertation: "I exhort you brethren to warn the unruly, comfort the feebleminded, support the weak, be patient to all men" (I Thessalonians 5:14).

When we see people who are not following the law of Christ, we should warn them of their mistakes. Now the "feeble minded" are those who have a "weak mind as a result of a cause". A person becomes feeble-minded when an event occurs in their lives that cause them to be weakened.

For example, my father died four weeks ago. Earlier today, my mother was rushed to the hospital and diagnosed with what the doctors termed an *acute neurological disorder*. In layman's terms, this means a *nervous breakdown.* Now, it must be said that my mother is one of the strongest Christians I have ever known. She is also known as one of the most Christ-like women amongst those who know her.

In spite of this, it was apparent that her grief had overcome her. She had dealt with my father's Alzheimer's disease for a number of years and then was crushed when he was taken to heaven so suddenly. Though I am in the midst of our busiest conference season and I am more strapped for time than I have ever been, I have the wonderful privilege to comfort somebody who for a period of time, I discern, has a temporary weakness in her mind.

The weakness in my mother's mind was caused by the death of my dad. And it is "but for a season", the Bible tells us in the book of Ecclesiastes. My mother's feebleness is well within the framework of an appropriate season as it has just been a few weeks since my father's death. Knowing this, how dare I refuse to comfort somebody who is so close to me and is experiencing turmoil thinking I am too busy? God wants me to help people, and He will sanctify my mind, body, and soul with the peace of God for doing so. Thankfully, my mother recovered within hours. Praise God.

So, we see then that we have two responsibilities given to us when faced with the turmoil of others. First, we are to warn them if it is a result of unruly behavior. Too often we want to just reject them or cast them out, but friends, this is wrong! The Bible tells us that we are to warn them of the consequences of their actions.

Secondly, we see that we are to comfort the feeble-minded. A lot of the time, we are too busy to take the time to really minister to a person in a terribly weakened state. We tend to rationalize: Oh they'll get over it sooner or later or expect others to notice their tumult and intervene. Friend, you *saw* it, you *thaw* it! Where is our compassion—the feeling of their pain in our heart?

The next phrase of this verse charges us with yet another

responsibility to the tormented, which is our third, Paul tells us to "...support the weak..." A person who is weak is one who is unstable. These people are unstable and are not able to stand up on their own without the support of another.

So we are commanded to stand in the gap for them. My friends, "gap-standing" is an outstanding opportunity to promote peace!

Finally, Paul concludes by giving us a fourth charge. He commands us to "be patient toward all men." The four exhortations listed in this passage are how God wants us to take the turmoil of others and use it to help promote peace in their lives. Now, in the verse 15, Paul tells us something we should not do. "See that none render evil for evil unto any man..."

He's saying do not retaliate with evil toward those who bring evil upon you. We all are pretty good at handling this when it comes to responding properly to those whom we love, but how about those people who are not in our inner circles? It is often very difficult for us to return good when evil is done unto us by those whom we are either indifferent to, or don't care for at all. The verse tells us we are to render good to all men—not just those whom we love.

So, in verse 14, he gives us four exhortations to produce the sanctification of our spirit, soul, and body. In verse 15, he tells us two things *not to do* so as to not disqualify ourselves from the peace of God. And, finally, in verse 16, he tells us how to respond to the adversity of others to maintain the peace of God, simply put: "Rejoice evermore."

First Thessalonians 5 continues on with more admonitions to prayer, giving thanks and fueling the flow of the Holy Ghost so that the God of peace may keep us blameless and at peace until the coming of the Lord Jesus Christ.

We are in no position, spiritually, to wage wars of frustration against those who cause turmoil in our life. This is why God wants us to restore the struggling, not wage war with the struggling! Friends, we are not in a position where we can critique those who are consumed with turmoil. In Romans 14:13, Paul states, "let us not therefore judge one another anymore."

Stop judging people! So when people come into our lives with turmoil, we should not push them away. This verse also commands us to not be a stumbling block for a weaker brother. I've got news for you, when somebody comes to us for help, and we reject them or rebuke them – that is a stumbling block!

In Romans 14:19, Paul concludes this treatise on judging people by saying: "Let us therefore follow after the things which *make for peace*, and things wherewith *one may edify another*." The word *make* is a key word here. Recall that God *made* peace in the beginning and has since then charged us with the responsibility to be peace*makers.* This is also known as our *ministry* of reconciliation that we spoke about previously. My friends, I've never seen a man at war who was in the midst of building up people.

Remember, those who bring turmoil into our lives often do so because they may need us. They need a release to be at peace and to be rectified in the eyes of God. This is what Paul is referring to as our responsibility to offer "things which edify another."

The late legendary newscaster Paul Harvey said it best: "At times like these, we have to remind people that there have always been times like these."

Purpose #2 for Strife: To Reveal Where We Are Struggling

Another reason that God brings turmoil into our lives is to reveal our own personal struggles. Recall the story given earlier about the apostle Peter and the three fires. God said that he had a ministry for Peter to "strengthen the brethren." This is the same type of ministry of which we just spoke: restoring others to peace who are tortured by turmoil.

But God knew that there was no way that Peter could have this ministry until he was emptied of himself; and when he was emptied of his pride, you'll recall, shortly thereafter he was enlisted to the ministry. And when Peter faced His final fire in Acts 2, he was empowered to change the world in Acts 2.

The Bible tells us that we ought to "glory in tribulation knowing that tribulation works patience" (Romans 5:3). So, we can deduce from this that if God wants to develop patience within us, He is *not* going to put us at peace, but rather he will place us in tribulation. The Bible tells a story in which the apostle Paul was in danger of becoming a proud man, so God gave him a thorn in the flesh. But why would He give Paul a thorn in the flesh to keep him from becoming prideful? Well, let's take a closer look…

Paul writes in II Corinthians 12:7: "And lest I should be exalted above measure through the abundance of the revelations, there was given to me a thorn in the flesh, the messenger of Satan to buffet me, lest I should be exalted above measure." You see, Paul was so illuminated by the Spirit, God considered that he would most probably be exalted above measure. Paul was so sure of it, he repeated the reason twice in one sentence!

So he says that because God sensed that Paul risked becoming prideful, God gave him a thorn in the flesh to save him from a high esteem of self. Paul called his thorn in the flesh a messenger from Satan to buffet him. The word *buffet* literally means to *rap with the fist.*

Now, the word *messenger* is an interesting word. It is used 99 times in the Scriptures including this time. Note that in the other 98 times, the word *messenger* is used to refer to a person. Granted, most people believe Paul's thorn in the flesh was some kind of physical malady or a habitual sin of some sort; but, friends, every other time the word *messenger* is used, it refers to a person. Knowing this, wouldn't it make sense to believe that perhaps Paul is referring to a person in this case as well?

To that end, it is my stance that the messenger that Paul speaks of is a person sent by Satan to buffet him, or hinder him. Now, when this person came into Paul's life, it was not him per se, but rather the turmoil that accompanied him that hindered Paul. Paul asked God to take this person's turmoil out of his life, but instead of doing that, God gave him His power to endure this messenger. This pleased Paul even greater as he reasoned he would rather bring God glory in his infirmities so that the power of Christ would rest upon him.

My friend, as He did in Paul's life, God wants to reveal to us potential weaknesses in our life by using the tool of turmoil. Paul said that when he is *made* weak, he becomes strong, and so could we, *if* we allow the power of God to come upon us in our times of difficulty!

Another apostle, Peter, said it like this in I Peter 3:10: "For he that will love life, and see good days, let him refrain his tongue from evil, and his lips that they speak no guile:" He says those of us who want to love life and see good days need to keep our words peaceful, speaking no guile, artificial lies, or hypocrisy.

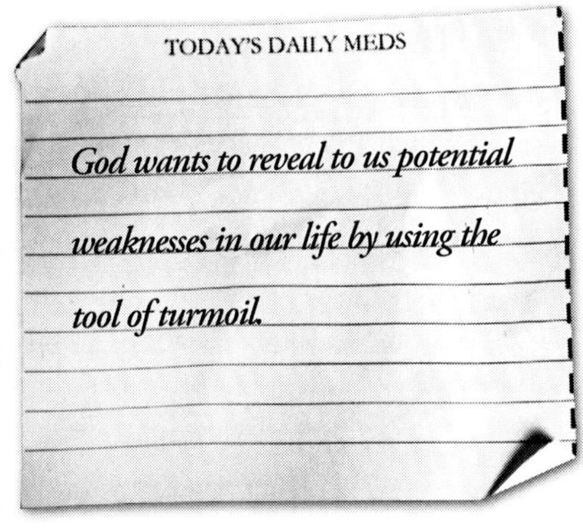

Peter goes on to say, "Let him eschew evil, and do good; let him **seek peace,** and **ensue it."** This is fairly self-explanatory, meaning those who want to love life and live good days are to avoid evil and seek peace and pursue it accordingly. Oh my friends, God wants us to restore the struggling, but also wants to reveal to us that with which we are struggling too!

Note in I Peter 4:12-13, Peter reiterates the joys that come from suffering by saying, "Beloved, think it not strange concerning the fiery trial which is to try you, as though some strange thing happened unto you: But rejoice, inasmuch as ye are partakers of Christ's sufferings; that, when his gl*ory* shall be revealed, ye may be glad also with exceeding joy."

Thus far we see that God brings turmoil into our lives via other people to accomplish two things. First, He wants us to restore others who are struggling to a position of pandemonium to a position of peace, and secondly, He wants to reveal to us when we are struggling by crowding us to Christ. Now take a look at verse 14 in I Peter 4: "If ye be reproached for the name of Christ, happy are ye; for the spirit of glory and of God resteth upon you: on their part he is evil spoken of, but on your part he is glorified." Now, note that most often this occurs when He takes us from a position of *turbulent* pride to a position of *tranquil* peace.

Do you remember the story of Laban and Jacob in the Bible? Jacob deceived his brother Esau out of his birthright by pulling the old switcheroo on his older brother, thereby fooling his father. Because of this, the Bible tells us that Isaac, Jacob's father, had to send him away into hiding to live with his brother in law, Laban, in a far-away land.

Now when Esau saw that Isaac had blessed Jacob, he decided he was going to go out and take a wife from the daughters of Canaan. Esau did this because he knew it would upset Isaac, his father. Esau had so much turmoil in his life because of what his brother Jacob had done. Note that Jacob was the original source of the turmoil, yet he was the blessed child!

The Bible says that Jacob obeyed his father and went to live with his brother in law but on the way, he stopped in the desert to have a dream.

At the conclusion of the dream, he called the place where he was, Bethel. In the dream God revealed to him that despite his mistakes, God was going to do something great with his life. At this point, Jacob made a vow that as long as God remained with him and would take away his worries, he would worship Him. Paraphrased, he said if you feed me, give me clothing, keep me safe, and restore peace to my parents' home so that it would be possible to eventually return; then he would make the Lord his God. That is four requests: food, clothing, safety, and peace in my family.

You may know the story of how Jacob goes on to live with Laban and quickly fell in love with Rachel, his daughter. But Jacob had become so full of pride because of what God had promised He would someday do through him. But yet, this proud man was homeless and running for his life. He was in complete turmoil because of pride and self-centeredness. So he was not only proud, but he was also in trouble!

When first approached by Jacob, Laban must have thought to himself: "Hey, I know exactly who you are. You're the man who swindled your own brother; you can't fool me. I am going to show you exactly what it's like to be tricked."

So Jacob worked for seven years so that he could marry the love of his life, Rachel. And just like the *brother* swap he pulled on his daddy, his daddy's brother-in-law did a *daughter* swap on him! Instead of giving Rachel to Jacob as his wife, Laban gave him his older daughter, Leah. And Jacob, for the first time saw first-hand who he really was, for he was deceived in the same way he himself had deceived.

The Bible tells us that from this point forward, God's power was upon Jacob. He worked for seven more years, the Bible says, and then came up with a plan that required faith, God's power and the creativity of his gift mix in order to get his life's love, Rachel. Most importantly, Jacob allowed the turmoil in his life to reveal to him where he had gone wrong and submitted to the humbling process that Laban instilled upon him.

In preparing to launch out into his own family business, he likewise honored Laban and did not steal from him, taking from him the worst of cattle he had to offer, rather than the best, and trusted God to bless his plan. Then he turned around and used creativity to cause an inferior flock whose eventual gross magnitude soon became a superior flock. The Bible says that Jacob then earned his way out of town.

Jacob had learned life's lessons and had kept his vow. Now God was fulfilling His part of the vows. As Jacob was finally released to build his family and personal wealth, he was truly a blessed man. He arrived there poverty-stricken, running from his parents and brother, fearing for his life and having no food or anywhere to sleep. And when he left his taskmaster, Laban, he had wives, handmaidens, and dozens of children as well as thousands of cattle. He departs with his proverbial cup spilling over to make his claim to fame in life.

At this point, he has only one more promise left undone from God's vow to Him—to be at peace with his family. On his way back to his homeland, word came to him that his brother Esau was coming toward him with 400 of his men. Jacob trembled and feared upon hearing this, but he ultimately trusted in the Lord. At the same time, he separated his family and put the youngest and the weakest in the back of the lines and the strongest in the front, as he prepared for what he thought was surely an impending family feud of all-out war!

Though he was terribly outnumbered, he still trusted in the Lord because he had already learned to call out to God, saying "Lord, save me from this trouble!" And when Esau finally showed up, shockingly there was a wonderful family reunion and peace was restored. Why was there peace and a reunion in light of the turmoil within the family? It is because God in His amazing grace had equally blessed Esau, while at the same time revealing to Jacob the error of his ways. God used the turmoil coupled with unmerited favor to show Jacob how to get right with his family.

To review, we see that two of the reasons God puts struggling people into our lives is to restore the struggling and to reveal to us what we may be struggling with. There is one final and key reason for turmoil in our lives; let's take a look…

Purpose #3 for Strife: To Remove Others From Our Life

The third reason God puts turmoil into our lives is for us to learn to avoid those who are bringing the turmoil. The Bible tells us that sometimes there are people in our lives who are struggling, and if we keep them there, they will steal our peace while we simultaneously hurt them. Though we ought to always strive to, we can't help everybody.

How do we try? Well, we warn them when they are unruly, and we comfort them when they are feeble-minded. We do good to those that do evil. We don't give up on them until the time appointed. And when that time is appointed, the way to keep our peace and to eventually even help them restore their peace is to remove their strife from *our* life.

Remember that Romans 3:23 says, "As it is written, There is none righteous, no, not one; There is none that understandeth, there is none that seek after God." Paul is saying there is nobody who does good. He goes on to say that all men's throats are an open sepulcher, their tongues are nasty, and their mouth is full of cursing and bitterness: "Their feet are swift to shed blood: Destruction and misery are in their ways: And the way of peace have they not known." Why are these people so bad? It is because they don't even *know* the way of peace, much less the way to find it. Why? Well, these verses conclude that there is no fear of God before their eyes, and this is what keeps them from changing.

Praise the Lord, for the Bible has a prescription to treat this spiritual sickness: "By mercy and truth iniquity is purged:" (Proverbs 16:6). My pastor recently wrote a book on mercy and truth entitled *Mercy and Truth: Discovering God's Perfect Blend for Balance* that really opened up our ministry's collective eyes to this phenomenal truth. Our housing ministry has always used mercy and truth as its platform in that we strive to not give people what they deserve, but rather mercy coupled with the truth in love. And since the recent teaching upon this topic by our pastor, we have sought to operate by this tenant all the more.

The definition of mercy and truth is withholding judgment while simultaneously speaking that which is strongly held to be right, in love. The Bible, in the next verse, also tells us that if we will do that, the fear of Lord will keep us from evil. The entire verse reads, "By mercy and truth iniquity is purged: and by the fear of the Lord men depart from evil."

It must be said, however, that when people fail to develop a fear of the Lord, they will not know the way of peace because it is the fear of the Lord that grants us our peace. Knowing that God is in control, our respect for and awe of God allows us to relax. But if one does not know this and he rejects the fear of the Lord, then mercy and truth will not impact him and they must be avoided.

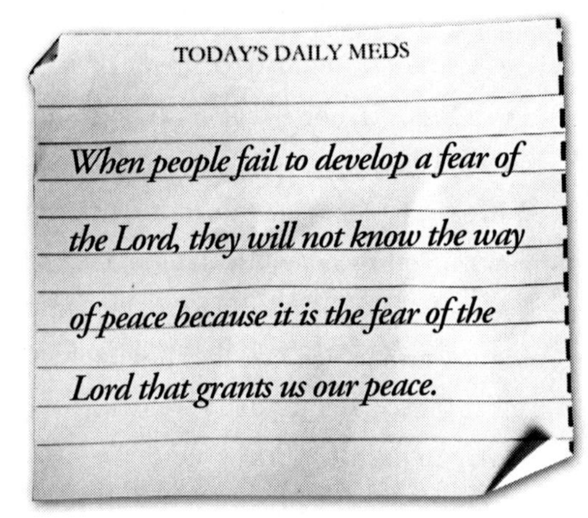

In this type of unfortunate circumstance, the only thing that can help this person is to be cast out. That is to say for us to be removed from the person or circumstance that is rejecting our efforts because otherwise they will not develop the fear of the Lord. Psalm 120:6-7

says it best: "My soul hath long dwelt with him that hateth peace. **I am for peace**: but when I speak, **they are for war."**

Here the psalmist is talking about people who literally hate peace. Those of us who hang out with them for a long, long time recognize that these people are not even interested in peace. Rather, they're interested in turmoil. That's right, they like turmoil. They want their turmoil. They know of nothing else but turmoil. And, my friends, they want their turmoil to be your turmoil. They bring their turmoil to you because they don't like your peace either!

The Bible says these types of folks are *for* war. However, I would say that not everybody who brings you problems with consistency—and does nothing about them—are for war or even that they dislike peace. It's still nonetheless true that if they do not develop a fear of God, they may need to be removed from our lives.

Now, friends, this is not reason to cast out all that are unruly or feeble-minded. Nor is this reason to cast out those who are struggling with some sort of tribulation or temptation. Oh no, my friends, we have the responsibility to help those types until further notice, and **further notice will always be much longer than you and I would prefer.** The simple truth is that when people do not develop a fear of the Lord as a result of our months and months or even years and years of ministry, it is our job to avoid them.

Romans 16:17 begins, "Now I beseech you, brethren, to mark them..." This literally means to put a spot on their head. Now obviously we can't walk around putting spots on people's heads, but this phrase is really just to indoctrinate it into our minds that these types are divisive people and when we see them, we'll quickly recognize them for who they are.

This, of course, begs the question: who are these *marked* people?

The second part of the verse refers to "them which cause divisions and offenses contrary to the doctrine which ye have learned; and avoid them." Now what is the doctrine that we've learned? Well, of course, this is Romans, so we're talking about the gospel of justification, then transitioning to the gospel of sanctification that someday will produce the gospel of glorification.

However, some people think that this doctrine is referring to only those who teach another way to get saved (justification alone). But there are some who believe that there are other ways to glorify God and live in His peace other than through the Spirit of Jesus Christ (sanctification). These people are focused on will-worship, trying to worship God in the power of their own soul. Because of this, these people will always cause division and interrupt any and all peace. They cause offenses contrary to the doctrine which you have learned, and this is exactly why we need to avoid these kinds of people.

Why do we have to avoid them? Verse 18 reads, "For they that are such serve not the Lord Jesus Christ, but their own belly; and by good words and fair speeches deceive the hearts (the meditations) of the simple" In other words, these people need to be avoided because they are wolves in sheep's clothing.

We must recognize that these types of individuals tend to come in unawares and use their many good speeches to deceive the hearts of the simple-minded to sour a congregation, or our organization, and even in our families. We must avoid these kinds of influences at all costs or else risk division and tumult in our lives.

The next verse then tells us if we do this—avoid such divisive people—"the God of peace shall bruise Satan under **your** feet shortly" (Romans 16:20). He's simply saying that if you'll keep them out of your life when they keep creating strife, that the God of Peace will empower **you** to bruise Satan under **your** feet.

Yes, my friends, there are troublemakers out there. Those troublemakers aren't only causing divisions and offenses to our peace by creating turmoil, but sometimes they are teachers among us. They are people who create division in our ministries by not challenging us to the Spirit-filled, Hidden life.

To take these yet a step further, notice II Timothy 2:22 where Paul writes, "flee also youthful lusts". Recall that lusts are our designer desires that we have personally forged throughout our lifetime. More often than not, ladies possess a lust that causes them to have a void of gratitude for people and circumstances around them. Likewise, men tend to harbor a lust that leads them to rebel against authority. So what Paul is essentially telling us here is to not only avoid, but to also run from our tendencies toward ingratitude and rebellion. If we break it down even more, what Paul is actually saying is to remove ourselves as much as possible from the pride that precipitates our lusts. This can be applied to our discussion because it is our pride, my friend, which keeps us from ridding ourselves of a hopelessly turbulent person. We feel that we, in our own ability, possess the means to change them and are blinded to the fact that they are unchangeable—at least as a result of our ministry to them.

Moving on now, once we have successfully turned from our prideful ways, the Bible commands us to follow after righteousness and peace. Specifically, we are called to maintain peace with God, ourselves, and others. BUT, we are only told to maintain peace with others who are willing to call on the Lord with a pure heart. Now, know that people do not necessarily have to call on the Lord and be pure-hearted for us to maintain peace with them, but they have to be WILLING to do so! He says, "But foolish and unlearned questions avoid knowing that they do gender strifes" (v. 23). Here Paul is saying that unlearned questions, or foolish questions, need to be avoided because all they do is produce strife and hinder our peace. In verse 24, he gives us a dissertation that most people take wrong. "And the servant of the Lord must not strive; but must be gentle unto all men, apt to teach, and patient."

The word *apt* literally means to *be willing*. You see, my friends, everybody wants to go fishing for men, but all we really want to do is go gold-fishing! Paul tells us to fish for *all* men! He goes on to say that we should in meekness instruct "those that oppose themselves....that they may recover themselves out of the snare of the devil." Too often we are not really interested in teaching those who oppose themselves and present us with any type of difficulty or show ingratitude. But Paul is telling us in this verse to go after these types of people, because although they present challenges, they still can be helped.

However, some may seem to be easier to work with but in reality they are not interested in loving the Lord, nor are they willing to change. And it is these types of individuals that we are to avoid, we are told in verse 23. Why is this, you ask? It is because they do not serve the Lord, but rather they serve their own bellies; therefore, we cannot help them!

The Bible tells us that if we are careful to focus our attention only toward those who truly desire a change in their lives it will save us from wasting our time on others who refuse or are hurt by our help, thus freeing our efforts to be maximized for the glory of God.

What typically happens in a case where we may stand in the gap and help out a fellow brother is this: the devil senses a person's weakness and will seek to destroy them at their moment of infirmity. God, Who wants to strengthen us through our times of weakness, will often allow the enemy access to these people in their state of weakness. When this happens, the weakened individual typically will yield to the devil's temptation rather than seeing God's examination, and hence, they fall prey to the enemy's trap and are taken captive, so to speak.

Now here is where we come in. It is at this point that we, as strong, seasoned Christians, can step to the plate and do our best to restore the infirmed person. However, know that there is one large caveat to this equation, my friends. Sometimes we will find that we are not fully qualified to restore another person through a particular turmoil laden circumstance. When this occurs, God will reveal to us that WE are also struggling and then proceed to help US find restoration. Once we are restored and adequately equipped we may then go back and restore the hurting person. This example is a fine demonstration of two of God's uses of turmoil. We see that first we sought to help another through turmoil, but as a result of their turmoil, God revealed to us a struggle of our own! Can you see how God uses something we perceive to be negative for tremendous good? How incredible!

Granted, it must be reiterated that we can sometimes make an error in our judgment and mistakenly invest our time in a person who proves to not grow and continues to persist in bringing us a constant flow of turmoil. And again, it is these types of people whom the Bible advises us to avoid, my friends. We must accept the fact that we cannot help them!

This is just like we saw previously in our discussion about the devil's devices. Recall the young man whom we studied in I Corinthians who was involved in fornication with his mother-in-law. What did Paul exhort the Corinthians to do? He told them to turn

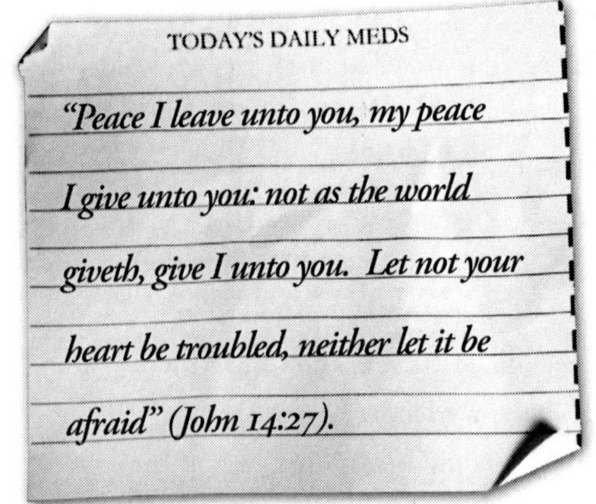
TODAY'S DAILY MEDS

"Peace I leave unto you, my peace I give unto you: not as the world giveth, give I unto you. Let not your heart be troubled, neither let it be afraid" (John 14:27).

him over to the devil for the destruction of his flesh. The Corinthians heeded Paul's advice and decided to remove this man from fellowship because they came to realize they could not help him anymore. We saw that it was not until this man was removed from the church that God was able to begin to work on his heart. Eventually, this wayward man transformed and was then restored back into the church. The key step here, however, was that he was purposefully avoided. This man needed to experience the humility of being cast out before he would get right with God.

You see, once sin is dealt with in these people's lives, we can restore them. However, we must do what can often be difficult and avoid them until God is able to reveal their own struggle to them. Friends, we must not enable a person PAST his mistake if God can enable him THROUGH his mistake.

In closing, Jesus leaves us with this: "Peace I leave unto you, my peace I give unto you: not as the world giveth, give I unto you. Let not your heart be troubled, neither let it be afraid" (John 14:27). WOW! God doesn't want us troubled or afraid. We know this must have been a VERY important truth that Jesus sought to convey given the fact that these words were some of the very last that He spoke to His disciples corporately.

Jesus promised us, in verse 26, of His return in the form of the

Comforter, or the Holy Ghost. The Bible says that God will send us the Comforter in Christ's name and He'll teach us things, and bring to our remembrance the things that Christ has previously taught us. What comfort – He will send us a Comforter! My friends, we are empowered with the peace of the Holy Spirit. This is **not** a peace that we can get from the world, for the world doesn't offer it. Only the peace of Jesus Christ can sustain us through the seasons of strife in life. My friends, we never need to be afraid. That's right! Rather, we can simply trust in Him!

Peter and Paul together said the phrase "peace be with you" a very impressive 22 times! Furthermore, these men opened and closed almost every one of their letters with a call to peace. Peter learned to have peace with God because he had peace with himself. And because he had peace with God and himself, he learned also the value of having peace with others. This is why he could exhort us towards the end of I Peter to humble ourselves under the mighty hand of God, that He might "exalt us in due time". How does He exalt us, you ask? Well, He does this in many ways actually, but perhaps none more pivotal than by bestowing us with His peace.

Oh my friends, prepare for peace, protect your peace, and promote peace! These are steps that will allow for a Christian life of which most of us have only dreamed! Let me close with Peter's great admonition that he formed in the crucible of the three transformative fires:

"Be sober, be vigilant; because your adversary the devil, [with many devices] as a roaring lion, walketh about, seeking whom he may devour:" And may the *peace of God* that comes only from the *God of peace* be with you. Amen and Amen!

NOTES-

Chapter One: RU Ready for Your Temptation Examination?

1. worldofquotes.com/author/Thomas-a-Kempis/index.html.
2. Gardner, Christine J. (March 5, 2001) Tangled in the worst of the web. *Christianity Today.*

Chapter Three: RU Slack During Attack?

1. Bill Wilson, *Alcoholics Anonymous* (New York: AA World Services, 1939), 64.

Chapter Four: RU Ignorant of Demonic Attacks?

1. Words and music by John M. Moore, copyright 1952.

Chapter Five: RU at Peace?

1. quotationspage/com/quotes/Edmund_Burke/

Chapter Six: RU Reconciling?

1. Billy Graham, *Peace with God* (Dallas: Word Publishing, 1953, 1984), 214.

Chapter Seven: RU Keeping Peace?

1. Words and music by Bobby McFerrin, copyright 1988.
2. Words and music by Tom Petty, copyright 1994.

Chapter Eight: RU Positioned for Peace?

1. Leo Tolstoy, *War and Peace*, 1869
2. users.erols.com/mwhite28/warstats.htm

Chapter Nine: RU Pending or Depending?

1. cbn.com/entertainment/sports/kurtwarner_2002.aspx

Chapter Thirteen: RU Still Struggling?

1. dickb.com/AAsJamesClub.shtm